A WOMAN'S HEART WAS A FRAGILE THING

"I am curious about what it must be like to feel a man's gentle touch," Mattie said. Then she surprised herself by asking, "Would ya kiss me, Gordon?"

"Most people hardly find my touch gentle."

Her pride flared. "I'm asking for a kiss, nothing more."

He stood, propped his rifle against the wall, and walked toward her.

She held up a hand. "Wait. I didn't mean for you to—"

"Will you shut up?" He took her raised hand and pulled her to her feet. Placing his big, scarred hands on either side of her face, he drew her close.

Then she felt his lips touch hers with such infinite tenderness. She ceased to breathe. Ceased to think. And for the first time in years, she let herself feel.

Also by Parris Afton Bonds

For All Time
Dream Time
Dream Keeper

Available from
HarperPaperbacks

Tame the Wildest Heart

 PARRIS AFTON BONDS

HarperPaperbacks
A Division of HarperCollinsPublishers

This is a work of fiction. The characters, incidents, and
dialogues are products of the author's imagination and are not
to be construed as real. Any resemblance to actual events or
persons, living or dead, is entirely coincidental.

HarperPaperbacks   *A Division of* HarperCollins*Publishers*
        10 East 53rd Street, New York, N.Y. 10022

Cover illustration by Doreen Minuto

First printing: November 1994

Printed in the United States of America

HarperPaperbacks, HarperMonogram, and colophon are
trademarks of HarperCollins*Publishers*

❖ 10 9 8 7 6 5 4 3 2 1

To Gary Rowland Summers
For the good times, for all time.

Acknowledgments

The author wishes to express gratitude to Dave Faust of the Arizona Historical Society's Fort Lowell Museum.

Author's Note

My great-grandfather was a cavalry Indian scout, and later in life owned a blacksmith shop and a corral in Tucson near Fort Lowell. Among his incredible adventures on the frontier was his rescue of a white girl who had been taken captive by the Indians.

At ninety-two, with an arrow-straight back, he was still performing saber drills. My grandmother's door is nicked from one of those performances. As children, my mother and her brothers and their friends would listen spellbound to their grandfather's spine-tingling stories about the Indians.

This story, then, is for my great-grandfather, Albert McAlister.

Parris Afton Bonds
Spring, Texas

1

John Nester, a squaw man and interpreter for the Sixth Cavalry, went to draw a card from the deck. His finger and thumb did not even get the card off the stack, when another gambler's knife whacked down a hair's breadth from the deck.

"Ye sonofabitch don't cheat when ye play cards with me," Mattie McAlister said.

All agreed that Mattie McAlister, nicknamed *Cimarrón,* Spanish for wild one, was a living legend in southeastern Arizona. There were some who maintained that her leather pouch was a man's testicle; that in the past she had actually severed fingers, and that she now carried those finger bones in her pouch.

She never said, and no one had the courage to ask.

The officers' wives of Fort Lowell considered

brown-eyed, brown-haired Mattie a wanton creature in the bargain. Could that be the reason the members of the recently formed Law and Order Society of nearby Tucson had neglected to extend an invitation for her to join their organization?

Her lips curled in a derisive smile. Before the astonished eyes of the other four players at the table, she rose, tucked her knife into the sheath strapped beneath her skirt at her thigh, and turned to walk out the swinging batwing doors of the saloon. Waiting outside, Reverend William "Buckskin" Bingham wasn't exactly ignoring her.

The Mormon circuit rider pointed his long, bony finger at her as she drove Sam Kee's buckboard out of Tucson's red-light district backing up to Pennington Street. "Jezebel!" yelled the bearded man in the soiled blue kersey trousers and buckskin jacket. From the rattlesnake band of his floppy, black felt hat protruded a single eagle feather. "Whore! A fiery hell awaits fornicators like you!"

He, alone, seemed unafraid of her.

Few of the pedestrians, most of them at one time or another solicitors of the fleshy wares to be purchased in the red-light district, paid heed to the ranting, rambling man.

Certainly not thirty-year-old Mattie. Since arriving in Tucson four years earlier, back in '78, she had armored herself with a solid steel shield of calculated indifference.

With a snap of the reins she nudged the two horses into a trot. They rounded the corner onto Meyer Street and headed for her once-a-week rendezvous at the Tombstone–Tucson stage depot. The sun was obscured by thin layers of gray, striated clouds. Another steaming day. May was a good month to bet on rain.

The buckboard, squeaking on its leather springs, squished along muddy ruts left by buggies and horses of the patrons of the Congress Hall Saloon. It was the most popular gaming place in Tucson. It reputedly had the largest mirror in the Territory, as well as the finest cigars and liquors. Mattie was one of the few females who could attest to the legitimacy of the claim.

The buckboard's team of horses clip-clopped on past Major Huffstuttler's wife, who was doubtlessly headed for the Tivoli Theater. Her operatic voice, as high as her bosom, was destined to entertain the territorial governor tomorrow night, according to the *Arizona Weekly Citizen.*

The May 19, 1882 edition lay folded on the slatted seat beside Mattie. The Personal Points column also announced that "Gov. J. C. Frémont has leased the residence of Mr. J. J. Hamburg on Main Street. Mrs. J. J. Hamburg leaves tomorrow morning for New York, accompanied by Mrs. Ed Hudson. They will spend the summer in the East."

Mrs. Huffstuttler shook her closed umbrella at Mattie. "You . . . you vile beast!" Of course, she didn't say it very loudly. Only loud enough to make herself feel brave. With a gloved hand she wiped furiously at her mud-splattered walking skirt.

The back of Mattie's sun-cooked neck reddened. She popped the reins. The team broke into a faster gait, flicking clots of mud onto the nearby boardwalk.

At the stage depot, she hopped down from the running board. Her butternut-colored skirts caught on the break and exposed a length of high-top moccasin, rolled below the knee, before she tugged them loose.

Old Cyrus ambled out of the mud-bricked building. Seven thousand souls, damned and otherwise, were crowded into such houses in Tucson. Most had dirt floors and roofs that collapsed under hard rains. Hers was one of them.

"Howdy, Cimarrón," he shouted. He wore a faded derby hat to shade his eyes. Equally faded white hair hung from beneath the derby.

"G'day, Cyrus. The tea come in?" One never knew if the daily stage from Tombstone would arrive. The cast of characters who made forays on the gold-carrying Concord was magnificent, ranging from Chiricahua Apaches to ex-cavalrymen to Chinese coolies.

"Five bags," he shouted.

She followed him into the storage shed beside the depot's corral and its remuda of spent horses. Flies swarmed around the dung. "Any news of interest from Sin City?"

He put his ear trumpet to his ear. "What's that you say?"

"Anything happening over in Tombstone?" she shouted again. Cyrus knew more gossip than the Personal Points columnist. But even he had never inquired about her leather pouch.

"Some fancy dude from back East arrived on the stage today," he shouted back. "Said to have killed some man in a boxing match on a sandbar in the Rio Grande. He's laying low, over in Gay Alley."

Mattie hefted a twenty-five-pound burlap sack, its contents procured from Tombstone's Chinatown. She was strong for one who looked so slight. "A better place he could not select."

The amorous peccadillos and predilections of the Gay Alley section of Tucson far outdid anything Abilene or Tombstone had to offer.

Cyrus followed her to Sam Kee's buckboard. "How's your Albert?"

She tossed the tea sack into the wagon bed. "Hasn't taken any scalp locks. Though I think his teacher isn't convinced he won't one day go renegade."

"Lemonade, you say?"

With a chuckle, she turned to him. "No, tea. Come by for tea sometime, Cyrus. Compliments of Sam Kee."

He waved, and she went on her way. Before leaving town, she stopped off at the Southern Pacific Railroad Depot to collect sacks of rice and sugar, imported from New Orleans.

Inside the new yellow depot, Mrs. Hamburg and her companion, Mrs. Hudson, awaited their train. By the big clock over the counter, it wasn't due for another forty-five minutes, at 9:50 AM. She nodded at both women.

Mrs. Hamburg stared at her through the white Swiss veil of her toque hat and cooled herself with an ivory-and-lace fan that she brandished furiously. Mrs. Hudson whispered something behind a spotlessly white-gloved hand.

Mattie passed a blanketed Indian; a businessman sporting a huge gold chain that dangled across his flowered vest; two fat, mantilla-draped Mexican women; and a bandy-legged man shod in cowhide boots. She continued on toward the freight counter.

The station master, Hiram, peering up at her from beneath his visor, slid the bill of lading under the window grill for her to sign. "Something else for you, too."

"It came?"

He nodded. "Three days ago."

With reverence she took the small, brown-paper-wrapped package he passed her. She had ordered the book by Sir Walter Scott for Albert. She hoped her nine-year-old son would enjoy the tale of the Scottish bandit, Rob Roy. Hoped even more she could give him a glimpse of the other half of his unusual heritage. Enough, at least, to whet his appetite for knowledge of the wide world stretching beyond the mudhole-and-sand oven that was Tucson.

After hefting the rice and sugar into the wagon bed, she then gave the horses their lead. They knew well the seven-mile drive to the fort and actually broke into a full gallop for that last quarter mile of Fort Lowell Road, lured by the hay and respite awaiting them at the stable behind Sam's restaurant.

An adobe plastered over with lime stucco, the little restaurant was located on the road that ran behind the post. It had become a mecca for gourmet diners, military and civilian alike.

Old Sam Kee hailed from Canton in south China. He had toiled in the coolie labor camps of the

Southern Pacific Railroad, where he had learned to cook. Not just line-camp slum-gullion but delicious things like pressed duck, wonton, egg foo-yong and other Chinese favorites cooked on the outdoor, open fireplace behind his adobe.

The little man greeted her at the restaurant door. Topping five feet including the thickness of his socks, he was not much taller than she. He was one of those lively types, always shifting, twisting, talking with his hands in the air. "Captain Jeter's wife, she need you, missy."

She carried the tea sack inside. A balloon ceiling of glue-stiffened, blue-checked cloth matched the restaurant's tablecloths. Sam and she had plastered the walls with laundry bluing. Shot glasses on the tables served as candle holders. The small, terracotta pots of hot pink geraniums on each table had been her idea. "Mick's been at it again?"

Sam's short pigtail bobbed with his nod. The elements had wrinkled his skin, but his old eyes mirrored the soul's inordinate dignity and the mind's innate intelligence. "By looks of captain's eyes, he drinky all the mescal in Gay Alley."

"Anything short of sulfuric acid is tasteless to Mick Jeter."

Weaving between tables, she put down the sack at the back of the room, near the tiny kitchen's half-door, next to canned goods by cases: tomatoes, corn, peas, pickles, corned beef, condensed milk, even shellfish. "How bad is Jessica?" she asked.

"Bleeding at the nose. A few bruises. All hell break loose. You go. I'll get other sacks."

Taking a detour between the guard house and the adjutant's office, she set out for her mud-brick shanty, just off the road into Tucson. She followed a path worn through salt grass and clover, purple-pink after the wet winter.

Her door was never locked because, quite simply, it wouldn't. It was a converted pine table top she had rescued from a bonfire. She had turned out a resident burro to claim her shanty.

When she entered, she was, as always, enveloped by the subtle sweet aroma of snakeweed. Three years before, when repairing the roof, she had wedged the herb between the roof and the ceiling, which was made of small cottonwood timbers with the bark left on them and hard-packed dirt.

She put down the paper-wrapped book for Albert and collected her leather pouch of medicinal herbs. The pouch was never far from her bed, which was a Wabash bed built into the corner with only one post.

She was on her way out when an object on Albert's rumpled bed caught her eye. He hadn't taken his *Olendorf's Grammar Book* to school with him.

She sighed. Old Miss Brayton would be pleased. The infraction would be just one more reason for her to request that Colonel Carr discharge the boy from school. After four years teaching a recalcitrant Albert, the spinster schoolmarm looked as if she required the services of a mortician.

Captain Jeter of the Twelfth Infantry, Company H, lived in adobe-and-pine-log quarters shaded by the cottonwoods that lined officers row. Mattie entered the back door to Jeter's quarters. For Jessica's sake, she could abandon her pride.

"Jessica?" she called out.

The answering moan drew her through the kitchen and down the wide, dark hallway to the bedroom. Jessica lay in the high tester bed, with her dark hair spilled over the sheets. Mattie sat down on the bed and, gently taking Jessica's chin, turned the woman's narrow face toward her. There was a bit of dried blood below her nose, and a tear seeped from the inner corner of one puffy eye.

Mattie drew opened her leather bag, stained and worn by years of use. "Looks like ye need to write back home to mamma, love." Her voice was light, easy. It always was when her mind raged. Soft and very controlled. She wanted to kill men like this. She carried her own hatred for Nantez and his ilk bottled inside her. Sights like this uncorked the bottle.

"You toughed it out for . . . all those years," Jessica whispered through swollen lips.

"Nantez didn't have as easy access to liquor." When the Apache subchief did, he would usually drink until he passed out, though not always. "Mind if I borrow your kitchen?"

The young woman shook her head and turned her face back to the wall.

Mattie found a bowl, a beautifully painted porcelain, one such as her mother had possessed, and dumped a handful of wheat bran, wormwood leaves, chamomile flower petals, the oil of roses, aniseed, clear lye of ashes, and pounded them together.

When they were well mixed, she took the bowl of

paste back to the bedroom and sat down beside Jessica again.

"How do you . . . stand it?" the captain's wife asked. "Everyone staring. Talking."

"Is that what ye fear most? The talk? More than this? The beatings?"

She had learned that each person had her own private fears. Monsters, fears were, like the monster of Loch Ness. You might not see it, but that didn't mean it wasn't there.

Mattie herself wasn't afraid of talk. Or beatings. Or even being alone. She was afraid of not liking herself, her real self. She was afraid of pulling the wool over her own eyes. In trying to be what she thought Mattie McAlister really was, was she denying what she had been? Or worse, denying herself the opportunity to be more?

She smeared a dab of the unguent on the lump on the woman's forehead.

"If it wasn't for Albert, you . . . could go East, where they didn't know that—"

"—that I lived with the Indians for seven years? Sometimes, when I look at Albert, I think to meself, Mattie ye should have remained a virgin."

"How can you . . . joke about such horrible things that happened when you were—oh, that smells awful, Mattie."

"But it works miracles. By tomorrow morning, the officers' wives will be exclaiming what a marvelous complexion ye have." She stood up, her medicine bag in hand. "Ye really should see the doctor."

"Doc Reilly is as big a drunk as Mick is. You know that."

Doc Reilly, Tucson's first doctor, had arrived two years earlier. One doctor to treat seven thousand people! He was competent when sober—and loose of lip. No secret was sacred with the rotund man.

Mattie took her leave and returned to Sam Kee's. Already a few diners had drifted in for the noon meal. Back in the kitchen, Sam greeted her with a concerned expression crinkling his parchment-paper skin. "Man out there, he asky for you, missy."

"Ye don't know him?" She tied on her apron, a bleached feed sack, over the brown-striped waist of her sturdy cotton and butternut skirt.

He shook his head. "No. He dressy like baritone in San Francisco Opera House."

"I'll see what he wants. Could I have a wee draught of tea, please, Sam?"

That was one thing Sam did as well as she, make a cup of tea. Oolong tea, no less! After Nantez had captured her, she had missed high tea and crumpets—crumpets with big dollops of butter—more than she had the luxuries of bed and bath.

She looked out through the half-door at the scattering of customers. Cyrus was sitting at the table nearest the cast-iron stove. Old Man Foster, owner of one of Tucson's numerous saloons, was talking with Miss Dolly, who ran a boarding house. And Bishop Salpointe sat with Lieutenant Gil Wood.

Then she saw the other man. Sunlight, shining through the single shutter-framed window, revealed a man dressed more for the drawing rooms and salons of the world's capitals than he was for that desolate, dirty backwash of the West.

His slightly crooked nose (evidently from a past break), scarred face, and brawny body clashed with the ruffled silk shirt and single, delicate gold earring. Long, dark, glossy hair framed a face that was a little too broad to be considered conventionally handsome. A drooping mustache graced his wide, sure mouth. His big, battered hands looked out of place, resting on the malacca cane's gold head.

So, this man had asked not for wonton but for the wanton, herself. He had to be new in town.

"Sam, kill the tea," Mattie said. She plucked two glasses from the bamboo drying rack and grabbed up a whiskey bottle from the narrow shelf of brown liquor bottles.

With a hard smile, she headed for his table. Well, she would make him squirm while he propositioned her. The Mexican prostitutes of Tucson were far gone in disease, and only the rawest recruits from Fort Lowell sought them out. Few of the prostitutes' patrons could appreciate the quiet charm of good taste.

She saw his eyes alight on her. Brownish-green eyes, the color of a deceptive desert at high noon and just as intense, watched her. Over the left eye was a puckered scar beneath the raven brow.

Mattie plopped one glass in front of him and, pulling out the cane-woven chair opposite, poured the amber nectar into her own glass. It was her contention that the peddlers of this tarantula juice, known as whiskey, showed a callous disregard for the palates and internal workings of their clientele. "Ye wanted me?"

She saw him take stock of her dry, rough hands and broken nails as she filled his glass. Her mother's admonition, "White, soft hands are much sought after," triggered the fleeting memory of her mother spreading oil of sweet almonds and two egg yolks into gloves that she wore to bed every night.

Mattie could tell that the man was repelled by her coarseness. No soft curls fringed her face to lighten its harsh lines from the sun. Her wild hair, dry and frizzy, looked like a dirty, ragged mop after too many years' use. That's what she had been. Used. But not anymore.

Her lack of obvious feminine attributes found disfavor in the deepening of the furrows below his mustache. "Mattie McAlister?"

She drew a match from the rolled-down folds of her buckskin moccasin, then lit up a Mexican cigarette. "Among other identities," she said, the cigarette tucked into one corner of her lips. She narrowed her eyes and stared at him through the stream of smoke. "And yourself?"

"Gordon Halpern. From Pittsburgh." He stared at her as if she were subhuman.

She plucked from the window ledge a fan with pink flowers on one side and E. J. Smith's funeral parlor advertisement on the other and waved it lazily. "Hot in here, isn't it? Sweating like a Salem witch, I am."

"People in Tucson say you're a witch, all right. A witch doctor." He batted at a buzzing fly. "That you learned healing from a medicine man of the Netdahe band of Apaches. That you know the Apache language and Apache ways."

She eyed him steadily. He was older than she had first thought. The ebony hair had been misleading. Up close, it and his mustache, were flecked with gray. Lines at the outer corners of his eyes suggested he was in his mid-thirties. His facial bone structure was powerful and suggested an equally powerful will.

Mattie clashed with powerful wills, which was not in her best interest. So, she had learned detachment. "Ye wanted to discuss business with me?"

He leaned forward, those battering-ram hands cupping his glass. "You lived in Mexico as Nantez's squaw?"

She downed half the contents of her glass. She probably drank more than was good for her; certainly, she could match any man drink for drink. His expression hinted that he found her about as appealing as a punch in the face. "Ye might say I took the cure in Mexico. Ye killed a man in a boxing match?"

He didn't look surprised that she had heard about him. "I'd like you to guide me down into Mexico—to Nantez."

She smiled and flicked a cigarette ash into his whiskey glass. "Sure, and I'd like a glassful of ice chips."

Beneath his mustache, his lower lip flattened. Both his hands tightened, so much that she feared he would shatter Sam's glass. He seemed to struggle to quench a volatile temper. Then, with the calm of an Indian meditating on a vision, he poured his polluted drink into the small, potted geranium, which she had placed on each table and devotedly nurtured.

She wanted to slap him. One of those slaps that sent the lips flapping, like in a Mark Twain novel.

"With what I am willing to pay, Miss McAlister, you can fill the glass with ice chips. My glass, yours, every glass in Tucson. I'm willing to pay three thousand greenbacks to get back my wife. Last month Diana was captured by Nantez's warriors."

She controlled her surprise. It was a trick she had learned well during her captivity. Emotions betrayed one's vulnerability.

Still, for one soaring moment, she was tempted. Three thousand dollars was an astronomical sum. With three thousand dollars, she could return to a life approximating the one she had once lived. She could even go back East, where no one knew her.

She stabbed out her cigarette in the geranium pot. Whom was she kidding? One look at her son, with his fierce, Indian features, and ruinous gossip would start again. For every Reverend Bingham and Mrs. J. J. Hamburg in the Arizona Territory, there were a thousand more like them back East.

"Not any amount would tempt me." She tossed the fan back onto the window ledge. "Not even all the ice in the Arctic."

She started to rise, and he grabbed her wrist. "You're the only one who can help me."

"Hire yourself an Indian scout from the fort."

"You know they all work for the Sixth Cavalry headquarters and field staff."

That was true, which meant that the military and those on its payroll were forbidden to cross the border to search for warring Apaches retreating into Mexico. "Like I said, I'm not interested."

"Look, I've been told that you lived with Nantez for seven years and know well the chief's habits."

"The man is a will-o'-the-wisp. No one knows him. That's why he is still terrorizing Mexico and lower Arizona and New Mexico."

"But if any white person could understand Nantez's thoughts and actions," Gordon Halpern persisted, "it would be you."

His hold on her wrist made her nervous. She shook off his manacling fingers. Obviously, he hadn't heard the stories about her pouch. "I know him well. I don't know the countryside, but I do know I shan't return to it. I'd as soon drink tea with the major's wife, and that's not a prospect I would relish either. She's pompous and boring. And besides, the old biddy lets wind. Abominable stenches if I do say so meself. G'day to ye."

Later, as she helped Sam Kee wash the dishes from the midday dinner, she recounted the story of Halpern's visit. "He's the same Eastern dude who Cyrus said supposedly killed a man in a boxing match held on a sandbar in the Rio Grande."

Old Sam fished a cracked dish from the cast-iron tub's wash water. "What do you plan to do, missy?"

She took the dish and dried it. "Nothing."

He eyed her. "You are one hot-damned good healer."

"If I wasn't," she joked, "ye wouldn't be around to say so."

She had found Sam down by nearby Rillito Creek, where she had gone to collect the medicinal oil of sage. He had been snakebitten and delirious with fever, and his forearm was swollen as big as a saguaro trunk. She had treated him at her house, and he had healed completely, except for two withered fingers. Afterwards, he had offered her a job working for him in the restaurant he had started five months before. It had seemed infinitely preferable to washing long johns for the soldiers and selling her body on the side, as many post laundresses did.

He dried his hands on his apron and faced her, arms crossed. "I say you this, missy, you needy to heal yourself. You Americans, you put periods at end of your sentences. You needy to put period at end of sentence."

She shelved the dry dish. Intuitively, she knew that Sam was telling her that the only way she could heal her pain was not to resist it but to replace it. But with what? She pushed from her thoughts any inclination to earn the staggering sum of three thousand dollars. "Any contact with Nantez is enough to dampen the allure of bettering me position."

Besides, she didn't like Halpern. Not only could she tell he was hot tempered and eccentric, but his almost brutish appearance triggered the most unpleasant memories of Nantez.

Albert was due home from school shortly. She removed her apron and, carrying a box of lunch leftovers for Albert's dinner, started homeward. She didn't have to be back at Sam Kee's until just before evening supper was served.

Back at her shanty, she thought about how very nice it would be if Albert could come home from the post school just a little less sullen. He had problems adapting to the Anglo regimen and was an outcast at Fort Lowell. Every few months, she had to straddle her son just to snip the hair he was determined to wear long like an Indian's.

Her heart went out to her nine-year-old son. All she could do was be there for him; console him and assure him that he was perfect, whole, and complete—just as he was.

She picked up his strewn clothing, filled the lamp, emptied the coal scuttle into the stove, and put some tea on to boil.

Then she sat down in the cane rocker to remove first one of her high-top beaded moccasins, then the other. With a sigh, she stared down at her feet. The skin was weather-cracked and covered with corns, bunions, and scars . . . not a sight that set a poet to penning verses of adoration.

From her medicine pouch, she withdrew the corked jar and rubbed some of the jar's contents, glycerin and rose water, onto each foot. Feet that had been cut and burnt and bruised during her years of captivity were now secretly pampered, her one admission of feminine vanity.

With the daily ritual completed, she donned again her moccasins, then poured a tin cup of tea to savor before returning to Sam Kee's.

The time came and went for Albert's arrival from school. The remainder of tea in her cup grew cold as Mattie grew worried. Something niggled at the back of her mind, as it does when one knows something isn't quite right.

Staring past the cast-iron stove, she realized what it was. Behind the stove, the wall where she kept a butcher knife pegged was empty.

She strode to the shelf where Albert stowed his personal belongings. His tattered deck of playing cards was missing!

She recalled how an old sod, a cavalryman due to retire, had found Albert and her as they had wandered dazed in the desert after their flight up from Mexico and Nantez. They had been detained at Camp Huachuca until they could be transferred to Fort Lowell. At Huachuca, the old cavalryman had taught Albert to play solitaire. From that time on, the boy was rarely parted from his deck, school being one of the few exceptions.

Until now.

Sam presented himself at her door. His normally stoic demeanor was clearly in a state of agitation. "Buckboard, missy! It's gone! Soldier, he say he saw Albert driving it."

At once, she knew. He had taken his deck of cards and Sam Kee's buckboard and God knew what else. Albert was returning to his father! He had threatened as much when she had insisted he go to school that morning.

She pushed past the startled Chinaman and set out in a rapid gait toward the post.

In her mind ran a litany of those times, those times of weakness, when she had wished she weren't saddled with the burden of an Indian baby. Then shame at her disloyalty would always overcome her. At those times, she would ask herself if Albert wouldn't be better off with what he knew and understood.

Now, a frantic and fierce protectiveness surged in her blood and thundered in her ears. She would not give up on Albert. He was as much white as Indian. He was *her* child! Worrying about her son's disappearance, she wasn't even aware of the looks given her by the soldiers she passed—looks of wariness mixed with disgust. Judgments. Who were they to judge? Their opinions were as valid as desert mirages.

Even though evening was nigh, a group of military prisoners were still scything the grass that clung tenaciously to the perimeters of the parade ground. There drilled the almost two-hundred officers and enlisted men posted to Fort Lowell.

Troopers, bent on errands, came and went from post headquarters, which was a long, low building with thick adobe walls and a veranda that offered meager shade. Inside, the outer office was stuffy, as was the balding aide-de-camp, who sorted through the paperwork strewn across his desk. His appearance was spiffy. He looked startled at hers.

"I want to see Colonel Carr. Now!"

His glance strayed to the door to his left, which was banked by a potted fern. The plaque on the door was stenciled with *Commanding Officer.* "That is impossible, miss."

Though his tone was neutral, the look in his eyes was not. After eleven years, she had learned to read emotions as well as conceal them. And in him she read contempt.

She planted her small rough hands on his desk. "Either ye announce me, or I shall announce meself."

"I can't permit that, miss." Not "ma'am" or "madam." Just "miss."

She straightened and stared down at him, watching something deep inside him begin to squirm until it manifested on the outside in the nervous flicker of his lids.

Her hand smoothed over the oblong object outlined beneath her skirt. "Lieutenant, your bowels will jolly well be hanging out before ye can summon help. Do ye believe me?"

"What's going on here?" Colonel Carr asked from his office doorway. He clutched a sheath of papers in one hand.

"The woman here—"

From behind his bifocals, Colonel Carr fixed her with his imperious gaze. "Mattie McAlister, isn't it? Step inside."

She followed him into his office. He left the door open, as if he thought she might commit mayhem before he could summon help. Leaning back against the front of his desk, he said, "You wanted something?"

"Me boy, Albert, he has run away." She tried to control the panic in her voice. "I want ye to send out a patrol to find him."

"Miss McAlister, if I sent out a patrol every time someone—"

"Please. Albert's all I have left." In that awful instant, she realized she *was* afraid of being alone.

The colonel's voice hardened. "My soldiers are too damned busy chasing Apache warriors this side of the border to have time for half-breed kids, Miss McAlister."

Her heart pounded heavily, like the rhythmic beat of a funeral dirge. "I see." She summoned her dignity. "Then g'day to ye, and may God have mercy on your soul."

Just outside his doorway, she paused to spit into the fern's clay pot. "Needs watering, ye dolt."

She strolled out and stopped beneath the veranda's lattice awning. Eyes narrowed, she stared across the parade ground at the setting sun. The clouds had deserted it, and now it was blood red.

Apaches believed a blood-red sun was an omen. It could be good or bad.

She, too, believed a blood-red sun to be an omen. Changes were afoot. She hoped that Reverend William "Buckskin" Bingham felt the same. If not, she meant to convince him.

2

The right Reverend William "Buckskin" Bingham removed his hat in public rarely. Only inside a church, and that was rare, too, since he entered a church about as often as he joked. His services were held in the great cathedral of the outdoors.

At sunrise, the trickling Santa Cruz River, which ran just west of Tucson, was the locale of his latest service, a baptism. The neophyte was a boy of Pima Indian/Mexican heritage. A potpourri of relatives and the curious of Tucson and Fort Lowell had gathered to observe the solemn ceremony.

Mattie was among them, but she wasn't there for any religious reasons. She waited beneath a stunted cottonwood tree while Bingham finished his benediction over the shivering copper-skinned boy who wore only his breech cloth. The desert still retained remnants of the night's coolness.

Arms spread wide, head thrown back, Bingham announced in his stentorian voice, "'After John had proclaimed before His coming a baptism of repentance to all—'"

He lowered his head, his fiery gaze scanning the paltry crowd to find her beneath the tree. His accusing finger pointed at her and he began to quote from the Bible.

"'All you who bend the bow, shoot at her; do not be sparing with your arrows, for she has sinned against the Lord. Reproofs for discipline are the way of life, to keep you from the evil woman, from the smooth tongue of the adulteress. Do not desire her beauty in your heart, nor let her catch you with her eyelids. For on account of a harlot one is reduced to a loaf of bread, and an adulteress hunts for the precious life.'"

In twos and threes, the onlookers turned toward her until she had the rapt attention of the whole crowd. She had been expecting them to shrink from her as if she had smallpox. Instead, chuckling erupted among them. The good reverend had painted a seductress, and they beheld a crusty, hard-bitten woman who they thought was unlikely to stir lust in the most ardent heart.

She straightened her thin shoulders and walked toward the Mormon preacher. The crowd parted for her. She stopped in front of him and stared up at those eyes of brimstone. "Ye are afraid of me," she said in a low voice that those nearest had to strain to hear.

"I am a God-fearing man."

"And I don't even fear hell." She glanced at those around them and lowered her voice even further. "Do you want to earn half of three grand? Think of it, fifteen hundred dollars!"

His gaze darted over the watchful faces. He took her arm and drew her away from the dripping boy and the others. "You would seduce with money where charm fails?"

"Me bairn has run away." They continued walking, their shoes squashing in the riverbank's soft mud. "Albert's returning to his father. Remember Nantez?"

In less than the flickering of an eyelid, a visible shudder came and went through Bingham. His ash-colored eyes stared at her with skepticism. "Where would you get that kind of money?"

"A man wants me to lead him to Nantez, because his warriors have captured the man's wife."

He stopped, glanced back at the people still milling around the baptismal site, still watching. "Why me?"

"I know Nantez, but not the countryside that he operates out of. Not that well. Not well enough. As a circuit rider in Mexico, ye know the paths crisscrossing the Sierra Madres as well as the scars crisscrossing your scalp."

He fingered his beard. After a minute, it parted to show tobacco-stained teeth. "I want it all. The entire three grand. Nothing less would induce me to return to Mexico."

Money was nothing to her. But Albert . . . if she could bring him back . . . money meant a better life to him. "Ye'd never find Nantez without me, Bingham. He'd find ye first."

"All right." He spat a stream of tobacco juice into a muddy footprint. "But I want half of it up front— $750. And we'll need financing for an expedition of this sort."

"Our employer will take care of that, too." She could only hope that Gordon Halpern hadn't found someone else crazy enough to guide him down into Mexico's treacherous Sierra Madre Mountains.

Gay Alley could be dangerous at night. But then, Mattie had little left to fear. She said as much as she stood before Gordon Halpern in his rented room.

"There are things worse than torture or rape, Mr. Halpern." When he made no offer for her to take a seat, she sat down in the spooled-back chair opposite the small table from him. He was playing solitaire. "I'm sure your wife will agree." *If she's still alive*, Mattie added to herself.

He tipped back his chair and propped the heels of his black patent boots with suede uppers on the rickety table. Civilization's garb—cream-colored trousers and vest, brown striped shirt, and ivory silk cravat— belied the primal man it clothed. "Like what? Death?"

"Death!" she scoffed. "Death is a blessing—if it is our own. But now watching someone else die . . . ." She stopped, still unable, after all these years, to talk about the heartbreaking horror. "So," she went on briskly, "if ye still need a guide . . . ."

The candlelight in the center of the table reflected his saturnine features: the broad sweep of his cheekbone, the curling sensuality of his lip beneath the raven mustache, the slightly brooding slant to his hazel eyes. "What made you change your mind?" he asked.

"Yesterday, me bairn ran off. I believe he's returning to his father. Nantez."

Looking into the dark depths of those eyes, she could almost see Halpern flinch. Did he fear that Nantez or one of his warriors would get Diana with child also?

"He can't be very old," he finally said.

"Nine."

His expression was one of incredulity. "You really think a nine-year-old can find his way back to his father over hundreds of miles of desert and mountain?"

"The question is," she said calmly, "can we?"

He shifted his feet on the floor beneath the table and slapped his thighs with his palms. "How soon can you be ready to leave?"

Taking the action as a cue of his impatience, she rose. She had noted that he moved quickly and with determination. Which, she had learned, often signaled a person uncertain of his decision and anxious to act before he could change his mind. But this kind of person got things done.

"We will need supplies for an expedition of this sort," she said. "Also, I'm taking a guide along. A Reverend Bingham. He was a circuit-riding preacher in Mexico and a captive of Nantez for several months. He wants half of his share of the reward up front."

Gordon Halpern raised an eyebrow. "Why don't I just hire him instead?"

"Like you said, I know Nantez's habits. For instance, Nantez and his warriors have a mysterious way of vanishing completely. I'll explain that secret later. We'll have plenty of time to discuss how we're going to find him once we're on our journey. Right now, it's important that we get the expedition under way. Ye are prepared to finance it?"

He leaned forward, those large, menacing hands clasped in a most businesslike fashion. "I've made a deposit with Wells Fargo. You may draw upon it for anything—within reason."

"The Arctic better have a hell of a lot of ice."

The next morning, she learned that Gordon Halpern was as good as his word. Zechendorf and Co. provided an array of supplies from which she selected what was essential for traveling light and far and fast, as well as a canvas tent by Phoenix Tenting Company.

She also purchased two repeating rifles, a Marlin and a Winchester, and an old single-shot Civil War-vintage Springfield.

Most of Nantez's warriors, numbering upward of seventy-five, were equipped with the Springfield and an assortment of handguns that had been taken in raids on the settlements or in attacks on travelers on the lonely roads of New Mexico and Arizona.

From E. F. Colton's Livery Stable and Corral, Mattie purchased a pack mule and a mount for Halpern, a five-year-old bay gelding that was fairly well muscled in the pants and with plenty of bone and balance. For herself, she had a spotted Indian pony an old miner had given her two years ago in trade for treating his gout.

The pony, Pepper, had proved capable of great endurance. Pepper and Sam Kee provided the ears that listened to her own occasional ravings. Neither the pony nor the Chinaman ever betrayed her soul's torment. She was tired of being ever-vigilant. She was furious at not verbalizing her rage at the injustices of life rather than merely showing it. A childish thing to do, she knew.

She could only pray that she and Bingham and Halpern equaled Pepper's endurance. And pray was something she rarely did.

Mattie, Bingham, and Halpern met before sunup the next day outside Sam Kee's. Bingham was astride his stout mule. He had already appropriated the old Springfield, and it lay across his lap, ready for use. For herself, she had reserved the Marlin, slung on a strap from her shoulders. It didn't carry a lot of kick.

With Halpern and Bingham watching, she bade farewell to the old Chinaman, who held a lantern against the indigo darkness. The presence of the other two men, along with her own discomfort in expressing affection for any male, hampered any emotional good-byes. "If I don't come back within three weeks, Sam, me place is yours—its bucket-brigade toilet facilities and all."

He bobbed his head. "I keepy the lantern lit in your place for you, missy."

By dawn's rapidly brightening light, she cantered with the two men along the Tucson–Tombstone road. Bingham's squint-eyed assessment of Gordon Halpern clearly indicated mistrust. Halpern had given the preacher only a cursory glance and then, as if dismissing him, turned his attention back to his mount.

The gelding had a mind of its own, but Halpern had a good seat. "For a dude, you ride well enough," Mattie observed.

He flicked her a glance that, however fleeting, did not miss her floppy sombrero, red bandanna knotted around her neck, and her shabby, navy wool-serge riding jacket that some woman had left in Sam Kee's. It was trimmed with brown leather straps, which were cracked with age. One was missing its buckle. Her buckskin skirt was soiled and had lost more than half its fringe decoration.

"I belonged to the Philadelphia Riding Club," he told her.

"Oh, did ye now?" Her censuring gaze took in his black broad-brimmed Charro hat, spurred Wellington boots, suede jacket, and buff riding britches. His cane was tucked into the saddle scabbard, where resided the latest model of Winchester she had purchased. "Well, we don't ride to the foxes here, but the coyotes may provide a source for your amusement."

"Look, Miss McAlister, this expedition doesn't promise to be easy. Don't make it more difficult."

"Expect it to be more than difficult. Expect it to be hell. Am I right, Reverend?"

Bingham fixed her with his condemning gaze. "God is judging you."

"And you are that judgment." She tugged her own sombrero brim lower. They were going east, toward the rising sun. The day promised to be hot.

The horses' hooves kicked up puffs of alkali dust. Cholla and saguaro cacti painted a stark and barren landscape, but the yucca was sending up wonderful clusters of cream-colored flowers, and the bright green, spindly-branched ironwood bore an abundance of lavender and purple flowers.

Their path paralleled the new Southern Pacific Railroad. The horses' heads were held high, characteristic of a good walking gait of the cavalry, which would average four miles an hour.

As each traveler was preoccupied with thoughts of the journey ahead, conversation was less than scintillating. A white-hot sun had beaten back yesterday's clouds. By midday, heat waves were rising off the floor of Sulphur Spring Valley, and a wide, rolling plain lay just ahead. The wagon-wheel-rutted road stretched out before them. Deeper ruts indicated the caissons that had transferred cannon from Fort Lowell to Fort Bowie earlier that spring.

"We could make better time," Halpern called out at one point.

She knew if he had his way, he would gallop the horse all the way to Mexico. "When ye march a horse at high speed, either a sustained trot or a long gallop, ye cost yourself and your horse a lot of sweat. In the desert that equals death. Our objective is to get there."

Bingham called for a halt in the shadow of a limestone ledge, a precursor to the Chiricahua Mountains rising to the south. Tufts of blue gramma grass and shoots of mustard primrose signaled that there was water nearby. The spring that gave the valley its name was only a thin thread burbling from the sand, but it was enough to ease the thirst of the mounts.

The three travelers brought out their Civil War-issue canteens, along with hardtack and canned peaches. Heartier meals would come only when they camped for the night.

"Lord God bless this humble food," Bingham intoned before chomping into his hardtack. Mouth full, he said, "We should reach Fort Bowie by some-time tonight." He swallowed. "Tomorrow morning, we'll travel on to Stein's railroad station, then turn southward."

Her back propped against the rock-striated wall, Mattie uncorked her canteen and wet her neckerchief to dampen her face. In her own way, she was as anxious as Halpern to make good time. Heading directly south through Apache Pass was the quickest route to the northern end of the Sierra Madres. And the most difficult. No rougher terrain could be imagined.

But with Albert traveling by buckboard, she figured he would probably stick to the main road that snaked on eastward toward Mesilla, the territorial capital of New Mexico.

On the other hand, the Apaches were fast moving and adept at blending into the landscape. Trying to sight an Apache was like trying to see the wind. Albert may have already abandoned the wagon in one of the numerous box canyons that gouged the area and vanished into the Chihuahua Mountains.

"Ye think the road to Stein's will be safe enough?" she asked Bingham. It was difficult for her to be civil to him, since he was partly responsible for her tainted reputation. But they had one thing in common: They were both survivors.

"I hear tell the troops at Fort Bowie have been reinforced by a detachment from Camp Huachuca. They'll be watching the road through the pass."

"So will the Apaches. They're watching us even now."

"How do you know that?" Halpern asked her, as he turned the tin can's key to open its top.

"They're the world's greatest fighters. They keep the element of surprise on their side."

Halpern braced a forearm on one knee. "What's this Nantez like?"

She shrugged. "Short. Squat. Ugly."

"No, I mean his behavior."

"He's the Nobleman of the Neolithic." She wished he wouldn't keep asking questions. They stirred up unpleasant memories.

"What do you mean?"

"I mean he's cruel. I watched him torture a victim to death by cutting small pieces out of his feet." She could have said much more, but there was no point in alarming him too much.

"You told Sam Kee we'd be back in three weeks," he said. "We've got to make better time than that."

"If Diana survived the first few days, time is on her side."

She knew he took her bluntness for a lack of compassion, but she had learned that the truth was better than holding out false hope. False hope only cracked the heart.

She sipped the metallic-tasting water slowly, then said, "Mr. Halpern, it's been almost a month since your wife was captured. Even a week spent as a captive changes one. Forever." She paused. How could she tell him delicately what to expect?

His gaze drilled into her. "Are you trying to hint that I won't want my wife back? That if Diana's been . . . defiled . . . I'll not love her or desire her? There's more to a person, Miss McAlister, than the physical body. If that were—"

"I'm trying to say that she may not want you." She corked her canteen and stood up.

Bingham was eyeing them both with grizzly amusement.

She stared down at Halpern. "Do ye understand what I am saying, or should I be more explicit?"

"So that's what turned you into the sexless, pitiful creature you are," Halpern said with no malice and the barest hint of compassion.

That compassion was what threatened to shatter her. Feeling her chest tighten, she swallowed her pain. So many horrendous memories crashed in on her. The worst of them came, not from her years spent in captivity, but from these four spent in a society that considered itself civilized. With her own people, she felt less than human, different from everyone else, tainted and worthless.

Nothing she could do would change their opinion of her. So she had stopped trying. Now, at least, she was true to herself. She hoped.

Before she could retaliate, Bingham said, "You willingly satisfied the lust of those red devils, girl." He took a swig from his canteen, then wiped his mouth with the back of his sleeve. "For that you will burn 'til your very soul shrivels to ashes like newspaper in a fire."

She stalked to where her pony stood placidly munching the tufted grass and swung up into the western saddle. She had learned to ride sidesaddle in Scotland and then bareback in Nantez's camp.

Mattie stared down at Bingham. "I was willing to gratify the lust of an extraordinarily cruel man. I did so for seven years. I often wondered if I wasn't becoming crazier than you."

She glanced at Halpern then. "I survived, Mr. Halpern. Let's hope your Diana can do the same. Coming?"

3

The journey resumed in strained silence. Halpern broke it when he pointed to a plume of gray smoke in the hilly distance, where the road crawled toward Fort Bowie and Apache Pass. "Have the Apaches spotted us?"

"They've been watching us since we left Tucson," Bingham said. "You can count on that."

Bingham was right, Mattie knew. Warriors kept watch from rocks and mountain lookouts across wide stretches of country, observing sometimes for days their intended victims before striking.

"Does the fire relay word that they have sighted us?"

"No," she said. "It's absurd to think that Apaches carry on regular conversations by means of smoke signals. They use smoke fires on mountaintops mainly as signals of distress. That fire isn't from a mountaintop."

"But it's likely to mean distress, all the same," Bingham said. "And trouble for us. I suggest we avoid the area. The terrain'll be rougher, but maybe we oughtta head south into the Chiricahuas and drop on down into Mexico now."

She shook her head. "No. For all I know, that could be me son in trouble."

"If we find your son first," Halpern said, "the deal still stands, right?"

"I keep me word, Mr. Halpern."

"Did you ever think you might be doing your son a disservice, trying to mold him into Anglo ways?"

"I think about it every day of me life." She looked over at him, then returned her gaze to the road. Hot sand, hot wind, fierce sunlight. "What about yourself? Did you ever think ye might have molded yourself into something you're not?"

His eyes swerved to her. After a speculative moment, he said, "Every day of my life."

"When do we collect for our services?" Bingham asked.

"When my wife is safely across the border. I can give you vouchers drawn on Wells Fargo at that time."

The plume of smoke grew more distinct, swirling gray at its top, a darker black at its base. At the sight of half a dozen gliding buzzards, encircling the plume, her scalp prickled.

In a quarter of an hour, the source of the smoke

came into view: an overturned stage. From the looks of the scene, a band of Apaches had surprised the regular mail wagon from the East. One of its wheels had come off and had rolled to a stop in a mound of nearby rocks. Two of the stage's lead mules lay dead. The others must have been taken by the war party.

Halpern dismounted and, cane in hand, approached the still-smoking wagon. The heat reached Mattie, a dozen yards away. With his cane, he nudged a small, blanket wrapped object. A child's doll rolled out. Eyeless sockets stared up at them.

She remained where she was. Where were the occupants of the stage?

"Where now are Fort Bowie's brave soldiers?" she asked of no one in particular.

She remembered bitterly that when an opportunity for escape had presented itself, she had fled Nantez's camp in Mexico with five-year-old Albert and eventually had arrived across the border, first at Camp Huachuca, then at Fort Lowell.

The welcome that Fort Lowell's soldiers had given her had been less than sympathetic. In some of the troopers' expressions she had seen ogling interest. Doubtlessly, they had entertained lurid visions of taking advantage of her.

Bingham climbed down from his mule, Jughead. She watched him move with cautious steps and Winchester held ready toward the overturned stage. "Damned heathens!" he said.

Halpern looked up at her. "Can you tell who's responsible? Nantez's band maybe?"

She knew he was hoping the subchief was in the area. Her gaze ran over the ground, looking for signs, but she couldn't tell by the tracks. The ponies, maybe a dozen of them, were unshod. She shook her head. "There's at least half a dozen different Apache bands in southeastern Arizona on the warpath right now."

Bingham walked over to the wheel that had rolled free and surprised her by prying loose two spokes. Then he started back to the wagon. She watched as he sawed off a length of rein that still tethered the dead mule and lashed the spokes into a cross.

He jammed the improvised cross deep into the sand, then removed his feathered hat. Sunlight glistened off his scarred pate. At the grisly sight, Halpern's dark brows raised, but he said nothing. Hands resting on his cane, he waited for Bingham to finish.

"Ashes to ashes, dust to dust," Bingham pronounced. "May the Lord God Almighty have mercy on these missing souls." He stood and said, "Let's skedaddle. Quick."

"Well?" Halpern asked, remounting. "Do we try and make Fort Bowie—or strike out into Mexico now?"

She looked to Bingham.

"At this point," he said, "Fort Bowie will probably mean a large portion of a night march for us. I say it'd be safer to head straight for Mexico. Make camp in the safety of the mountains."

"Safety?" Halpern drawled. "Miners in Tombstone claim the mountains are crawling with Apaches."

"What Bingham means is that we're fair game here on the plain for Indians doing sentry duty. In the mountain ravines, we have about as much a chance being seen by an Apache scout as we do seeing one."

Halpern shrugged. "The mountains it is then."

The sky turned purple in anticipation of evening before they reached the Chiricahua foothills. By the time the heavens were black with thousands of stars, the hills had grown so steep as to necessitate dismounting, and the threesome led their horses through the treachery of darkness.

Mattie hadn't bothered to tell Halpern how hazardous traveling in the mountains at night could be. His occasionally muttered, "Damn!," told her he was finding out. She smiled.

In addition to thorns, cactus, yucca, and other spearlike plants to scratch the flesh, one had to avoid knifelike rocks that were practically invisible, holes and crevices in the ground, and cliffs of all kinds.

Doing so came easily for Mattie. She had developed a sort of sixth sense over the years of traveling the Southwest with the Netdahe band.

Like most Apaches, the Netdahe were warfaring nomads. As wide and vast as was the extent of the territory controlled by the Apaches and many as were the streams, mountains, and forests where they camped and hunted, regular supplies of water and food in that arid and crabbed Southwest were not easy to secure.

Constantly, she strained to listen for noises that

didn't belong. The yip of a coyote made her pause to listen. But when no responsive yip followed, she began moving again, as quietly as possible considering the crunch of pebbles under foot and hoof.

The moon was lost behind turreted peaks, when Bingham led them into a deep U-shaped ravine where they could set up dry camp. The tent would not be needed tonight.

While Halpern unpacked the mule's camp gear and Bingham unsaddled the horses and hobbled them for the night, Mattie gathered twigs and branches, the kind that made for a smokeless fire.

This had been but one of her myriad, menial duties as Nantez's captive. Gathering piñon nuts or mescal for roasting, building wickiups, weaving burden baskets, and making pottery jars were only a few others.

Those and satisfying Nantez's lust. When he was in one of his foul moods and she failed to do so, she could expect a boxing that left her ears ringing.

Bingham elected to take the first watch from the rimrock above. It was a precaution only. At this point, unless a war party traveling by night stumbled over them, they were unlikely to draw attention. Raiding Apaches were interested in the more extensive booty they could get from robbing ranches and wagon trains.

At dinner, she and Halpern passed the rations to each other in silence. She knew he was as uncomfortable with her as she was with him. Propped against his saddle, he sipped his coffee and eyed her across the small smokeless fire she had built.

His expression of distaste for her mirrored her own for him, with his air of elegance. He represented all that she had been, and she was both contemptuous and envious of him.

With his forearms braced on his knees, he leaned forward and asked, "I noticed your brogue—you're Scottish?"

She pushed her floppy hat off, so that it was suspended from her neck by its leather thong. "Aye, that I am." She was wary of conversation with him for conversation's sake alone.

She remembered when a cavalry patrol officer had discovered her and Albert, half-starved and dehydrated, wandering the desert south of Tucson. He had brought them to Fort Lowell, and she had found it inordinately difficult to communicate in English. Even a few English words strung together in coherent fashion had required great concentration on her part. Further, she found English now full of empty and excessive phrases.

"Born in Scotland?"

"Ayrshire."

"What were you doing in Mexico?"

"Me father was a mining engineer. He worked for American Smelting and Refining. Twelve years ago they sent us to a mining town, Santo Tomás. Outside of Chihuahua."

She could tell he was trying to figure out her age. She made it easy for him. "I was eighteen at the time."

His unwavering gaze didn't betray that he might think she looked older than her thirty years. "How did you come to be . . . captured by Nantez?"

She noted he did not use the demeaning term of "Nantez's squaw." "Nantez and his warriors struck Santo Tomás, looking mainly for horses, cattle, arms, and ammunition. They took four hostages. Me parents, me, and the reverend there." She nodded up toward the rim, where spiraling pines were silhouetted against the rising moon.

"Me parents were tortured to death."

"And the reverend?"

"Our preacher survived because he was rambling and ranting about what God would do to Nantez and his warriors. They thought he was crazy. Touched by the gods. He was released after only a few months of captivity."

"But not you?"

She focused on stirring her sea of peaches and tomatoes. "Not me.

"Do you mind?"

Was he daft? She looked up. He was rustling in his supply pack. "Mind what?"

He fished out a pad and a small leather sack. From the sack he extracted a wand of pastel chalk. "I'm a portrait artist."

"Really?"

"Do you mind if I sketch you?" he asked, propping the pad against one raised knee. "In this altitude, without the distraction of city lights, the night has its own magic lights and shades."

She shrank back. She hadn't glanced in a mirror since before retiring for bed on that muggy night in August of 1871. "No!" The refusal was more a hiss of her breath than an actual word.

He arched one black brow. "Why not?"

She scraped off her tin plate. "Why not?" She recalled the occasional photographers and artists who painted Tucson's blanket Indians and poncho-wrapped Mexicans as caricatures. She knew what she had become. She certainly did not want to add to descriptions like pathetic and disgusting the term of laughable. "I'm simply not interested in posing."

"You're afraid!"

She packed away the plate and took out her leather bag. "I most definitely am not." She unlaced one high-top moccasin, then the other. The tin ornaments on the fringe seaming their sides clinked as she tugged off each. "Maybe I believe in what Geronimo always said. Something that makes your likeness steals your soul." She took a jar from the pouch. "Then ye get ghost sickness."

He was watching what she was doing with curiosity written in his expression, but he only said, "Tell me about this ghost sickness."

She uncorked the small terra-cotta jar and scooped out a fingertip glob of the precious cream. "The Apache fear the ghosts of the dead."

She concentrated on massaging the salve into the cracked skin of her left heel. "If a relative has kept anything that belongs to the departed, he would fear that the ghost of the dead person would come back to claim it. They believe that ye might arouse or anger the ghost of the dead if you speak his name."

"How does the person get sick?"

"They become nervous. Agitated. Sick to their

stomach. Ghost sickness is brought on by the hooting of a nearby night owl. You see, the Apache have an obsessive dread of the owl. If one hoots near the camp, it is an omen of the worst sort. The Apache believe that the spirit of the dead enters into the owl and comes back to warn or threaten them." Her lips curved in a smile. "Like a Scotsman, they are afraid of the supernatural. That's why after awhile, the Apache women stopped tormenting me."

"Why is that?"

She lifted her other bare foot and inspected it by firelight. Hard skin. Dead skin. Scar tissue. She applied another dab of the unguent to the ball of her foot. "Oh, I began watching the medicine man. His cures seemed to work for the most part. Ye must understand that those who traffic with the supernatural for evil purposes are witches. Evil beings who work their spells through things like the snake and the coyote, clouds and lightning. The Apache have a superstitious dread of a witch."

"And they thought you were a witch?"

"I never let on either way. The shaman taught me the art of healing after I helped him when he was in a bad way. But I also took care to fast and keep lonely night vigils and act as though I could interpret omens. A precaution, mind ye."

"What did you do for the shaman?"

Now she grinned. "Most Apache medicine men believe special virtue resides in their hair. They take care that no one should touch it. When a warrior in a raiding band of renegades, Commancheros, tried to scalp Ramos, he thought he had lost his power. I told him about the Biblical Samson and convinced him that with new hair growth his power would return."

"There."

At the single word, she looked up at Halpern. He held the pad up for her to see. The fire's smoldering embers glowed beneath the portrait of a woman she did not recognize. His hazel-green eyes watched her steadily. "Well?"

The woman in the pastel portrait was neither youthful nor particularly pretty. Dirt smudged her cheeks like a whore's rouge. Her hair was lackluster and looked as if it could use a good washing. All this against the background of the squalid trappings of her attire.

The long, dark eyes, framed by eyebrows shaped like hummingbird wings, glinted with unmistakable anger. How he had managed to capture her inner rage with mere colors and lines was remarkable.

The woman in the portrait, though, wasn't remarkable.

Yet in the tilt of the square chin there was a certain strength. The broad forehead suggested an intelligence the wild image rebuked, and in the direct gaze and the set of the wide mouth could be found a certain integrity. The overall tone was one of innate dignity.

She had seen a jaguar once, prowling the perimeters of the family hacienda. She had been picking blackberries. Both she and the jaguar had frozen and stared at one another, waiting. Then the jaguar had gone on its way.

The portrait Mattie stared at now could be a human rendition of that jaguar. "That's me?"

Gordon Halpern's gold earring glinted in the firelight. "That's what I see."

She corked her jar. "Ye do have a measure of talent, Mr. Halpern."

He might have chuckled. She wasn't sure. After putting away pad and pastels, he rose and swirled his jacket about his shoulders with the grace of a matador. "I'll relieve the reverend of his watch."

She watched the man use his cane to scale the boulders with the agility of a goat herder with his staff. She thought of Halpern's deadly fists. That they could deftly wield a fragile paint brush was unimaginable.

When he was out of sight, she stepped around the fire to his supply pack and drew out his sketch pad. She held it up to catch the firelight. What she saw in the portrait was not the young girl she remembered and still thought she was in her mind's eye.

She had been a fool to hope she could escape unchanged. Tears trickled paths through the dust coating her cheeks. And for the first time in eleven years, Mattie cried.

4

Mattie, minus her riding jacket, was already stretched out in her bedroll when Bingham slithered down the boulders and approached the campfire. "You asleep, gal?" he asked.

"I'd like to be."

"What do you think about the gent up there?"

She raised on one elbow and stared at the bearded man. "Do ye even sleep in your hat?"

"He made more noise up there than a mescal-drunk Indian. Greenhorns like that could land us in more trouble than the three thousand dollars is worth."

"Give him time, Buckskin. He's smart." She knew that sobriquet irritated Bingham.

"Are you lusting after him, gal? Is your harlot's heart plotting how you can destroy his soul?"

At another time, she would have ignored him, rolled onto her stomach and gone to sleep. But the image of the woman in Halpern's sketch lent her insight. "Ye remember me as I was, don't ye, Bingham?"

He eyed her suspiciously. "What makes you ask that?"

"Ye remember me as a young, attractive woman. Ye sat at me parents' dinner table and drank our wine. Ye admired the Goyas and Mirós hung on our walls. Ye knew me mother, Lady Morgan, and knew that I was the granddaughter of a Highland earl."

"I don't remember anything from those days at Santo Tomás—and right after. Best you don't either. Memories can kill."

He was right. Memories killed self-esteem. Emotion. The ability to love. They could also heal, though. At least, that's what she wanted to believe.

She lay down again, her back to him, and propped her head on her saddle blanket. Her jacket she spread over her chest against the early morning cold that settled over the mountains even on summer nights.

"If that's true," she said as she stared off into the darkness, "then why return to Nantez's camp? Like ye said, three thousand dollars wouldn't be worth risking another scalping, would it?"

"That is true, gal. But a cache of gold nuggets is. Found it when I was fleeing Nantez's camp. A placer mine on the Yaqui River. Big enough to last several lifetimes."

So, she thought sleepily, Bingham was putting his own period on the end of a sentence. "Remember, me good man, that the mines men find are never so rich as the ones they lost."

Her lids grew heavy. Kaleidoscopic memories of her childhood in Scotland, revived by her conversation with Bingham, were woven into her deep sleep:

Of Hogamany, when her parents permitted her to toast in the new year with hot spiced claret, the cinnamon smell of plum pudding, the evergreen decorations.

Of high tea at six o'clock and crumpets dripping with great dollops of butter.

Of her father teaching her to use the mayfly for trout bait. "'Tis nae wee thing how ye cast, Mattie. Drag your line crosswise. So that 'tis like the way a mayfly flutters upstream just before their wings are dry and are unable to lift off the surface."

Of Wappinschaw, when games were held, of tossing the caber and curling and shinny.

The Apache women played a game like shinny, but that was the only way her life with the Apaches ever paralleled her old life in the Highlands of Scotland. Unless she counted the Apache male's white breechcloths that looked for all the world like kilts.

She realized that what she missed was not so much her family, but family memories. They gave color and warmth to her harsh, austere life.

She was finding out that memories were inaccurate, that they changed with vicissitudes and prejudices. A sorrowful thing when not even memories could be trusted.

When she would have drifted deeper into sleep, the image of Nantez loomed before her, as often happened, turning her dreams into nightmares: his broad head on his short, muscular neck; his thick coarse black hair with its few streaks of silver, smelling of smoke, sweat, and grease; his powerful torso and spindly legs.

The hands shaking her shoulders ripped a scream from her throat.

"Sssh!" a male voice warned.

Her eyes snapped open to see Halpern kneeling over her. "What is it?" she asked, sitting up.

"Bingham. He's gone, damn't!"

She brushed her tangled hair from her eyes and tried to blink the sleepiness from them as well. "He's probably just scouting—"

"Scouting—hell! That's not all. He took the pack mule and supplies."

"What?" She scrambled to her feet and almost tripped on her rolled saddle blanket.

By the light of the moon, she could see that his grim gaze was accusatory. After all, it had been she who had suggested hiring the Mormon preacher.

She felt like demanding why, since it was Halpern's watch, he had not noticed Bingham stealing out of camp. True, Halpern may have been unaccustomed to distinguishing the moving shadow of a branch from an animal, but surely he had heard something. She supposed she shouldn't have let herself sleep so deeply that she was oblivious.

She brushed past him to where only Pepper and Halpern's gelding were now tethered. She dropped to one knee and studied the ground. Apache could learn a lot from the manner in which a twig or branch of a tree had been broken, the way horse manure dropped in camp or along the trail, even the way in which three sticks had been placed.

She could tell little from the rocky ground. A few overturned stones told her that the preacher had been careless in covering his tracks. But then, he had little to fear from her.

From the looks of Halpern's thunderous expression, Bingham might have to fear either flying lead or a leading left if the Easterner caught up with him. "Now what?" he asked her.

"Now what? Why, 'tis up to ye. Ye can head back and keep your money. As for meself, I'm going on into Mexico."

Something in his eyes changed. The accusing gaze gave way to reluctant . . . well, maybe not admiration, but perhaps reluctant acknowledgment of her grit.

"The question is," she said, "are ye still bent on going?"

He turned back to the campfire, now nothing but a few glowing embers. "If I have to crawl on my knees like a penitent on pilgrimage, I'm going after my wife."

"Well, then, we'll need supplies. We've got enough with us to last maybe through tomorrow."

"We can replace them at the first Mexican village we come to."

Now was not the moment to tell him that the Mexicans liked Americans only a little more than they did Apaches, which was about as much as the Mexicans liked rattlesnakes. "Ye'd better get some rest. I'll stand guard."

The night was intensely sharp and the air chilly. She wrapped her arms about her knees as she perched atop a massive stone buttress overlooking the ravine, where gigantic, rough-barked cottonwoods grew. Behind her, oak and hackberry branches formed a canopy for her.

Night was Mattie's time. She had an affinity with the moon and the stars. From the rim, she listened to the sounds of nature. To the noise of rocks creaking and speaking aloud. The nocturnal serenade of the coyote awakened that wild part of her soul. Not wild in the sense of being out of control but more akin to living at one with nature, as she had with the Netdahe Apaches.

She missed dancing barefoot in the grass, the campfires with their billowing incense, the scent of burning piñon, the sound of the tom-toms and the crackling of resinous pine logs.

That freedom had become domesticated with her return to Fort Lowell's civilization. She had lost track of her wildness. She knew that when that happened to the Indian, when they became blanket Indians, they often died without even getting sick.

She was sorry to see the rose hue lighting the ridges to the east. She slip-slid down the boulder trail to the bottom of the ravine. Halpern was beginning to stir. With a minimum of motion, he coiled up his bedroll.

After finger-combing the leaves and twigs from her hair, she tugged on her sombrero and started packing her own gear.

"Do the wolves run in big packs?" he asked.

"T'wasn't the yip of wolves ye heard last night." She tossed her saddle blanket over her mount. "Coyotes.

Wolves do prowl the Sierra Madres, though. Sometimes, they'd come to the clearings near our wickiups. I'd wake up and see them dancing in the moonlight."

Over the back of his bay that he was saddling, he regarded her with bemusement. "Such a wild woman I have hired to guide me to Nantez."

She jerked her saddle's latigo and slapped down the stirrup leathers. "Look, Halpern, I don't have the foggiest notion of where Nantez is right now. He's always on the move. But his favorite stronghold is the area around the brink of the Big Canyon."

"The big canyon?"

"The Mexicans call it Barranca del Cobre. There's an abundance of water and wildlife. Jaguars, mountain lions, wolves, and grizzly bears. If ye can imagine the end of the earth, that's it." She swung up into the saddle. "While I'm not pleased as punch about riding into a Mexican town, I'd not like to strike out for Barranca del Cobre with the wee supplies we have left in our pack saddles. I think there may be a village, Frontera, not far from here, down on the desert floor."

"Think?" He mounted up. "What if—"

"Me knowledge of the area isn't the most reliable. I already told ye that." She nudged her horse onto the narrow path that dropped down between two steep limestone walls. Wisps of sunlight were already dispersing the night's chill.

"Maybe we can hire someone in this Frontera to—"

"To shoot us in the back when we're not looking," she said grimly. "Bingham was our best bet, or I wouldn't have dealt with him. Believe me."

"Bingham vanished," he reminded her, falling in step behind her. "Just as you said Nantez was capable of doing. You were going to tell me how he accomplished such a feat, remember?"

While talking didn't come easily for her—and especially to Halpern, who made her feel most uncomfortable—she decided it would make the hours in the saddle pass more quickly. "When Nantez is on the move, which is most of the time, he has his band travel in groups. He designates an assembly point for nightfall of the next day. If the camp is attacked, everyone scatters."

"So the scouts have a hard time tracking down Nantez and his people because of the many diverging trails?"

"Aye. Most of which disappear in the rocks anyway."

"But eventually, Nantez has to make camp again, doesn't he?"

The trail widened, and she made way for Halpern to ride up beside her. The pines and firs were giving way to oaks and willows dotting the shallow canyons that laced the foothills.

"True," she said. "But at a predetermined rendezvous point the next day, the women build an imitation camp. They erect several wickiups and small campfires. An old worn-out horse is tied to a tree to make it look as though the camp is occupied. Then the band moves on for several miles and establishes its real camp elsewhere. The cavalry scouts lie in wait all through the night ready to attack at daybreak—when their attack lands upon a fake camp!"

"Cunning," Halpern said. "Which makes me wonder if you are, also."

Her head swiveled toward him. "What?"

"Cunning." He arched a questioning brow. "Did you and the preacher set me up?"

"I don't know what you're talking about."

He pulled up ahead of her, blocking the path of her horse with his own mount. He leaned forward in the saddle, those powerful hands resting on the pommel comfortably. But she wasn't deceived. His hard-edged smile confirmed her wariness. "Did you think to relieve me of the entire three grand early on, Mattie?"

She cocked her head, trying to figure out what he was thinking. Then she knew. "I didn't take ye for a fool, Halpern—to bring the three grand with ye. Ye didn't do that, did ye?"

"No, but enough to keep the three of us in supplies—your suggestion, remember? Well, it's gone, too. Nearly two hundred dollars. I want it back."

She could feel the heat creeping up the back of her neck. "Ye want it back, do ye? Then go after Bingham. But make up your bloody mind. Do ye want the money or your wife back? Which is it?"

A vein in his temple began to throb.

Life with Nantez had taught her to watch for signs. Her gaze dropped to his hands. But they didn't ball up into mighty fists.

Something that had happened in his life must have taught him to watch for signs, as well. His eyes, flecked with gold in the sunlight, studied her face. What was he looking for?

At last, he grasped the reins. "I've got enough tucked away on me to replace the essentials. After that—well, I hope you can pull a rabbit out of a hat."

Right now, she'd settle for pulling a bucketful of water from a well. The morning was growing hotter as the sun climbed the sky's blue dome.

They stopped in the foothills to shed their jackets. Beyond stretched an ocean of desert with only olive-green tufts to break the white landscape. Farther to the south rose the jagged, granite walls of the formidable Sierra Madres. From her viewpoint, the Mexican mountain range looked like an enormous, crenelated castle.

Since their confrontation over the missing money earlier in the day, neither of them bothered to speak. There was nothing to say.

Actually, that wasn't true. She wanted to know more about him. He might be a greenhorn as Bingham claimed, but this man also seemed fearless. She couldn't help but admire his sterling endeavor to save his wife. "Ye've been married to your wife a long time?" she asked.

"Seven years."

"Any children?"

"No."

"You're as parsimonious as a Scotsman with your words, ye are."

"What is it you want to know exactly?"

"I want to know about this woman who commands such devotion from ye."

"She believed in my work, my painting, when I wasn't sure I believed in them myself. She led me to myself. She was a pathway for my lost soul."

"Oh." There was nothing subtle about the man. Mattie wished she hadn't asked. Comparisons with a virginal goddess, for all consideration, could only make her feel less than worthy.

She shrugged off further curiosity and conserved her energy for the grueling pace required if they were to reach Frontera by sunset. She knew it was to the southeast, but wasn't certain how far. Or exactly where.

She must be crazy, a female Don Quixote, to charge off into Mexico with as little information and resources as she had.

But, then, what else could she have done? To let Albert go back to Nantez meant giving up hope of something better for her child. Even if she were wrong—that she could provide that hope of something better—she loved her wee one like her own life.

She had carried her son beneath her heart and suckled him at her breast. No, she couldn't give up on him. Not now. Later, when he matured into his manhood . . . then, if he still wanted to return to the Indian way of life, he could.

But, first, she had to find him and bring him back to her world. Did she even have a world anymore? A world that she fit into?

The day seemed interminable. A bouncing tumbleweed was the only movement on the horizon. The monotonous rhythm of the horse hooves crunching into the sand was the only sound. Sweat trickled down Mattie's ribcage and dampened the shirtwaist under her armpits. The air was so hot and still that her mouth felt like cotton.

They had ridden two days without seeing another human being. The entire area had been ravaged by Apaches over the years. Few settlers were either courageous or foolhardy enough to live outside the protection of a community. The few split-shake cabins and log corrals she saw were obviously abandoned.

The mauve-hued mountains seemed to retreat capriciously from her, but, at last, the terra-cotta belfry of Frontera's Jesuit mission came into view. Its sun-bleached stone arches were hung with drooping vines. Further on, wrought-iron balconies were festooned with flowers. The dusty little one-street village possessed a raw charm that Tucson lacked.

A fork of the Bavispe River, flowing beneath the pueblo's foundations, attributed to the town being established in the middle of the desert. A trickle of the underground river ran into the plaza's fountain.

Pistoleers on horseback shared the narrow street that blocked off the plaza with a wood-laden ox cart, a string of pack burros, and dusty-faced miners from nearby mines that had once financed the Spanish armada.

From arched doorways Mexican women in long cotton skirts and blazing kerchiefs hawked pottery and baskets and *nopalitos.*

Mattie had sworn if she ever reached civilization, she would never eat cactus again.

Every corner and niche of the pale, rose-colored adobe houses and buildings contained talismans: a poker-faced wooden mask, a rough-hewn cross, a wreath of thorns, a statue stained with purple berry juice, representing the blood of Christ.

As she and Halpern trotted their horses around the central square, with its three mountain madronas that sagged sadly, the belfry's big, black-iron bell began to toll for evening mass. That meant the *tiendas* and *mercado* would be closed.

Brown water beckoned her thirsty pony to quaff noisily from a nearby tin horse trough. She swallowed back her own thirst and had to restrain herself from dropping down before it to douse her heat-reddened face.

Other than the mission, a cantina with batwing doors turned out to be the only public establishment open. The knife at her own thigh and the Marlin slung across her back vastly reassured her.

When she dismounted, her legs felt wobbly from her having sat in the saddle so long. She was more accustomed to walking long distances than riding for lengthy hours uninterrupted.

Halpern's hand at her elbow steadied her. It had been so long since she had been touched by a man, that she flinched at the chivalrous gesture.

His eyes turned as dark as his mustache. "I wasn't going to ravish you."

"That's a dirty thing to say."

He had the gallantry to look contrite.

She sidestepped him and headed for the cantina. Inside, her eyes had to adjust to the smoke-hazed room. Kerosene and candlelight showed brown bottles of pulque lined up like infantry soldiers on a mahogany bar. Vaqueros and campesinos with machetes roped to their waists hunched over the bar.

At the sound of the flapping slatted doors, the

shifty-eyed lot turned to stare at her. One face reminded her of a knife artiste who looked as if he would be delighted to carve her into an objet d'art.

She stepped back onto Halpern's boot, but it was too late for retreat. She looked up into his face, flashed him a smile and took his arm in hers. "A grand place, isn't it, husband, luv? Can ye see about getting us a room for the night? I simply must sit and rest."

He looked too astonished to tell her no. She watched him approach the mustachioed hombre at the end of the bar, then she sought out the nearest table. If possible, her legs felt even wobblier than they had upon dismounting.

At the bar, the third Mexican from the left was still watching her. He wore the pajamalike clothing of the common campesino. Strapped to his tooled-leather belt was that all-too-familiar pearl-handled knife.

Días muire, but she was fortunate her sombrero shielded her face!

His face . . . well, it wasn't one she would forget: it was weathered, with a hawk nose, fierce eyes, and sideburns that were as wild and bushy as desert chaparral.

Halpern came to her table, two bottles in one hand, cane jauntily carried in the other. In a lowered voice, he demanded, "All right, what's going on, Mattie?"

"The man at the bar with the beastly sideburns. I know him," she whispered.

"Yes?"

She half-turned away, so that she was mainly facing Halpern. In the cantina's murky candlelight, his earring gleamed like gold among coal. "He's Kiko O'Neil. Half-Mexican, half-Irish. He works both sides of the fence. Sells stolen Mexican and American weapons to the Apaches, and Apache scalps to the Mexicans, who pay a bounty for the grizzly souvenirs."

Halpern took a sip of the pulque, made a face at the pungent taste, and said, "Go on."

"I've seen O'Neil half a dozen times in Nantez's camp. And once more—here in Frontera. When Albert and I were fleeing Nantez, we stumbled into the *carnicería.*" She had tried hard to tell its butcher that she had been a captive of Nantez, but the words wouldn't come. She had forgotten English! Instead, the Gaelic words of her childhood had stuttered from her sun-blistered lips.

Not understanding her, and noticing Albert's obvious Indian features, the man behind the bar had thought her to be Indian and had summoned O'Neil to interpret.

"O'Neil recognized me. He told the local butcher he would take me and Albert over to the mission and the padre. I knew that Albert and I wouldna live to see the baptismal font much less the padre."

Taking Albert's hand, she had tried to run, but O'Neil had been quicker. He had yanked her back beside him and the butcher. Albert, only five at the time, had looked up in bewilderment at O'Neil, who was bragging about the latest string of scalps he had taken.

She knew they had belonged to a peaceful band of Warm Springs Apaches who had taken refuge in the Sierra Madres, rather than submit to being confined

at the desolate San Carlos reservation northeast of
Tucson.

"What happened?" Halpern asked, interrupting her
memories.

She shrugged and took a deep swig from her bottle. "I was desperate. I grabbed the butcher's big knife
from the chopping table. In that next instant, O'Neil
twisted to one side. The knife missed his bowels.
Embedded itself instead between two of his lower
ribs. Once again, Albert and I were on the run."

Thoughtfully, Halpern stroked his mustache where
it bridged the indentation of his lip. "The room has
cost us just about all that I—"

"I'm sorry. I didn't know what—"

"Nothing we can do about it now. Except make
use of the room. We both need the rest. By tomorrow morning, maybe our trader-in-humanity won't
be around. You go on up. Room Three. I'll get the
saddlebags."

She nodded and went to climb a narrow staircase,
which creaked with each step. The hallway, lit by a
single candle ensconced in tin, looked as seedy as
those she had heard about over in Tucson's Gay
Alley. Old newspaper peeled from the walls, revealing chipped plaster and mud brick beneath. The
stale smell of urine drifted from the corner.

Apache wickiups were more appealing. But what
waited downstairs wasn't.

She opened the door to Room Three. On a rustic
pine washstand sat a chipped porcelain commode,
along with an oil lamp. Its flame cast a yellow light
on the already dingy walls.

Then she noticed the bed. It had no sheets, leaving its mattress ticking exposed.

She felt herself go hot. Her stomach knotted. Her pulse pounded in her ears. She swallowed back painful memories. She was no longer a captive. She could leave at any time—and she would!

She swung around and collided with a man. Her gasp was nearly as loud as a scream. Blindly, her fist lashed out at him. Her sombrero tumbled off.

He dropped the saddle bags and caught her against him. "Mattie, it's me! Gordon!"

She tried to slow down her galloping breath. "I canna! I canna sleep there . . . with you!"

His gaze darted to the bed and then returned to her. His hazel eyes glowed softly, like the aurora borealis on a clear night in the Highlands. "You don't have to, Mattie. I'll take the floor."

She drew away, saying, "No, I'm meself now. Just keep to your side of the bed."

"My stomach is growling," he said, closing the door behind them. "At this moment, even canned peaches sound appetizing."

Her stomach still churned, but food was not a priority. She collected her saddle bag and sombrero and dropped them in a mound near the bed. She was so tired she could not stand. The mattress sagged with her.

He set his saddlebags down, then arranged his black hat and cane carefully atop. She watched him go to the washstand, pour water from the ewer, and begin to wash the grime from his face.

"An exercise in futility," she said. "The dust even

blows through the cracks in the boards. You'll wake up tomorrow morning, dust-coated."

"An exercise in the discipline of civilized souls."

His fastidiousness annoyed her.

"Besides, gathering dust has its own corrupt smell." He sat down on the opposite side of the bed.

She watched him forage around in his saddlebags for a can and fork. With his back against the wall, he peeled off the can's tin top and began to eat.

Feeling safer now, she took her medicine pouch from her saddlebags and extracted her jar of glycerin and rose water. She could feel his eyes on her as she removed her moccasins. The tinny tinkle of their decorative strips was the only sound in the small room. Sharing the supportive wall with him, she began massaging the precious ointment into her left sole.

"You're not hungry?" he asked.

She shook her head. "No." Leaning forward, she went to work on her other foot. Her eyes closed. Her sigh was almost a purr.

"It must have been awful," he said, placing the empty can on the washstand. "What you went through."

Finished, she dropped the jar back into its leather pouch and dug out the tin of papers and the small bag of Mexican tobacco.

"You're curious," she said, holding a thin rice paper between her fingers. "Like all the rest of the men." She shook out a plug of the tobacco and licked the rolled paper. "Well, I'll tell ye, now. A man doesn't begin to know what that kind of forced submission does to the spirit."

He reached for his saddlebags and drew out another bottle of pulque, which he must have purchased downstairs. "Then tell me what it does to the spirit."

She struck the sulfur match and held it to her rolled cigarette. "The spirit leaves the body. Stays away. So that the body is empty. Empty body, empty mind."

He took a deep draught. "I often wonder if that was how Diana felt."

She wasn't certain she understood him. "Ye mean what she's feeling now—as Nantez's captive?"

"No." He tilted the bottle again. "I mean what she felt—as my wife."

A pencil-thin column of blue smoke eddied from her parted lips. She looked over at his profile. It seemed as menacing as Nantez's. "Did ye be beating her, Halpern? Did ye rape her, now?"

His laugh was short, harsh. "No. The only beatings I gave were in the ring." He finished off the bottle. "Even that I found . . . distasteful. When I left an opponent comatose, I swore off boxing forever."

"I heard ye killed him."

"Killed—?" He looked at her with a puzzled expression furrowing his dark brows. "You're talking about the match on the Rio Grande? How do you think I raised the money to finance this expedition? Though, God knows, I certainly didn't mean to kill Jack Johnson. I only wanted to win the prize money and get back Diana as quickly as possible. I swore then I'd never fight again."

"Your wife is very fortunate," Mattie said. *If only she had been loved like that.*

"Diana, fortunate? She didn't think so. Once she had subdued the beast, she was no longer interested."

She heard the bitterness in his voice. "Interested in—?" She couldn't bring herself to complete the sentence.

"In me. Period. In my touch. Hell, even in my thoughts." The pulque was casting its spell on him. "I was the beast that the coal mines had belched forth. She had taken me to her very proper home and cleaned me up. And then she found me disgusting."

From below came the plunking of guitar strings. She dropped her cigarette stub into the bottle Halpern still held, making a quick hissing sound. "Would ye mind dousing the light?"

He tossed the bottle beside his saddlebags and gun holster. "My regrets to you, Mattie, but I like a light left burning at night."

Trying to figure out what was going on in his mind, she peered at him from beneath her lashes. He couldn't possibly be afraid of the dark, so why the light? Unless he was expecting company. O'Neil perhaps?

"But I will lower the lamp wick," he said.

For a moment its bright light cast a radiant glow on his face. From her angle, she got a glimpse of what he might have looked like without his battle scars. A Romanesque profile with sternly chiseled features. He must have been extraordinarily handsome.

Then the light shrank to a pinpoint. She turned over on her side. From the shifting of the mattress, she could tell that he had done likewise. The guitar was joined by a mournful trumpet.

She couldn't sleep. Judging by his restive breathing, he couldn't either. "Do ye still love her?" she asked softly.

He didn't reply, and she thought maybe she had been wrong about him being awake. The guitar abandoned its efforts. The trumpet continued its serenade.

Then, he said, "I don't know. Whatever I felt for her nine years ago . . ." The bed shifted, and she knew he had turned on his side, facing her back now. "An illusion? I'm not sure."

"And yet ye went into the ring again to raise money to rescue her."

"I suppose I still love her. She's a woman that consumes a man like the fire in the pulque here."

There was such an emptiness in his voice. She knew that feeling. And knew that no words, no matter how well intentioned, assuaged a pain that could literally crack the heart. "With luck, we'll rescue your wife."

"Have you ever been married?"

"Aye. For six months."

Mattie thought about Reggie. Before they were married, he looked upon her as something mystical, sensuous, desirable. "Ye are my magic," he would tell her. Then afterwards, complacency and familiarity and the distortion of pregnancy made her ordinary to him.

"He . . . died?"

"Reggie ran off and left me and my parents to face Nantez and his warriors. The raid had been cyclonic in its swiftness and destruction."

Her voice, she realized, sounded as hollow as

Halpern's had. "Later, maybe a year later, I learned Reggie was, indeed, dead. A Mexican woman from Madera had been sold to Nantez by a band of Chiricahuas. She told me Reggie had taken refuge in her husband's barn. Reggie had been wounded—an arrow in the thigh or something. Anyway, while he was recuperating at their *rancho,* the Chiricahuas attacked and murdered her husband. And Reggie."

Halpern touched her shoulder. "No wonder . . ." That was all he said, then his hand was withdrawn.

She was surprised she missed its comforting touch. When much later, in the deep of night, his arm encircled her waist and gathered her against him, she was even more surprised. Surprised at herself, that she did not resist. That she did not flinch. That her body yielded and melded itself against the cradle created by his body.

5

Mattie McAlister had a quicksilver tongue and Scottish brogue that delighted the ear. Her face intrigued the artist in Gordon: features that announced a strong-willed and seasoned individual. It wasn't even an attractive face, but nevertheless, it would weather the years better than the run-of-the-mill pretty ones.

Her wide mouth, with its asymmetrical upper lip, indicated both a whimsical and a passionate nature. The way she didn't turn her head toward you but rather let her eyes seek you out said something else about her nature. A confidence in her own self. Yet a certain wariness, too.

Yes, she was without a doubt an interesting person. Oddly proud. A wild creature.

Initially, Gordon had thought her only a little

above the savages with whom she had lived for so many years. A heathen, lacking in the rudiments of social graces. Now, he was figuring out that it wasn't that she was lacking in the civilities, merely that she chose not to utilize them.

Yes, she was definitely an interesting and quaint little character, he thought, recalling how during the night his hand had accidentally brushed the knife strapped to her thigh beneath her skirt.

Thinking about that knife reminded him of the finger bone she was said to carry in her leather pouch. He'd wager his best work, *Coal Miner's Kid,* that that finger bone didn't belong to a gambler who cheated her or a gent who had gotten too familiar. Nope, if that finger bone didn't belong to Nantez, he'd ride a Pittsburgh trolley buck naked. That is, if the finger existed at all.

He continued to hold the woman now, her back against his chest, even though the sun had already crested the Sierra Madres a good thirty minutes ago. He could say he held her because the bed sagged so badly that the two of them had perforce rolled together.

But there were other, more compelling, reasons why he held her. Even that tiny pinpoint of lamplight was not enough, would never be enough. So he held her as a talisman against the dread of darkness. Do we see our mates as talismans against our fears, he wondered.

And held her even though he continued to find her uncouth. Well, refinement wasn't everything. Or was it? In his soul of souls he knew he was repulsed by her because she represented to him all that he had been, and there was in the dark spot of his soul a fear that he could become that again.

It had been so damn long since he held a woman, much less Diana. There had always been only Diana for him. From the moment he had first seen her.

She and her mother had been standing before his portrait of an urchin whose face was covered with coal-mine soot. Diana's expression had been one of bemusement, her mother's one of critical study.

It had been a gallery show. Pittsburgh's Brighton Gallery had been highlighting him as an up-and-coming artist, as well as pushing an established artist who hadn't sold recently and a moneymaking artist who in the past had withheld some of his paintings. The theme was Pennsylvania People.

He had been as nervous as a miner whose candle has gone out. At last, Diana's mother had nodded her head and pronounced the portrait, "Excellent. The artist shows great promise."

Thus the tough kid from West Virginia had found a patron in the arts society of Mrs. Harold Ashley. And eventually, almost two years later, a wife in her lovely and refined daughter, Diana.

In his arms, Mattie stirred. Strands of her snarled hair enmeshed itself with the coal-black hair matting his chest and forearms. "What time . . . *Días muire*! I overslept!"

She half-turned to disengage herself from his embrace. The startled look in her eyes told him she had been unaware of where she was. "I . . . uh . . ."

"You slept deeply. You needed it."

At that moment, she reminded him of the urchin he had painted. A wild, rebellious, and lost child. Determination looked out of eyes that mirrored an old soul, in utter contrast to the childlike body that was slight but all lean muscle. Those eyes were deep enough to absorb a man.

Briskly, she swung her legs over the side of the mattress. Her little feet dangled above the floor. "And you didn't?" She tugged down her skirt and tunneled her fingers through her matted hair. "From the shadows beneath your eyes, ye look rather spent yourself."

He knew she was talking to cover her uneasiness. He rose, reached for his saddlebags. "I sleep in short stretches."

He fingered his stubbled jaw and determined he could forego shaving for another day. Funny, how the isolation of the West made you disregard some things that civilization deemed important.

Still, a bath would be most welcome. After the years of emerging from the mines, his skin black from the coal dust, he was almost fanatical about bathing.

"Do ye mind. . . ."

He turned back to her. "Yes?"

Her look was one of discomfort, even embarrassment. She nodded toward the chipped porcelain commode.

Enlightenment dawned on him. He had figured that once they were underway again, he would mosey off somewhere into the brush and do his business. "Uhh, yes. I'll take our gear on down."

Relief and gratitude eased the ever-present lines tensing her thin face.

He collected his and Mattie's effects and started down the staircase. He guessed she was as glad as he to put the shabby little room and the night of enforced intimacy behind them.

At the bottom of the stairs, someone was waiting, watching. It was too early for most people in a *cantina* to be up and stirring. In the semi-dark of early morning light pouring past the slatted batwing shutters, the man was silhouetted, making it difficult to identify him. But the lanky build and the brush of sideburns told Gordon that this was O'Neil, Mattie's Trader-in-Humanity.

Gordon continued down the staircase with the easy grace of a pugilist. The demanding movements peculiar to a fighter had been second nature for him as a kid growing up in the poverty and soot of a coal-mining town.

Sheer determination to rise above his station in life had brought him from the coal mines of West Virginia to the boxing arenas of Pittsburgh, where he had discovered he had a flair for painting, especially portraits. Once abreast of O'Neil, he nodded. "'Morning."

O'Neil nodded but said nothing.

Gordon kept on walking toward the doorway, but behind him he heard the stairs creak as O'Neil started up them. In midstep Gordon pivoted and dropped his gear.

The bounty hunter must have heard him coming. O'Neil spun back toward him and went for the knife sheathed at his waist. The man was damnably quick.

But so was Gordon. In boxer fashion, he ducked

to one side and swung his cane like a claymore. The cane snapped. The knife clattered on the stairs.

O'Neil's eyes widened. He drew back his fist, but Gordon popped up under the man's striking arm. The right hook impacted O'Neil's jaw with a jarring thunk. O'Neil staggered back, lost his footing on the stair. He swung out at Gordon, but Gordon dodged, taking the punch on the side of his head. O'Neil's next one didn't even connect.

Gordon didn't wait. A winning fighter displays neither indecisiveness nor mercy. He pummeled his opponent's face. Right. Left. Right again. Blood spurted. The face sank lower. The battering was distorting what once had been distinctly human characteristics. Eye sockets, lips and cheekbones blurred into a lumpy mass.

"Halpern! Halpern! Halpern, for God's sake, leave off!"

Only then did he realize that someone—Mattie— was tugging at his shoulder, trying to pull him away from O'Neil.

"Leave off, Halpern!" she was saying. "We've got to get out of here! Now!"

She might have said more, but he didn't hear her if she did. He was wheezing, and his ears were ringing. He shook his head, trying to restore completely his peripheral awareness. He had that survival knack for focusing solely on vanquishing the foe. In an uncivilized place like Mexico where no rules governed the sport of bloodshed, that knack could be dangerous for both combatants.

He straightened, staggered, regained his balance

and his breath. Mattie took his hand. He let her tug him down the stairs, where they collected the gear he had dropped.

Like a puppy, he followed her out to the corral out back of the *cantina*. A boy in *huaraches* strad-dled one of the corral's mesquite-wood bars. "Your horses, señor, they're still here. I watch them good."

Gordon dug a bleeding hand into his shirt pocket and withdrew the last of his coins to flip into the boy's palm.

Now a mere fistful of currency stood between him and poverty. And they had yet to replenish the stolen supplies. Frontera was certainly not the place to do it. Not now.

She began saddling their mounts. "Just grand, Halpern. Ye acted like a wild man back there. Now we have to watch our backs for not only Apaches and Mexicans but for O'Neil as well."

"You're right." He took his gelding's reins and led the bay through the gate that the grinning boy held open. "I should have killed the man." With a wince, he mounted. "Or maybe I should have just let him kill you."

"Then ye wouldn't find Nantez," she said, mount-ing. One of those superior smiles tipped her lips. "Ready to go after him?"

Hell, he could barely sit straight in the saddle. But he didn't relish lingering in Frontera. "After Nantez? No. We're going after Bingham, my two hundred, and our supplies. Without them, we won't have a Chinaman's chance of continuing the expedition."

Her laugh was just short of disgust. "Finding Nantez will be easier than finding Bingham. I know Nantez. He's intelligent and practical. Bingham's unhinged. As unpredictable as a jenny."

"A what?"

"A jenny—a female donkey."

"I grant you, female anythings are unpredictable. Furthermore, men are predictable about certain things." He stared out into the scattering of tall cacti that were lifting their fluted arms and headless necks to an already white-hot sky. "Like money, for instance. Bingham obviously could be bought. He agreed to help us find Nantez, didn't he?"

She nodded. "I see what you're getting at."

"He has $750 now. As well as my two hundred. The question is, where would he go next? Back to the States? Or would he—"

Beneath her sombrero, her eyes lit up. "Halpern, Bingham's headed for a spot where he found placer gold when fleeing Nantez's camp years before! That money would serve as his grub stake."

He reined in on his mount. "Do you have any idea where that mine could be?"

The light in her eyes as quickly faded. "No."

"Think about it. At the time Bingham ran away, do you remember any prominent land marks?"

"Well . . ." Her eyes took on a faraway gaze, and he knew she was going back in time. The lines around her mouth seemed to deepen with the tension of the memory. "It seems it was before we reached the Big Canyon. The Mexican *federalistas* were pursuing Nantez, and we climbed down inside it and waded across its river in order to lose them. The descent was terrifying—slipping and sliding down rubble and pebbles."

"So, that means that this placer gold would have to be on a bed of a river or creek between Barranca del Cobre and the border. In a desert, there can't be too many rivers."

It turned out Gordon was wrong about this. When he and Mattie paused for rest and food at an arroyo whose bank offered shade, they dug out a tattered map of Mexico. It had been drawn by scouts for the Mormon colonists thirty years before and was not all that reliable.

He stared at the dozens of lines dotting the Mexican state of Chihuahua, indicating dry creek beds that could become raging torrents in the rainy season.

When they finished with the last of the hardtack and sausage, Mattie settled back against the gravelly bank and deftly rolled one of those God-awful Mexican cigarettes. Her deer-hide skirt was hitched up above one of her high-top moccasins, revealing a shapely knee.

She tilted her head and let out a helix of slow-swirling smoke. "Sonofabitch, here we be traipsing after not one but three missing persons. We must be sunstruck!"

He watched her fingertips wipe a trickle of perspiration from the hollow created at her throat by her collar bones. She was totally unaware how sensual the action was.

That he could find this wretched female sensual, even for a mere moment, amazed him. Her stubby fingernails had half-moons of dirt beneath them.

Had she no dignity, no sense of propriety? He had hoped to leave women like her behind, back in the childhood years of blight.

He forced his gaze back to the map. The only thing more wrinkled was the surrounding landscape. "The way I figure it, our best possibility for finding Bingham and his cache is along the San Miguel River. One end empties near the Barranca del Cobre, the other runs north through the Sierras to the border and Apache Pass."

"What does she look like?"

Gordon glanced up. Head canted, she was peering at him over the glowing tip of her cigarette. The sight of her smoking was incongruous with her childlike frame.

He put away the map and flexed his hands. They hurt. He was getting too old to be throwing punches. "Diana? Golden like a Greek goddess. Gold skin. Gold hair. Gold eyes. So much light, it almost hurt the eyes to behold her."

Mattie stubbed out her cigarette in the sand. "Gold always did blind the beholder." She rose and tugged the rumpled skirt down over her narrow hips. "Better be putting some miles behind us, Halpern."

He didn't know whether to be angry or amazed. Wisely, he kept silent. He had little recollection of his mother, so his childhood experience with women was limited. Perhaps, because of this, he found the species fascinating. And he found Mattie McAlister especially fascinating. She was so maternal. When discussing Albert, her features took on a protective, aquiline fierceness. Yes, she was most definitely a fascinating creature.

As the day wore on, his fascination with her was in inverse proportion to the climbing heat. Ahead, on the western horizon, gray-brown humps and mesas of the Sierra foothills promised shelter and shade.

Midafternoon brought the distinct shapes of trees. Only scruffy mesquites and scraggly cottonwoods in shallow canyons. Heavier timber in the higher ridges required several more miles of riding and several more hours.

A sideways glance toward the northwest told him that he wasn't likely to make it to the security afforded by the mountains. A stew of brown clouds bubbled and boiled on the horizon. It hadn't been there a quarter of an hour before. "Mattie—"

"I know. I've been watching it for some minutes now. A dust storm. 'Tis moving fast and furious." She pulled her red neck scarf up over her nose. She looked like a bandit, by God, if ever he saw one.

She was the kind that could steal one's certainty about truth and alter one's philosophy of life by twisting it into an irreverent yarn. She confused him, by making bad seem good. And all the while laughing at the pomposity of manners. A bizarre character, she was.

She pointed beyond the curve of a hill toward a rocky wall of a rising cliff some distance ahead. A darker area appeared to be a hollow in the limestone. "There," she shouted through the flannel material. "Shelter!"

Before he could knee his horse, she spurred hers. The Indian pony broke into a trot. His bay balked, then followed suit.

Incredibly, within the space of a couple of minutes, a blast of wind and corrosive dust buffeted him. Mattie's sombrero was whipped off, as was his own hat. Only the tie strings kept their hats from accompanying the tumble weed and other brush sweeping past them. The wind's sudden roar obliterated all other sound.

Immediate darkness the color of sandstone shrouded everything. Gordon couldn't see more than a few feet in front of him and had to trust that his mount would instinctively follow Mattie's.

For a harrowing moment, he thought he had lost her. Then she materialized out of the biting alkaline haze. Her hand grabbed his reins and tugged his horse forward. In the lee of the cliff, the force of the wind dropped sharply. After he rubbed the grit from his eyes, he could see why—he was gazing into the cyclonic eye of a mine shaft!

"Get down!" Mattie yelled.

The dust storm might just as well have been an Arctic storm. He sat frozen in the saddle. Nothing short of the Second Coming was persuasive enough to beckon him enter that black portal.

Mattie stared up at him, uncomprehendingly. "Halpern, ye got to get out of the storm!"

She jerked hard on his arm, and like a block of ice he fell from the saddle. When she would have nudged him forward into that gaping hole, terror welled in his chest. His lungs felt like collapsed bellows.

His terror must have communicated itself. At once, she stopped pushing and slipped around in front of him. "What is it, me love?" Her voice was still loud in order to make herself heard, but there was a cooing in its tone. Her rough hand caressed his cheek. "Come along with me. 'Tis a grand place to keep us safe. Like bairns in the womb. Come along, now. We'll not be going any farther than just inside the opening."

She lured him into the mine shaft entrance. He felt her hands on his shoulders, pressing him to sit. His back scraped against the rock wall. Sagging timbers coalesced in his vision. The sight should have made him bolt, but with her hand holding his, her shoulder buttressing his, he felt okay. An overturned wheelbarrow all but blocked his flight from the mine's black maw.

"Something ye said made me wonder," she said, her voice soft now, "if your fear came from working in the coal mines. 'Tis so, isn't it now?"

"Yes." Cool air wafted across his face, like the fingers of death.

"Well, now. We all have fears that cramp our spirit. Me, I fear fire. I keep an eye on the hearth even. Just to make sure the fire is banked afore I sleep."

He knew she was talking to take his mind off his surroundings. He tried to respond intelligently, but words were on short supply. "Your house ever catch fire?"

"No. Nothing so easily replaced."

Her little hand tightened in his. "Ye see, it happened six or seven months after Nantez took me captive. By then I had given birth to Alicia. Me daughter by Reggie. Nantez's band was on the move again. He had attacked the Mexican town of Galeana."

She paused, and he heard her rasp of breath.

"Mexican soldiers from Casas Grandes had tracked us down and attacked that portion of the band traveling with Nantez. Thirty-two warriors and a few women and children. He directed us to take cover in an *arroyo*. The men stood off the Mexicans while we women dug holes for the warriors in the dry little creek bed. Nantez and his men are good shots. They picked off the Mexican soldiers as fast as they appeared.

"Then the soldiers disappeared. Nantez suspected a ruse. After dark the Mexicans set fire to the grass, hoping to burn us out. We were surrounded by a prairie fire, the circle of it drawing closer."

"And?" he asked, caught up in her story.

"Alicia was crying." Her baby's cry had had that same low keening as the wind outside. "Nantez told me that if I didn't quiet her . . . he would choke her. I . . . I couldn't get her to stop crying. I was forced to watch him choke her. So that her squalling wouldn't give away our movements. We all crawled through the fire. Got away without being seen."

She was trembling. He released her hand and put his arm around her thin shoulders to draw her against him. Her head drooped against his chest. Her hair smelled of wood smoke and dust.

He didn't know how to comfort her, so he talked. As she had. "Just after my eleventh birthday, my mother abandoned me. Ran off with a Methodist minister. I was big for my age. I got work in the mines. High-grade ore, we mined. Three candles a day to keep the darkness at bay for ten hours.

"Day after day, year after year of darkness. It got to where only my sheer will forced me go down into the mines. The poverty, the soot, the dark depths of the mines became nightmares that I beat back by boxing.

"One day a dynamite cap went off in the tunnel I was working. Two other men and I were trapped. They died from their injuries before rescue came. Three days I lived with their bodies, their rotting bodies touching mine."

"I assume that at that point, ye had wee desire to pursue the underground profession?"

The light tone of her voice eased his panic. "I never was more sure. When I emerged, I kept going. All the way to Pittsburgh before a promoter saw me boxing and offered to stage a bout for me. In my off hours, when I wasn't training or fighting, I began a self-education program. Read all the classics at the local library, then—"

A muted neighing interrupted him. "Sonofabitch! Sonofabitch!"

He looked down at her. "What?"

She was already shooting out of his clasp and charging toward the mine entrance. "Pepper!"

"What?"

"Our horses!"

He caught up with her just outside the entrance. Driving dust got into Gordon's nostrils and inside his mouth and ears. Searing wind hurled him against her. "Are you crazy? You can't find them in this!"

She tried to pull away. He held her tight against him.

"Don't ye understand? Without horses—out here—how long do ye think we'd last afoot? Without water or food?"

He half-pushed, half-dragged, her back inside the rocky cavity. Grabbing her shoulders, he whirled her around to face him. "Listen to me, Mattie. Don't be so damned hardheaded. If anyone goes after the horses I do. I have an affinity for the darkness. I can feel my way around—I guess it's like a second sight. I just know."

Her compressed mouth didn't indicate a readiness to yield.

So, he added, "Besides, I'd rather go anywhere than back inside the mine."

The resistance seemed to leave her body, that small body. She was no taller than he had been at nine-years-old. "All right, Halpern. I give ye half an hour. Then I'm going out meself. After the horses, not yourself, ye understand?"

His laughter was short. "So, it's come to this. I'm not even a match for horseflesh."

He left then, before she could change her mind. With his neck scarf over his nose and his chin tucked against his chest, he leaned into the wind and started walking. It was foolish, because the two horses could have wandered off in any direction.

Still, he hadn't been lying to Mattie. Call it blind instinct, but he had learned to rely on another sense. That sixth sense that had no name.

He stumbled over something, a cholla cactus, but

caught his balance in time. The land rose and fell beneath his feet with gullies and hills. After a few minutes, his eyes began to detect and distinguish shapes. Trees that looked like scarecrows. Boulders that were blobs.

Sand abraded his skin and stung his eyes. The resulting tears formed tiny mud cakes on his face. Something moved across his field of vision. The horses?

No! Someone!

He shouted. The wind stole his voice. He staggered into the wind. Drew closer to the other person. Shouted again. The other turned, saw him, then began to run in the opposite direction. In that fraction of a moment, he got a glimpse of the ghostly figure's features: Indian. Unmistakably Indian and unmistakably a boy in western clothing.

"Wait!"

The kid charged ahead, into the shroud of sand.

A dozen thoughts darted through his mind. The kid might not be Albert. Even if he were, he obviously did not want to be found. To go after the kid meant losing track of the horses. Hell, it might mean getting lost himself.

He turned his steps back toward the familiarity of a rock-crusted ledge, rising out of sight in the dust. The wind pushed at his back, hurrying him.

Abruptly, he spun around, cursing his foolishness even as he trudged back into the unknown. There was one chance in a hundred of stumbling over the kid again. He had to have lost all sense of good judgment out here.

Despite the face handkerchief, he inhaled sand

through his mouth and nostrils. "Damn you, kid! If I catch your red hide, I'm . . ."

His words couldn't be distinguished from the growling, rasping wind, but yelling made him feel better. "You little shit, you haven't—"

His boot struck something. He went sprawling. Quick as lightning, the kid was atop him. A butcher knife, no less, pressed against his throat.

Surprise had been on the kid's side. Strength and experience were on Gordon's. He jackknifed to one side. The kid was thrown off.

They both scrambled to their feet. Dust swirled around them as they circled each other. Admittedly, the kid was agile. He glared at Gordon with what had to be centuries of accumulated hate.

"Give me the knife," Gordon ordered.

The kid lunged at him, swiped, and missed.

Gordon didn't. He chopped the kid's wrist with the side of his hand. The knife flew beyond his vision. The kid's face showed panic. This time he didn't give him a chance to bolt. He snared the kid around the waist and hauled him up against his side.

"Put—me—down!" Kicking, punching, squirming, howling. "—cos—Naat'-aani!" Indians words mixed with English.

Gordon couldn't help it, he started laughing. This infuriated the youngster even more. Gordon continued with his burden in the direction that he could only hope led to the area of the mine shaft.

Now, he wasn't so sure. All his declarations to Mattie about his affinity with the darkness had been vainglorious. The tussle with the kid . . . he had lost his sense of direction. Damnit, had he passed that depression in the rock before? Was he gradually climbing? Or, mayhaps, descending?

"Goddamnit!" he cried. The kid had bitten him.

Taking advantage of his loosened grip, the kid struggled free and took off at a Kentucky Derby gallop. *Let him go! Good riddance!* Gordon thought.

Yet, if Zwigenhut hadn't gone after him after he had lost that first fight, hadn't brought him back, hadn't encouraged him. . . .

He had been only a few years older than this kid. And someone *had* cared about him. Just not his mother. That scrap of humanity known as Mattie McAlister cared about her child. That was enough.

He took off at a lope, his long legs covering twice the distance as those of the kid's. Ahead, the boy was a blur. He tackled his quarry, smacked it hard against bedrock, heard the breath whoosh from the boy's chest.

Then he half-dragged, half-propelled the kid back in the direction of the mine shaft. At least, in the direction he hoped was the shaft. He grunted. "If I had your mother's knife, kid, I'd scalp you!"

He couldn't see anything by now. His world was reduced to an hourglass, and the sand was running through its waist faster than he could move. Where in the hell was the mine shaft?

Just when he was cursing the run of his luck, he collided with Mattie. "Oh my God, Halpern, I thought ye were a goner!" She tugged him inside the mine shaft, where there was no wind, no sand. It was a womb. "Sonofabitch, where have ye—"

He deposited the kid before her.

Her reaction surprised both Gordon and the boy, but probably not the species of humans known as mothers. She glared down at the seething mound of bones and flesh and black hair. The boy's longish hair, hanging over the collar of his fringed leather shirt, was matted with dust.

She jammed her fists on her hips. "Albert! Do ye realize that ye haven't done your sums and you're missing school to boot?"

The kid grinned up at her with genuine contriteness. New ragged-edged teeth made his smile look like a picket fence.

She dropped onto her knees, grabbed him against her breasts, and began rocking, crying, crooning.

Gordon stared down at the two. How had he gotten himself entrapped with this pair? He had wanted only to rescue Diana. He would do anything to get her back. The possibilities were looking dimmer by the moment. As dim as the sand-blasted sunlight.

Should he even stumble upon Nantez's camp, as he had stumbled upon the subchief's son, how could he even begin to hope to carry Diana away when seventy-five or more warriors stood ready to carve his heart from his chest?

And then an idea lit the darkness of his hopes. Before him, he had the answer. An exchange of one soul for another.

6

Mattie trudged along beneath the sun's broiling light. Behind her, Albert dragged his feet. Beside her, Halpern's long strides indicated his impatience.

Impatience could be a deadly thing in the desert. Ahead lay steep mountains, rugged canyons, cliffs, rough lava beds. In between, a burning, bleached desert. A goat skull they passed attested to the land's sun-struck fierceness.

The sandstorm had driven them farther from their quarries—Nantez, Diana, Bingham—and their mounts. The driving wind had obliterated any hoof tracks. Reason pointed to the refuge the mountains offered.

Thirst parched Mattie's throat. Blisters bubbled on her feet. Hunger rumbled her stomach. Occasional dizziness distorted her vision. Sweat and her body's salt had dried her calico shirt. She knew she smelled rank as a wet mongrel.

Her thoughts naturally turned to her present folly. As of yesterday afternoon, she had her son back. But she did not have, would not have, any recompense for pursuing Nantez and his captive, Diana Halpern. She, Gordon Halpern, and Albert were without mounts, food, and water. To continue would be to court death. Anyone with half a mind could see that she should turn around and return to Fort Lowell.

Yet she had Albert at her side precisely because of the very same man who was dependent upon her to get him to his wife. She felt obligated. She had a debt to pay.

She squared her shoulders. "Mister Halpern, I'd like to suggest we repair to yon cactus."

He looked down at her, as if the sun had indeed fried her brain. "What?"

"That agave. We'll find—"

"Shade? I doubt that, seriously. Cool water? I doubt that, too. And my stomach growls for something more than cactus pulp. A thick, juicy steak would be more to my liking. The kind served up in the American Restaurant at Philadelphia's '76 Centennial Exhibition. Now if you think you can—"

"Your palate will be satisfied, I assure ye," she interrupted him, directing her steps toward the agave. Actually, it was a scattering of the cacti. Hardly an oasis.

When they were within a dozen yards of the cacti, she signaled Albert and Gordon to wait. Wordlessly, she proceeded on, hoping that all the training of her life as an Apache squaw would at last bring something good, other than her bairn.

She scanned the area. The sand, the foothills crusted with sparse vegetation that clung to rocks like leaches, the shadows created by the agaves. There was nothing, nothing that moved. She hadn't expected any sign of life. Not yet, anyway.

Slowly, she went down on all fours, then flat onto her stomach. With movement as infinitesimal as a glacier, she glided forward like a serpent in Eden. Except in no stretch of imagination was the vast Chihuahua Desert a resemblance of Eden.

When tips of the agave shaded her fingers, she lay still. She could feel the sun sizzling a patch of her flesh above the top of her moccasin, where her skirt had hitched up midthigh. Sweat beaded from her right temple, slithered over her cheekbone, and fell onto the sand. The droplet evaporated at once.

Minutes stretched out endlessly. She could only hope that behind her Albert and Gordon mimicked her stillness and silence.

Then, her patience produced results! A salamander. How long it had been there, she didn't know. It was as if it had poked its head from beneath the sand. Or maybe, her sight finally accommodated itself to the illusive blending of her surroundings. The salamander's black eyes stared at her and she stared back at it, waiting.

Please, come closer, lizard.

The lizard was her totem. It was a symbol to the Indian of silence, wisdom and good fortune. The dreamer who basks in the light of the sun. The seeker of the shadow, who finds there the fears and hopes of the future. The lizard was teaching her to welcome life's darkness as well as its light.

Her patience was infinite. As was Albert's. Could Gordon sustain his own?

Then, one of the salamander's forelegs moved forward. Hesitated. The other moved. Quickly, all four flashed as it scrambled past perceived danger.

Mattie was quicker. Her hand shot out. The captured salamander wriggled wildly. Without conscious thought, she rendered up a traditional Indian blessing. "Thank you, Lizard, for sharing yourself with us, that both you and we may live on."

"Sonofabitch, Mother!" Albert said, coming forward.

"Albert, please."

His full lower lip thrust out. "You say—"

She cut him off. "When you're an adult you may say what you bloody well please." She turned to Gordon. "Would ye say a light repast is in order?"

He swallowed and looked at the salamander, then at her. Repugnance was reflected in that brutish face.

"You need to eat, Mr. Halpern. Or you won't get where you be wanting to go," she added as an ominous but truthful inducement.

His normally deep voice became a croak. "We eat it raw?"

"Oh, I should hope not. I have, mind ye. But I never got used to it. Albert, would ye mind starting a fire?"

"A fire?" Gordon glanced around at the treeless plain. "You're joking."

Her sullen son was already collecting the desert debris: slivers of mesquite and cottonwood along with tufts of dry beargrass washed down from the foothills, clumps of withered cacti, a scattering of seeds, a small pile of antelope droppings.

She set Gordon to lining a depression in the sand with small stones. Meanwhile, she took her knife and dispatched the salamander. Gordon watched, half-fascinated, half-repelled.

To her dismay, she had no matches left in her moccasin folds. Resorting to the primitive method, she knelt and, using her knife, fashioned a round, hard stick of wood.

"Let me, Mother."

She peered up into the face of a boy determined to be a man. Without a word, she ceded him the wood.

He twirled it between his palms. The rounded end bore into a cup-shaped hollow made in a flat, softer piece of wood Albert had collected. The trick was in cutting a little notch in the end of the round stick, so that the friction quickly generated heat to cause the softer piece to smolder.

Soon, little wood shavings glowed. He blew upon them, and they burst into a small flame. At that, he was ready to add a little heap of dry materials. He sat back on his haunches, pleased with himself.

Mattie was pleased for him. So little opportunity existed in the confines of the fort to prove himself a man in the way of his Indian forebears. He rose to his feet, his head coming no higher than her breasts, and actually smiled up at her. So long since she had seen that boyish smile.

When Gordon had hauled him back to the mine shaft, Albert had been afraid. Anyone else would have seen in the child's face features as impassive as an Olmec statue, but in the depths of his black eyes she had seen a fear that had beat at his throat like the small wings of a hummingbird. He had been almost joyful to be reunited with her, if the way his grubby little hand tightened in hers was any indication.

She had tried to explain to him why she was with Gordon Halpern. That he was financing the trip in order to recover his wife, that the woman was apparently with Albert's father, that Mattie herself had contracted to help so that she could look for him, that their horses had stampeded in the sandstorm. . . .

But Albert had heard only two words. *His father.* After that, he had been almost compliant. Almost. She doubted her son would ever be the perfectly biddable child.

Quickly, she skewered the lifeless salamander. While it roasted on a spit of sorts, she and Gordon and Albert sucked dry the juice of the agave stalks. The pulpy head of the mescal-agave was cooking slowly in the stone pit. She nodded at it and said, "The agave tastes sweet, like the heart of artichoke. And it's nutritious."

"Yeah," Gordon said. "And the salamander tastes like chicken, I bet."

She laughed and saw that her laughter took him

by surprise. Even her son, startled, glanced up at her. Solemnly, he wiped his sticky fingers on his calico shirt. "Tastes like shit."

"Albert!"

This time, Gordon was the one who laughed. "Now, if only we had a good red wine. A fine claret of Bordeaux . . . '69, I should say."

He was being facetious, but she responded quite seriously. "Oh, no. With the salamander, I would suggest a white wine. At the most a light- to medium-flavored red wine. I would prefer a white burgundy such as Le Montrachet or Corton Charlemagne."

Gordon narrowed his eyes. "Who are you? Really?"

She shrugged. "I am what ye see, what ye drew on your pad."

"That and more, I suspect."

She squatted before the salamander. Its juices dropped into the fire and sizzled. "I am the grand-daughter of a Highland earl." She sliced away a portion of the cooked salamander and passed it, knife-tip, to Gordon. "Sir Colin Campbell, Lord of Glenorchy, Earl of Badenoch, and Thane of Cawdor." Her mouth curled with her sarcasm. "Difficult to imagine, isn't it?"

For her, what was even more difficult to imagine was the home of her childhood. Had it all been a fantasy? A castle carved of rose-colored stone; its facade draped in ivy, looking like a lace mantilla.

Gordon removed the sliver of seared meat and bit into it. Mouth full, he asked, "Can't you return to Scotland? Aren't any of your family left back there?"

She passed a piece of the meat to Albert, who immediately popped it into his mouth. "Aye, the side of the family who supported the Hanovers in 1745. Me father's side supported the Jacobites and Bonnie Prince Charlie."

She tilted her head and eyed the man. "Take a look at me, Mr. Halpern." With the back of her sleeve she wiped a droplet of the salamander's fatty grease from her chin. "Do ye really think any of the Campbell clan would want to lay claim to me as a relative of theirs? Much less Albert here?" She motioned to her son, who was tearing at his meat like some prehistoric primate.

To Gordon's credit, he did not lie or try to flatter her. "The Old World aristocracy, eh?" He shook his head, and the sunlight glinted off his earring. "Too often we trade our souls to try and measure up to their yardstick of propriety."

She passed around the last of the meat, saying, "Albert is bright." She felt more than saw her son's attention shift from his food to her. "Me only hope is that he learns to adapt."

"The world's only hope," Halpern said, "are people like Albert, who can combine the best of his two worlds and discard the rest."

Still eating, Albert eyed Gordon. His disdain toward the Easterner had been obvious to her. Only now, she caught a glimpse of her son's reluctant willingness to view other aspects of the man.

"By me estimation, I think by nightfall we should reach the foothills of the Huachineras."

He flexed his scarred fingers. Powerful fingers. "I want to reach Bingham."

She grinned. "Ye want to box his ears?"

He gave her an amused glance. "Hell, no. I want to sketch. I want my pad and pastels back."

"And I want me jar of cream back. And Pepper." Her Indian pony was loyal and loving, and did not care if she smelled like gardenias or cow dung. Pepper asked nothing more from her than a gentle hand.

The sun was edging toward the western half of the sky. Mattie wanted nothing more than to sit where she was. Yet the longer they sat the less chance they had of catching up with either their mounts or Bingham or both.

She scooped sand onto the fire, then rose and stretched the kinks from her legs and arms. At that moment she happened to glance down. Gordon was staring at her with a fiery look in his eyes. It was as if he had just realized she was a woman.

At once, her outstretched arms dropped to her sides. She had forgotten she was a woman.

Just as quickly, Gordon came to his feet. "Let's get started then."

Albert, ever mindful of man and earth being brothers, restored the area as it had been before their presence had disturbed it.

Then they walked again, placing one foot in front of another. She noted that her moccasins were wearing thin. She also noted things that were not as obvious.

Where previously she had concentrated on survival, she now had the dangerous diversion of Gordon Halpern to contemplate. He was but a mere man. And a man who was worthless in terms of survival. A man who had abandoned a chance at finding the horses in order to rescue her son.

She cast him a sidewise glance. His profile looked as powerful as his hands. Was his temper as powerful? The thought made her inwardly shrink. As an adult, her relationships with the male sex had not been satisfying.

Discounting Albert, of course. Living with her son in virtual ostracism, she had gradually learned that the male was as vulnerable as the female.

For all his taciturnity, his inexpressiveness, Albert was hurt, she knew, by the rejection of kids his age. The sting of their taunts was worse than the sting of their fisticuffs when several boys would gang up on him. One on one, he could lick the toughest of the youths. Yet that didn't bring him friends. In fact, his disdain for all that was white only alienated him more from society at the post.

He couldn't see that his mother was white, and that he was half-white himself. She ached to comfort him, but her words would not heal him. He would have to heal himself.

Gradually, the sand hills yielded to rocky inclines and slopes peppered with stunted mesquite and spindly willow that indicated a presence of water. Eagerly, Albert pushed on ahead. Mattie kept his little silhouette in sight, although she didn't think he would attempt to flee again, not when they shared the same goal: Nantez.

He was the first to find a creek bed. "Mama!" he called and pointed proudly. Water surfaced at intervals just barely above the alluvial gravel.

Her pace and Gordon's became much more ambitious. Amid the bracken fringing the water, she fell sprawled on her stomach. She didn't know which to be more thankful for—the shade or the water.

A voice behind her cut short her elation. *"Manos arriba!"*

Cursing beneath her breath, she whirled.

Gordon didn't keep his curses beneath his. "God damn, what the—"

Three Mexicans stood with rifles leveled at her, Gordon, and Albert. The three mustachioed men wore the gray-brown uniforms of the Sixth Mexican Infantry and bandoleros crisscrossed their chests. "Ahh, americanos?" one said, the slimmest of the trio.

Gordon lowered his hands. "We have lost our way, sergeant."

"Put your hands up, my friend," the same Mexican said. "How do we know you are not bandidos, eh?"

"Come on, sergeant. Do we look like—"

The captain jerked the point of his bayoneted rifle in the direction of Albert. "Indio?"

Fright squeezed Mattie's heart. The inimical tension between the Mexican and the Indian was unsurpassed. She stepped in front of Albert. "My son. *Mi hijo.*"

Next to the sergeant, a soldier almost as round as he was tall grinned. A gold tooth gleamed. "The woman beds down with the Indian? Maybe she should see what a Mexican has between his legs."

She had learned to show no fear. "A worm. Am I not right, *gordo?*" She taunted him by using the Spanish word for fat. The Apaches had not been reticent about showing their genitals, and it had been her experience that the fatter the male, the smaller his genital. "Do you have a big snake, eh?"

The sergeant chuckled. The other Mexican soldier slapped his fat friend's back and guffawed. "Show her your snake, Diego!"

Diego's swarthy skin took on a red undertone. "*Sí,* I will show her what a real man is."

He took a step toward her, but the sergeant said, "No. I outrank you. Come with me, *señora*. Mine is not a worm, I assure you."

"She stays with us," Halpern said, putting a restraining hand on her forearm.

As if she would go with the officer. If she did anything, it would be to turn and run. Her heart was beating so hard. Here it was, beginning all over again. That helplessness. Where the woman had to submit. If even one more time she had to make her mind blank . . . to leave her body. . . .

Albert understood the implication of what was going on. He grabbed her other arm and clung to it.

That was what lent her immediate courage. Had she not endured his father's sexual assault and lived to enjoy things that others took for granted? Like sunlight on her face? The sound of bird songs? Her son's small hand? A warm bath?

Their lives were worth far more than that submission of the body. Her soul was far stronger than any physical infliction. She shook off the hand at either side of her. The man's hand, the child's hand. "I will be back, soon."

She turned toward the Mexican officer. "Sergeant? I prefer privacy, if ye don't mind."

His handlebar mustache lifted with his grin. "But that is part of the sport. Spectators, *entiendes*?"

Yes, she understood. But she would hurl her body against the bayonet before she would acquiesce to her son's watching the officer rape her. Her heart hurt for Albert. Why must his spirit be bruised and battered over and over again? Was there no respite?

The sergeant passed his rifle to the fat soldier and began removing his holster. "*La blusa, señora.*"

She didn't move at the order to take off her blouse.

The captain grinned. "Your son will find the bayonet a painful way to die."

The fat soldier took the hint and nudged Albert's stomach with the bayonet's tip. She saw the boy tense, as if to spring forward like some mountain cat.

Her hand flew to her shirtwaist's looped buttons that ran upward to her small, lace collar, dirty and torn. Her fingers fumbled.

All three soldiers laughed. From the corner of her eye, she saw Gordon's hand draw back into a fist.

"Don't try that, *señor*," the sergeant warned him with a congenial smile.

What in God's name did Gordon think he could do? He was as helpless as she and her son.

She often thought that being helpless had to be so much worse on a man, who was oriented toward action and aggressiveness. A woman was trained to accept pain from the onset of her first monthly through the birth of children and the eventual loss of her monthlies.

All this she thought as she pulled the calico shirtwaist up over her rib cage, over her head, and—

Something exploded. A gun shot! "Sonofabitch!" she yelled. She couldn't see. "What—"

Gordon grabbed her arm. "Duck!"

She was jerked to her knees. Gravel abraded her flesh above her prized muslin chemise. She had decorated the muslin with Ayrshire embroidery, that small eyelet, needlepoint type made famous by her Scots forebears.

On her other side, Albert crouched, as if both seeking protection and protecting her. Above her, she could hear one of the Mexicans pleading. *"Señor, por favor, lo siento—"*

"Well, well. If it isn't the harlot with her wares displayed."

That voice! She tugged the blouse back down and struggled to her feet. "Sonofabitch! 'Tis Bingham."

Beneath the big, floppy black hat, his answering grin briefly parted his beard. He was eyeing her with desire. "Yours truly, gal. The Lord God Almighty has sent me to make certain you tempt no more men."

"I wouldn't call ye an angel of mercy, Bingham, but ye sure—"

"Bingham, watch what you're doing!" Gordon nudged the preacher's Springfield rifle back toward the two Mexican soldiers left standing.

Only then did Mattie notice the man crumpled on the ground with a bullet hole through his forehead. She put her arm around Albert's shoulder, perhaps more to steady herself than to insulate him from a sight with which he was certainly familiar.

"God's wrath," Bingham said and spit a wad of tobacco juice into the gravel.

"God's wrath will be mild compared to mine, Bingham, if you have spent my money."

"The gal's lucky I happened upon the sight."

"Tell the two soldiers to drop their pants," Gordon told her.

"Quítenselos!" she said. *"Quítense los pantalones!"*

Quickly, almost comically, the two men lowered their trousers around their ankles.

"It is a worm," Albert affirmed in an adult's judicious voice.

Laughter erupted from her.

"Can't say the Indians don't have humor," Bingham drawled.

"I don't have much humor," Gordon said, training one of the Mexican's pistols on Bingham.

"What the hell are you—"

"Taking back what you stole from me. For the moment, though, I'll take that Springfield."

Bingham hesitated only long enough to make up his mind that Gordon would shoot him, then passed him the rifle.

Gordon flicked a glance at Mattie. "Find the soldiers' horses."

"Oh, *señor,*" the fat one cried out, *"por favor, no nos deje—"*

Gordon didn't ask her for a translation. He could discern the soldiers' fear at being left stranded without mounts. "Albert, get their rifles," he said.

She expected some show of resistance, and her son did not disappoint her. He simply stared at the Easterner.

"You heard me, kid."

No movement from her son. Not even the blink of an eyelid. The salamander could not have remained as motionless.

"Albert," she said, "do as—"

"Mattie." More than any words, Gordon's tone told her he would handle his own challenges. Including those issued by a boy. A boy who would be a man.

Keeping his pistol trained on Bingham, Gordon dropped down until he was eye level with Albert. "I am in charge here. So you will do what I say. If you are able to be in charge, then I will do what you say. Understand?"

Albert surprised her by nodding. Only once. But she knew once was enough. For now. He collected the remaining weapons from the soldiers, who had obeyed Gordon's motion to sit.

The horses, including Bingham's and the supply mule, were rounded up and watered. Somewhere along the way, the tent had taken a wrong turn and gotten lost—according to Bingham.

When they had refilled their canteens, they set out again, leaving the two half-naked Mexican soldiers behind at the creek bed.

Now a party of four rather than three, she and Albert and the two men, were once more traveling in the direction of the Huachineras. The mounts of the Mexican soldiers had been hard run and ill fed and would be better off put to pasture. They began blowing wind puffs as Bingham, in the lead, prodded his horse ever upward.

The slopes were shalely, and often Mattie's mount,

a chestnut with a white star and white sock, slipped and fell to its forelegs.

Gradually, the trees grew denser along a nearby stream, with juniper and piñon to offer scented shade. When the western peaks hid the sun, its afterglow filtered through the branches like a shower of gold dust. The place seemed magical.

By unspoken agreement they made camp for the evening. The fire wreathed them with a thin haze of mystical, pinecone-scented smoke.

Over his bowl of beans, Bingham complained about his lack of armament. "If we're attacked by Indians, there's no way I can protect myself."

Gordon swallowed a spoonful of his beans and replied, "Did you think about that when you left us without supplies and weapons?"

"For good reason."

Mattie hooted. "To be sure. I'd wager God spoke through a burning bush and told ye to abscond with our pack mule."

Bean juice glistened in his beard. "Like I told you back there that first night we camped, Halpern here is a greenhorn. I could see that teaming up with him was going to cost us our scalps. Now, if I went after his wife on my own, I'd stand a better chance of finding her—and keeping my scalp."

"Why go when you already had my money?" Halpern demanded.

Bingham looked affronted. "You entrusted me with it, and I wouldn't—"

"Oh, is that what I did? Entrust you with my money?"

"Hey, I saved you three back there at the creek bed, didn't I?"

Halpern picked up Bingham's Springfield and tossed it to him. "Well then, I will entrust you with first shift tonight. I'll be sleeping lightly. Don't try to make off again."

He leaned forward, the empty bowl in his hands dangling between his spread knees. His eyes, tonight the color of sage, gave no quarter. "I want my wife back, Bingham. I had to kill once in order to go after her. If you stand between me and my finding my wife, then you had better start praying to your God."

There was a glint in Gordon's eye. Even those who didn't know him, like Bingham and herself, had to know he meant what he'd said.

Reluctant respect for the Easterner was taking root in Mattie. And she wasn't the only one to experience a change of opinion. Bingham was sizing the man up by a new measuring stick. Albert, she could tell, was wary, but she suspected he was coming to regard the man as something apart from either Indian or white settler. With this man, nothing was black and white.

Gordon Halpern was not weak either in body or spirit. And he was a quick learner. From what he had told her about his childhood, she could surmise that, like herself, he was a survivor. Like herself, he was a *cimarrón,* a wild thing, for all his polished veneer.

She felt uneasy about the loss of antagonism she had immediately felt for the man. Antagonism made for distance, safety. But it almost meant fear.

Was she losing the fear of men that had become

so much a part of her? Why should that loss make her uneasy?

Unless it wasn't that at all. What if, instead, her uneasiness was a result of that emotion that made one the most vulnerable?

What if she was falling in love with Gordon Halpern? "Sonofabitch!" she groaned beneath her breath.

7

Bingham, *his head* and face covered by his hat, snored in spurts and accompanied by body twitches.

Albert slept solidly.

Mattie couldn't. She threw off her bedroll blanket. Then wished she hadn't. Mountain nights, even in summer, were cool.

Her night vision sought out the solitary figure standing sentinel. It was strange that she should find Halpern's moonlit profile reassuring when he was so inexperienced with Indian tactics. Still, he had proved himself resourceful and reliable.

At her age, and given her experiences thus far, she could truly say she had no illusions about men. She was no romantic soul. And yet . . . .

She rose and tiptoed across a granite slate toward the silhouette of the man cradling the rifle. She saw more than felt his gaze peel her away from the darkness. He was becoming more attuned to the noises of the night.

He sat down on a fallen cedar and watched her approach. "Relief time already?"

"Not yet." She sat down on the other end of the log, her arms locked around her knees. "I canna sleep."

"Happen often?"

She nodded. "I love the night."

"Yeah. The night makes no distinction between people, does it?"

She peered at him. "People hide in the light of day under clothes and rouge and rings." She recalled the portrait he had sketched of her. "Ye see with the eyes of the night, Halpern."

"Oh? Why so?"

"Ye look past the clothes and rouge and rings."

"I didn't." He leaned forward, forearms braced on his thighs. "Not when I was younger."

She knew he was talking about Diana. "And now that you do? You would change your mind?"

"I don't waste my time speculating about what's already done."

"Aye, the past is the past. What about now?"

He turned moon-gilded eyes on her. "Diana is a good woman."

The answer was a non sequitur, but they both understood that what was not being said was the real issue. "What brought ye two to the Arizona Territory?" she asked.

"A trip out West, to new environs. An attempt on my part to save our marriage."

She knew she shouldn't pry, but she asked anyway. "Because of her reluctance to . . . uhh . . . share the marital bed?"

"The very thing that she said had initially attracted her to me became a repulsion to her. In the early stages of our courtship, she was more fascinated with my boxing than she was with my painting. It was as if my sweating, battered body magnetized her hands. . . ."

Embarrassed, she remained silent. *Días muire!* She wished she had a cigarette.

"Of course, there were other things that contributed to our marital problems," he said after a moment. "I, like most artists, do not earn enough to enable Diana and me to live in a style to which she was accustomed. In turn, I couldn't relate to her friends. My unvarnished opinions sent too many of them packing."

The way his mouth twisted beneath his mustache told her he was lost in unpleasant memories. "How did your wife become a captive of Nantez?"

"We had arranged a side trip to the gold and silver mines of the Territory of New Mexico. While in Silver City, I was approached by a store owner. A man named Roy Bean. He had noted my build, the way I moved. He found out my name. Told me he had heard about me and wanted to promote a boxing match. I turned him down.

"Later that day, Diana and I rode six miles north to a little town in the tall pines, Pinos Altos. A rough and tough town of gold bonanzas. It was raining.

We had ducked into the schoolhouse, a log cabin that leaked. The children and the waiting got on her nerves. She stepped outside for a breath of fresh air—and into the path of Nantez's warriors."

Oh God, but Mattie could imagine what the woman must have felt. The disbelief that it really was happening, then the monstrous terror that this was no mere nightmare.

"The next day, when I could get no cooperation from the command at Fort Bayard, I went to see Roy Bean."

"Made a pact with the devil, ye did."

"I think I made that pact when I let Diana's mother become my patroness. Mrs. Harold Ashley of Pittsburgh's Arts Society. At one time I had been impressed by the name. I was nineteen, and the name sounded like an incantation. With that name on my lips, I could summon all sorts of wizardry and magic and, yes, even realized dreams."

It was strange to listen to the man's educated speech and know that an untamed animal lurked beneath that civilized mask. "Was she in favor of your marriage to Diana?"

He didn't reply at once. "Diana's mother was more a philanderer than philanthropist. In other words, she specialized in affairs. I suppose my marriage to Diana was an affront to her own . . . desirability."

"I see." She wanted to say, *So ye, too, have let yourself be used in order to keep a dream alive.* "Ye must have loved Diana very, very much to risk your painting career."

He shifted the rifle nestled in the crook of his arm

and leaned forward to better study her face. "Why all the questions?"

She averted her gaze and looked around until she saw a shadowy form in the branches of a juniper. The ghostly whistle confirmed the apparition to be an owl. "I . . . I was curious about what it must have been like for Diana. For a woman to feel . . . totally absorbed, loved, desired, by a man."

"You never have been, have you?"

"No." The solitary word was so . . . so solitary. She elaborated. "Me husband . . . I fear he was more absorbed by me family's finances."

"After all these years, you must be very—"

Afraid that he might say something that would break down her wall of defense, she blurted, "Curious. I am curious about what it must be like to feel a man's gentle touch."

Then she surprised herself. "Would ye kiss me, Gordon?"

His eyes widened, but he did not betray by speech whatever had gone through his mind. "Most people hardly find my touch gentle."

Her pride flared. "I'm asking for a kiss, nothing more."

He stood, propped the rifle against the cedar and walked toward her.

She held up a restraining hand. "Wait. I didn't mean for you to—"

"Will you shut up." He took her raised hand and pulled her to her feet. Placing his big, scarred hands on either side of her face, her drew her close. "Mattie, for God's sake, close your eyes."

She complied. Her heart did a drum roll.

"That's better."

Then she felt his lips touch hers, with such infinite tenderness. She ceased to breathe. Ceased to think. She only felt. For the first time in years, she let herself feel.

Instead of trying to control her responses, she let them control her for once. Her legs trembled. Tears seeped from her eyes. *Días muire*, but the feeling was so good. So wonderful! Her breath broke from her in a sob.

At once, he released her and stepped back. Consternation showed in his lowered brows. "My God," he said softly. "My God."

Her hands balled. "If ye say just one word of pity, I swear I'll—"

He caught one of her knotted hands in each of his. "No. I wasn't going to. You just startled me. I had forgotten that people are capable of such pent-up passion. You see, mine has gone. And with its leaving, my creativity and my imagination went also. My paintings are as lackluster as my heart."

"Oh, no. The sketch ye did of me . . . it was grand." Feeling suddenly shy, she tugged her hands from his. "I'm tired now." She brushed past him, but after taking several steps, she turned and glanced back at him over her shoulder. "Thank ye, Gordon."

"For the kiss?"

"For reminding me that I am a woman. G'night, now."

A disgruntled pair eyed her the next morning. Did both Bingham and Albert know of her tryst with

Gordon during the night? Or was guilt making her unreasonably suspicious?

By the half-light of dawn, she studied the two across the breakfast fire. Albert wouldn't look at her. His lower lip was thrust out in a little boy's pout.

He had found her scrubbing her arms and face in the creek earlier. A ritual that she usually performed carelessly.

Last night had changed all that. After all these years, she was aware of her body again. She had rejected any aesthetic qualities about it, thinking of it only in terms of its functional dictates.

Bingham sipped from his tin mug. Occasionally, he spit coffee grounds into the fire. "Coffee tastes like the devil's brew."

She took a sip of her own and nearly spewed out the fire. "Ye gods, 'tis strong enough to float eggs! Must be the hickory nut."

"Hickory nut?" Gordon asked, smiling at her reaction. His own mood that morning had been quiet, reflective.

"A secret of old Sam Kee's. He uses it to flavor his tea."

"This ain't tea, gal."

She felt too lighthearted to let Bingham bother her. "Then ye fix the coffee tomorrow."

"How many more days of travel do you think we have before we reach Nantez's stomping grounds?" Gordon asked the preacher.

Bingham chewed thoughtfully on a piece of rancid bacon. "Depends."

"On what?" Gordon said, impatience edging his voice now.

"On how fast we travel, for one. You and the gal here were slowing me—"

He broke off whatever he had been about to say and stared past Albert at some fixed point. Slowly he set down his cup and picked up his Winchester. He brought it to his shoulder and looked down the sight.

Frightened, she glanced beyond Albert, saw in the dew-wet tufts of grass a snake.

"No!" her son said.

In a single instant, he bolted from his squatting position and knocked the Winchester from Bingham's hands. Then he whirled and picked up the snake that was slithering toward the next tuft. He held up the twisting reptile. "It does not poison." With that he tossed it into the underbrush.

Mattie sighed. Albert wasn't a bad boy, no matter what the teacher made him out to be. She believed that fervently. True he was wild and often distracted. When she would try to help him with his sums, he wouldn't listen, or at least didn't seem to care to.

She also knew he was sensitive and kind to all God's creatures. With the exception maybe of the white man. He didn't trust him. Why should he? The white man had been less than welcoming to the little boy.

She gave thanks at her inner altar that he had none of Nantez's cretin appearance. Her son was beautiful. Not in the usual child-fresh-beauty way. But with the strong, sculpted features and piercing, somber handsomeness of the Apache's Athapascan ancestors.

"Awful jittery aren't you, Bingham?" Gordon said, peering at the preacher through the steam rising off his own cup. A wry smile lifted the ends of his pirate's mustache.

"We're trespassing on Apache territory now. What's left of my scalp rises like a dog's hackles."

Gordon set down his half-empty cup and stretched out his long, muscular legs. "Never heard of anyone surviving a scalping."

Beneath the brim of his hat, Bingham's eyes were as hard as stone. "I survived because of the maggots."

"Maggots?"

"Yeah. Maggots. This gal here scooped them from a dead dog rotting in the sun. Put them on my exposed skull to eat away the rotting flesh."

Gordon swallowed. He looked as if he were going to be sick.

Mattie had to smile. "I had watched the shaman treat a warrior's wound the same way."

She glanced at the preacher, wondering if he would take her words with good humor. "Bingham was burning with fever and ranting about Satan's fiery hell. Looked to me like he was dying. I figured the maggots couldn't make him any worse than he already was."

Bingham turned his gray stare on her. "*You* made me worse than I was."

He had been idealistic. A young man full of life and love for all of God's creations. After his ordination, he had set out to change the world: to bless the poor and heal the souls of the sick and guide aright those who had gone astray. The portion of the world given to him to change had been the wilds of northwestern Mexico.

In his youth he was an intelligent young man and handsome in a slender, ascetic way. The third of nine children of a blacksmith from Ohio. And Mexico was a long way off. Still, with God in his heart, he knew the world would be his home.

In Santo Tomás, he was invited to dinner at the sprawling hacienda of the wealthy Scots engineer, Archibald Chisholm. Beneath the sala's hundred-candle chandelier, he first glimpsed the young woman he knew that God had selected to be his mate. Mattie was playing a Scottish air on a grand piano hauled all the way from Mexico City over the Camino Real.

She was a vision that had flitted through his dreams for years, all sparkle and light and loveliness. Warm brown eyes that tilted at the ends, matching that same tilt to the ends of her pale pink lips. Rich, cocoa-brown hair spilled in curls from a circlet of silver-wrought flowers atop her head. And she was small, standing no higher than his shoulder.

Her smile was given freely, but not so her affections. Those, William Bingham learned, were reserved for Reginald McAlister, the young civil engineer newly graduated from the University of Edinburgh, who was a guest of the Chisholms until he could find his own place.

Obviously, he already had, Bingham soon realized. In Mattie's heart.

That night, and for the thousand-and-one nights thereafter, William Bingham retired to his bed to pray and chafe and rail and pray again, humbled by his own rebellious spirit. He lusted after Mattie, who belonged to another. This unplucked flower, who was much purer in heart than he could ever hope to be.

"'Let us lie down in our shame, and let our humiliation cover us; for we have sinned against the Lord our God,'" he would pray each night, even as his flesh burned for her and his imagination ran riot: to hold her beneath him, to rain kisses on her skin, as white as the lily, to enter her and give her his life seed.

That sacrifice of sacrifices.

Soon, he found his prayers were little more than fantasies. Mattie had become his Vision, his Way, his Light, and his Life. He waited for her to visit his little adobe house with her basket of cast-off clothing or unused food that her mother sent weekly for the *campesinos* and blanket Indians to whom he ministered.

Could Mattie not see his suffering? That he suffered because of her? The fetes and soirees he occasionally attended at the Chisholm home were opportunities to glimpse his adored.

The night the pueblo's priest married Mattie and Reginald, William had watched with a heart that shriveled. Behind the priest and the bridal couple, the ivory statue of Saint Tomás, patron saint of the pueblo, glowed warmly from the brass niche in the west *crucero*. The heavyset priest gently nudged the couple, a prompt to indicate they were to go down on their knees. In adherence to tradition, a *rosario* was looped over the shoulders of the pair.

Crazy thoughts beat at William's brain. He could still rip away the *rosario,* carry her off into the night with him; make her his forever. She should have been his mate. Together, they could take God's Word to the world's four corners.

Like a man possessed by a demon, a wild animal turned loose, he whirled from the back of the chapel and charged out into the rain-misted night. He had no idea where he was going. For him, there was no Gethesemane.

A voice from an arched doorway called softly. "*Señor* Billy, I give you fun time."

Fun time? Had he ever known a fun time? At six years of age, he had pulled the plow—he, the mule the family couldn't afford. His nights had been spent learning to read from the family Bible. His toil-worn mother had been the strictest of teachers.

The plow harness of his youth had become the faith harness of his manhood. But on this night his manhood rebelled against this unfair yoke. He strode through that portal to hell and bedded the young Mexican *puta.* Over and over. Until his pockets were empty. His body was empty. His mind was empty.

Then, after only half dressing, he went outside. Turned his face up to the rain. And cried. For the first time. And the last.

He left Santo Tomás. Rode circuit through the numerous mining towns and pueblos scattered throughout northwestern Mexico. He didn't see

Mattie McAlister again. Not for almost a year. Not until some ten days after he and she were captured on the same sweeping raid Nantez's braves made in a twenty-mile range of the subchief's Sierra camp. When he did see her, he almost didn't recognize her.

She was bedraggled. Still wearing the cotton nightgown she had been wearing the night she was captured. It was tattered and blood-stained, and it clung to her distended belly. She was with child!

Her hair was matted. Her eyes looked haunted. At that moment, he probably felt for her the only pure love he would ever feel for anyone. It was uncontaminated by desire in any of its demonic faces.

He did not see her again for some days. At that time, he was feigning insanity. The deception permitted him to roam free within the camp. Left on his own, he had hopes of escape soon. Then bad luck intervened.

A contingent of Mexican soldiers approached Nantez's base camp with a white flag of negotiation. A misunderstanding occurred. He never knew what it was, but one of the soldiers fired on the mother of an Apache named Tsao. Tsao was so enraged that he turned on Bingham and scalped him on the spot.

He was left to die. Unattended, he would have. But Mattie ministered to his wounds, even at the risk of being cuffed, being battered was more like it.

He fell in love with her this time. Desire, love, lust all consumed him like a gigantic conflagration. During his circuit riding, he had witnessed a holocaust wrought by a wildfire. For those who were in its path, there was no escaping it.

He had been in Mattie's path. There was no escaping her. He was afire for her. All over again. And all over again, she chose another. Nantez.

Bingham's prayers included new biblical intonations. "'Behold, you have spoken and have done evil things, and you have had your way. Then the Lord said to me in the days of Josiah the king, *Have you seen what the faithless Israel did? She went up on every high hill and under every green tree, and she was a harlot there.* And I thought, after she has done all these things, she will return to me; but she did not return. . . .'"

When he could stand no longer her groveling beneath the heathen, he plotted his escape and looked not once behind him. Put the harlot from him forever.

Until that day she arrived at Fort Lowell with her bastard child. Not even all his condemnation would make her bend her head with shame.

He had put her behind him again when he left her and Halpern at that first night's camp. And after getting lost in a sandstorm, he had run upon her again.

Now he knew that Satan was a god he hadn't discovered yet.

8

The rain started and did not stop. Surely it was a curse of God, thought Bingham. Forty days and nights of rain.

The foothills had leveled out. Mattie and the others were traveling across a wide, endless plateau dotted with juniper and piñon. The trees by themselves did not offer sufficient shelter.

So she made her own shelter, just as she had for Nantez every time he moved base camp. She instructed the men, including Albert, who did not remember how, to cut saplings and brush. Next the long, slender poles where thrust into the ground about two feet apart, bent inward until they met and bound together at the top. A little hole was left to let the smoke out. She then proceeded to show them how to weave brush and branches into the framework. All this took a little less than two hours. By the time they were finished, the four were drenched.

Mattie huddled with the others around a fire that was more smoke than flame. She thought of other tasks she had performed for Nantez. Of tanning buffalo hides and using animal brains and tallow. Of more intimate tasks like fashioning the muslin strip around his smelly body, passing it between his squat legs and around his pelvis and adjusting the ends so that they fell to the knobby knees, both in front and behind.

He had seemed to take delight in watching her do this. Had it been because he had known she loathed him?

She had to be unbalanced after all those years of captivity. Proof was right here, right now: she was persisting in the search. She had Albert back. She hadn't taken any of Gordon's money up front. She had no responsibility to him.

And yet, she was going to help him find his wife. Help him find the very thing that would take him out of her own life. If he didn't find Diana . . . maybe, just maybe, he might come to find in herself the qualities that were worth loving. Except, after all these years, she didn't know what they were. If any, they certainly weren't those that would attract romantic love.

Why would she want to reject those very qualities that had sustained her during those nightmarish years? Her ability to withdraw from that outer brutal world even as she performed degrading tasks and received physical blows. Her desire to find beauty amid the ugliness.

Disgust at her weakness, coming now when she

had put the worst behind her, overcame her. She was more than her body! Abruptly, she leaned forward, clawed both hands through the mushy earth and raked them down her cheeks, painting muddy war stripes.

Her outrageous action elicited a variety of responses from her traveling companions. Albert glanced up and then away. His little face, as usual, betrayed little of what was going on in his mind.

Next to her, Bingham didn't even bother to look up from the stringy dried beef he gnawed.

Across the fire pit, Gordon stared at her through the eye-stinging smoke. His brows were raised in surprise.

She laughed. "Mother Earth." Explanation enough.

Later, much later, she left the wickiup and went to stand alone in the downpour, her face uplifted to the cleansing rain. When she allowed herself the luxury of feeling emotion, she had to be where none could spy upon her.

No, she would never be afraid again. At least, of change. Of loss. Of death.

Unless she was afraid of emotion. Love was something she didn't know if she was courageous enough to risk. The wise knew that love meant all three at once: change of the self, loss of the self, death to the self. That supreme sacrifice.

Días muire, what she wouldn't give for a cigarette!

She stared down at the gumbo mud, into which her moccasins were sinking. Neglected feet, she thought morosely, wishing even more for her lost foot balm than for a cigarette.

Reluctantly, she turned those feet back toward

the wickiup with its fragrant bed of pine needles and the man who had the power to make her panic.

Love was ecstasy and torment, freedom and captivity.

Captivity. That was what life on a U.S. government reservation meant to Nantez of the Netdahe band of Apaches. Instead, he would take his own captives.

The Netdahe were regarded by other Apaches as being true wild men, whose mode of life was devoted entirely to warfare and raiding the settlements.

The band was composed of outlaws recruited from other Apache bands. It included in its membership a few Navajos as well as Mexicans and whites who had been captured as children and had grown up as savages.

He stared across the fire pit at the two figures huddled in the corner. The woman he had taken captive more than a month ago in Pinos Altos had no spirit and bored him. But her coloring—gold skin, gold hair, turquoise eyes—was a living trophy. A symbol of his prowess.

The little girl, four or five years of age he judged, he had captured four days earlier in a raid on a stage outside Fort Bowie.

He had heard that Baishan, his son by the woman his people called *Cimarrón,* was somewhere in southeastern Arizona. He would yet find the boy. And the boy's mother. Nantez's rage at the insolence of the white woman continued after all these years to seek an outlet.

He raised a finger and crooked it. "Come here," he told the child.

The yellow-haired woman scrambled farther back into the wickiup's corner. The more compliant she was, the more contempt he had for her. *Cimarrón* had been hard-nosed, a scrapper with the pluck of a man. And much more amusing to torment.

Behind him, he heard his wife Pon-chie rise. "Where are you going?" he demanded as he turned.

She dropped her gaze before his fierce stare. "The deer meat. . . ."

He nodded his head and watched her depart in silent and rapid steps. Sometimes his vengeance could not be contained and directed at only the selected quarry.

He took pride in the reports that said he wasn't human. That he was invincible. People looked into his eyes and were spooked. Because they said they saw nothing there. Nothing. No light. Only darkness. No soul.

Good. Fear made them weak. Ramos was weak. The medicine man didn't show his fear, but the way he slunk around the camp was proof enough. Hobbled was a better word. Ramos had intervened once too often.

Nantez hated to admit it, but he needed Ramos. Like all great leaders, he needed a whipping boy.

His grin was contemptuous. His enemies underestimated him, all but the white woman *Cimarrón*.

He crooked his finger again. The little girl rose. He looked her over. Her swollen lips trembled. Tears made her eyes ugly red berries. She was obviously having trouble breathing. He thrilled at the fear exuding from her.

As a boy, his parents had claimed he displayed a mischievous nature. He used to go out into the woods with a few other young men to tease the girls who were gathering acorns. One of his tricks was to wait until the girls had done a lot of hard work, then take the acorns away from them.

This had come to the attention of the wife of Chief Mah-ko, who told her grandson Goyakla and some of his friends to waylay Nantez and give him and his gang a good whipping.

As the chief's grandson, Goyakla was always the favored boy. The weak and fearful boys sought the protection of his status. It was the only time Goyakla probably lost a battle. Now, under the Mexican name of Geronimo, Goyakla had become a noted leader and spent most of his time preying on the weakness of the Americans.

Nantez hated people for their weakness. He liked to believe it was his strength that made him succeed. But he sometimes acknowledged to himself that it wasn't that way at all. It wasn't his strength. It was the weakness of others that helped him. That, and his own ruthlessness in the face of truth and honesty.

Now, he lifted his fist and cuffed his captive. The little girl was an object for the hatred he felt for the weak, a target for the overwhelming hatred he felt for all those who were not on his level. The girl fell with a thud, and her head hit one of the fire pit's rocks. Blood slowly stained it red.

He shrugged, then shifted his gaze to the only one

remaining in the tent. He crooked his finger at the figure crouching in the shadows. "Come here."

The rain poured so hard that it was pointless even to attempt riding that day, especially considering the condition of their mounts.

That scrap of humanity known as Mattie McAlister curled up and dozed as easily as an old, mangy mongrel. The preacher read silently from his Bible. His hat's soggy feather still drooped from the morning's outing to relieve himself. The half-breed kid doled out his cards in four strips of solitaire.

As for Gordon, he decided a shave was in order. Without a mirror and only rainwater to serve as a lather, the shaving was turning into a bloodletting worthy of a medieval apothecary. The inconveniences imposed by the Wild West were beginning to irritate him.

"Nine of hearts goes on the ten of spades over there," he told the kid.

Albert fixed him with a baleful look but moved the card as instructed.

Gordon temporarily abandoned his effort at shaving to watch the kid. For a nine-year-old, he was good. Very good. "Ever play stud poker?" he asked.

Albert shook his head, and his long, black hair flicked against his copper cheeks. Though he was small, like his mother, there was little other similarity between them. He looked completely Indian.

"Any kind of poker?"

Again, the shake of the head.

"Then it's time you learned."

Bingham shifted his attention to them. His gray eyes were stormy with condemnation. "'The way of the wicked is an abomination to the Lord, but He loves him who pursues righteousness.' Proverbs fifteen."

"'But the mouths of fools spouts folly.' Proverbs fifteen also," Gordon said. He picked up the kid's deck and began to shuffle. "First, you ante up. Seeing as how we're short of coins, pebbles will serve."

He went on to explain the royal and straight flush, four-of-a-kind, and the rest of the ranks. "We'll go through a practice hand, all right?"

He dealt the hand. When the kid picked up his cards, he fanned them out. After a moment, confusion puckered his arrow-straight brows.

"What is it?"

The kid flipped the joker in the center. "What is that?"

"No one ever told you?"

Albert shook his head.

"It's a joker. A wild card."

Those acute dark eyes stared back at him. "A wild card? Then it is not good. Something wild."

"No, not at all. It's the highest ranking card." Then, he understood what the kid was really saying. "Look, Albert, a joker is good because it *is* wild. Besides cards, a joker is something that is held in reserve to gain an end or escape from a predicament. Understand?"

The kid displayed a jack-o'-lantern smile. "I hold five aces, then. I think you will not escape from this predicament."

Albert seemed so cocksure. Yet Gordon knew the kid was like him. Bewildered about where he was, and who he was. Like a leaf poised on its edge. Swirling, turning, blowing in various and opposing wind currents. Uncomfortable in his uncertainty. Needing to find where he was, but moving before he knew. Accepting without question the unpleasant, but somehow not believing the pleasant with equal certainty.

"That was nice of ye to take the time to teach Albert to play poker," Mattie said later that afternoon. She had awakened just as Gordon was explaining the purpose of the wild card, the joker.

"I was bored." He sat on a stump. The big lightning-hit desert willow bridged a ravine where it had fallen, some fifty yards from their campsite. Once the drizzle had stopped, he had deserted the crowded, stuffy wickiup. The bitter tang of wet sage scented the rain-washed air.

"Here, let me help." She knelt beside him. Taking his razor from him, she tilted his head at an angle to catch the sunlight, which was finally peeking through tattered curtains of clouds.

All too vividly, he recalled the tale of the finger bone she carried in her pouch. "Dare I trust a knife-wielding woman?"

"I'm good at this. One of me duties while captive was to pluck out Nantez's sparse beard. I used tweezers made of bent strips of tin."

Her voice conveyed absolutely no emotion. He studied her face. Her upper lip, full with only a hint of an indentation, was sheened with perspiration from the afternoon humidity.

"You talk as if what happened to you was commonplace," he said. "I don't know about you, but I would feel damned bitter. Resentful as hell."

"I hate Nantez with a passion equal to the love I feel for our son. For Albert, me heart is engorged with love, if that gives you any idea of what I feel for Nantez."

"I can understand that hate. For the longest time, I hated my mother for abandoning me. Later, I learned she had died in a western railroad town, Cheyenne. Died drunk, penniless, used up. Now I can only think how miserable she must have been. I guess I feel sorry for her."

Her hand worked deftly, using the same firm but light stroke of an artist. "She was free to choose."

"Is there nothing you fear, Mattie?"

For a moment she was silent. "Being alone. I know that now. I want to enjoy me life all the time without feeling guilty, Halpern. I want to no longer feel the need to judge meself for mistakes and failures. The flaws in meself that keep cropping up."

"The past is over."

"Your mustache needs clipping."

"Your hair needs combing," he said out of the side of his mouth. She was shaving his jaw line, close, maybe too close.

"Why?"

"Because–because–for the same reason my mustache needs clipping. Because a person has certain standards. Good grooming is one."

"I like me hair wild and unconstrained. It suits me nature."

She nicked his neck, just below his jaw. "Oow!"

"Hold still," she said.

He studied her face. Her expression was one of concentration. "Look, Mattie, everything changes. Even one's nature. You've got to surrender to life some day."

She rose like smoke. "The day I do, you'll see me hair coifed tighter than chicken wire."

9

No one talked now. Every sense was focused on being alert.

The air was cool and dry. The sky was light blue, the shade of the eyes on a China doll Mattie had had as a child. The double squawk of the ring-neck pheasant as it accompanied the whir of wing-flapping broke the monotonous sound of hoof on rock and hard-packed earth. Resinous scents of pine and juniper and firs tickled the nostrils.

All these were reassuring sights and sounds and smells. There was nothing to suggest that danger and even death waited at the end of the wide, chaparral-covered canyon or perched on its high, craggy rims like vultures. Even those birds of prey had deserted the sky for lack of warm air currents.

Or had they yielded their roosts to a more malevolent stalker?

Introducing
The Timeless Romance

Passion rising from the ashes of the Civil War...

Love blossoming against the harsh landscape of the primitive Australian outback...

Romance melting the cold walls of an 18th-century English castle —— and the heart of the handsome Earl who lives there...

Since the beginning of time, great love has held the power to change the course of history. And in Harper Monogram historical novels, you can experience that power again and again.

Free introductory offer. To introduce you to this exclusive new service, we'd like to send you the four newest Harper Monogram titles absolutely free. They're yours to keep without obligation, no matter what you decide.

Free 10-day previews. Enjoy automatic free delivery of four new titles each month —— up to four weeks before they appear in bookstores. You're never obligated to keep a book you don't want, and you can return any book, for a full credit.

Save up to 32% off the publisher's price on any shipment you choose to keep.

Don't pass up this opportunity to enjoy great romance as you have never experienced before.

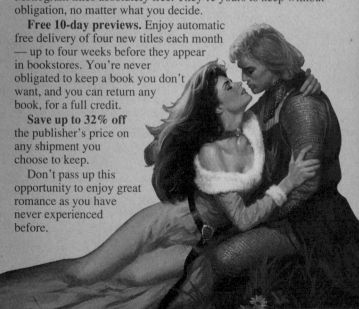

Reader Service.

Yes! I want to join the Timeless Romance Reader Service. Please send me my 4 FREE HarperMonogram historical romances. Then each month send me 4 new historical romances to preview without obligation for 10 days. I'll pay the low subscription price of $4.00 for every book I choose to keep--a total savings of at least $2.00 each month--and home delivery is free! I understand that I may return any title within 10 days and receive a full credit. I may cancel this sub-scription at any time without obligation by simply writing "Canceled" on any invoice and mailing it to Timeless Romance. There is no minimum number of books to purchase.

NAME

ADDRESS

CITY   STATE   ZIP

TELEPHONE

SIGNATURE
(If under 18, parent or guardian must sign. Program, price, terms, and conditions sub-ject to cancellation and change. Orders subject to acceptance by HarperMonogram.)

The travelers were now in definite territory claimed by the Netdahe Apaches, having crossed Rio Bavispe, which was actually more a meandering mountain creek than river.

Mattie's floppy sombrero hung from its string tie around her neck and bounced against the small of her back in cadence with her mount's measured gait. She was perspiring, but it wasn't generated by heat. It was purely from fear.

If Nantez should recapture her. . . . She mentally shrugged it off. Why was she worrying? Either he would kill her or she would kill herself.

No, that wasn't true. She had discovered life too dear to surrender. When once she could take pleasure in the sight of a painted-lady butterfly amid a stinking, flea-infested pile of dozing camp dogs, well . . . . life always had new meaning.

She glanced at Gordon. He reminded her of a sketch she had seen of D'Artagnan in Dumas's *The Three Musketeers.* That long, glossy hair and sweeping devil-may-care mustache. His black *charro* hat needed only a plume. The earring was out of keeping with the look, though. It belonged on a Caribbean pirate.

Was he as noble as D'Artagnan? As steadfast in love as Cyrano de Bergerac? As bold as Blackbeard? Aye, that Gordon Halpern was all that. Witness his hero's journey to the underworld to bring back his lady love.

Would that she were that lady love. Alas, such was not the case. She could vividly imagine the lovely Diana. Hair the gold-silver shade of moon dust. Eyes the prismatic blue of Mexican opals. Skin as translucent as Salome's veils.

Daydreaming as she was, she almost missed the way her mount's ears cocked suddenly. She hauled back at the reins. "Listen!"

At once, the other three heeded her call. Only Bingham's eyes questioned her.

"I'm not sure," she whispered in response to that unspoken inquiry. "Something's ahead, though."

"What now?" Gordon asked.

"If 'tis Apaches, they've already seen us."

"No use walking smack dab into their trap," Bingham said and spit a brown squirt of tobacco juice.

She lost her patience. "If they're here, we're already in it, fool."

The look he turned on her was like gray smoke swirling up out of hell. "A fool is it? Better a fool than a lost soul, gal. You—"

"Cut it, Bingham," Gordon said. "Now is not the time for a discourse on sins and salvation. Well, Mattie? Do we turn back?"

Días muire, she didn't know. Her horse's ears no longer exhibited that alerted position. "Maybe what was out there was something as harmless as a mule deer."

"Maybe as lethal as a steel-tipped arrow," the preacher growled low.

This was what she was getting paid for, wasn't it? To take Halpern to his beloved. "I'll go on ahead, see if I pick up any telltale signs."

"No," Halpern said. "We're in this together." He kneed his horse's flanks, and the mount started forward again. "What are we looking for?"

"Could be a hundred things," Bingham said.

She kept her gaze on the ground directly ahead. "Could be what ye don't see."

"Like what?" Gordon asked.

She talked, if only to ease her bowstring-taut nerves. "Try following the tracks of an Indian. Often, ye will find they end abruptly. As if Bingham's God snatched the Indian from the face of the earth in midstep."

Beside her, she saw Albert's mouth crimp in the barest of smiles. He had lost two teeth, and new ones were just coming through.

She knew he was taking delight in this particular trick of his father's people. Maybe even taking pride. As much as she resented it, she knew this pride was important to her son if he was ever to come to terms with his heritage.

Of course, Bingham and his God would condemn pride as a monstrous sin. Well, Bingham's God wasn't hers. When in the midst of her hell-on-earth, she had done a lot of praying at an inner altar. Her God was inside. And outside. Maybe, more like the Apache's concept of a Superior Power. Moving through all in all.

Surely, it was not in Nantez.

"What does the Indian do?" Gordon asked. "Swing up into an overhead branch?"

"Good guess. But not if ye are traveling on the plains or desert. In that case, the Indian simply back-tracks in his own footprints and takes a different path that is unlikely to be detected."

The canyon began to narrow. Its chaparral crowded the trail and forced their horses through its funnel of overgrowth. A definite site if ever for an ambush. The trail bent with the curve of the canyon walls then abruptly opened onto an abandoned cornfield. A flutter in the withered stalks brought her and the others up short. She put up a silencing hand.

A moment passed. Dry, silvery cornstalks rustled slightly. She studied a sycamore's leaves. No breeze stirred them. Signaling the others to wait, she dismounted, passed the reins to Albert, and approached the rows of cornstalks.

God, please let it be a raccoon. Not an Apache or a jaguar.

Behind her, she heard a noise. She gasped and turned to look. Halpern and Bingham had raised their rifles, cocked them, and trained their sights on the corn rows just ahead of her.

Reassured, she crept forward. She was careful to avoid stepping on leaves or old corn husks. She parted the stalks with a minimum of betraying noise. Silky corn tassels tickled her nose. She stifled a sneeze. Somewhere, a bee hummed.

When she was no more than four or five rows deep into the corn field, she heard more distinct noises. At once, she froze. Sweat instantly trickled down her ribs and collected at her waist band.

Then a sense of familiarity with the sounds she was hearing prompted her to part the corn fronds. Ahead, where the cornstalks lay flattened, two horses grazed. They were partially hidden by stalks, but she could tell they were saddled. She released her pent-up breath.

Still, she was careful. The visitors might not be Indians, but they could be Mexicans soldiers, who were just as formidable. Or almost. Macabre memories made her nervous all over again.

Her gaze roving from left to right and back again, she crept toward the two horses. Where were their owners? Nearby?

The gelding paused, looked up suddenly. Had the horse heard her—or something else?

Then . . . *Días muire*, yes! . . . those saddlebags, she had purchased them at Zechendorf's. Just beyond the gelding, she could identify the rump of her spotted pony!

In her joy, she stepped out into the clearing. Her sudden appearance spooked the horses. They turned and trotted off in the opposite direction.

"No! Pepper!" All she could think about was the disappearance of her precious foot balm.

She sprinted after them. They trotted down out of the field and along the dry creek bed of the Rio de Janos. Rocks jabbed through her thin moccasin soles. The faster she ran, the faster the horses' gait.

Then her ankle gave way beneath her. She stumbled, fell on all fours, and scraped her hands. She sat back on her haunches, looking at her stinging, raw palms. She started to cry. "Sonofabitch!"

Behind her, she heard hooves drum against gravel as they swept past on either side of her, and thundered on in pursuit of the runaway horses.

"Mother?"

She lifted her face from her hands and looked up into her son's face. There was confusion in his eyes. He had never seen her cry. "I'm all right, Albert. Really. Here, help me stand. I twisted me ankle."

With her son's aid, she took the reins he had held for her and mounted the horse. They rode for some fifteen minutes, and she began to fear the two men had run into more trouble.

Then, farther down the canyon, she could see Gordon and Bingham cantering back. They had the two runaway horses with them.

When Gordon was close enough, he called out, "Come along. We found a great campsite for the evening. On a knoll, overlooking a spot where the water runs."

The place was where the canyon emptied into a vista of mountains and river-carved valleys. A gradual descent of hills was contrasted with a sheer thousand-foot cascade of water.

The trail down took them away from thundering falls to a high plain, clustered with towering trees and bisected by a tributary of the falls.

By the time they reached the spot she had to hobble from Pepper to a mound Bingham had created of saddle, horse blankets, and packs. All pleasure in recovering her pony was lost in her pain.

Her ankle had swollen so much that the moccasin had stretched as tightly as animal skin on a war shield. She took the knife from the sheath at her thigh, and slit the moccasin from knee to sole. The deer hide fell open, revealing her already discoloring flesh.

Gordon dropped his own saddle and bags nearby. "In the creek you go."

"What?"

"I've had enough swollen hands and eyes to know whereof I speak, my dear lady."

His dear lady?

"The mountain-cold water will stop the swelling. Then, we apply heat to drain the blood back out of the area."

Before she could protest, he bent and scooped her up into his arms, effortlessly, gingerly, as if she were that priceless China doll of her childhood. Automatically, her arms went around his neck, but at once it seemed odd. She felt like both grinning and weeping.

She hadn't been cared for like this since she was a little girl and fell from the wrought-iron arch over a gate she had been climbing. Her father had carried her into the house. "Acch, me bairn, ye are *glaikit!* A foolish one. I shall have your bum tanned royally, mind ye!"

Gordon carried her to the river. Shading the rippling water were smooth, white-trunked sycamores, pliant willows, and dark, gnarly ash. He knelt on the edge of the bank, gently took her ankle and held it down in the shallow, swift current. She gasped. "The water! 'Tis freezing!"

"Bingham's starting a fire. A heated blanket ought to finish off that swelling." He probed the mounded flesh around her ankle bone. "Don't think it's broken."

She didn't either. "Ye are a kind man, Gordon Halpern."

He looked from her ankle up to her face. "No. I am not kind. Not totally. Understand me now. I am. That is all. I am. And I will do whatever it takes to get my wife back. Do you understand that, also?"

She nodded, thinking that she knew what she was doing. That she was going into this adventure with eyes wide open. That she would allow herself to fall in love, fully, for the one and only time in her life. That she knew this man was representative of all the base emotions and all that was fine in a human being. But that he sought to express the latter. That was all that could be asked of anyone.

"Aye, Halpern. I understand. More than ye realize."

He glowered at her, swung her up into his arms, and headed back to the campsite.

Albert appeared to be emptying cans from the mule's pack, but his gaze clung to Mattie and Gordon. If his already swarthy face could darken, it did.

Gordon eased her down onto the improvised chaise longue and passed her a plate of unsavory-smelling stew before settling across the fire from her with his own.

Bingham paused in ladling a glob of the burnt stew onto a tin plate and flicked her and Gordon a scowl. "I wasn't hired to do the cooking."

"I didn't hire you to make off with the supplies either, Bingham."

Between bites, Albert muttered, "Supplies? Supplies is for everyone. No one owns supplies in Apache camps."

Gordon cast him a sidewise glance. "You have a point there, kid."

Mattie said nothing, but she was perceiving how desperate Albert was to find his place. Apparently, he had made up his mind that it was going to be with his Indian bloodline. If and when they found Nantez's camp, she would have to keep an eagle's eye on her son.

"The Apaches defile all that is holy and sacred in

God's Book," Bingham said. "Pity is a feeling unknown to them. Cruelty is ingrained in them. A brave who can kill without being killed and can steal without being caught is the most respected and admired."

Disgust made the food even more unpalatable than it already was. She tossed her plate down beside her. "The only difference between the Apache and the Christian, Bingham, is that the Apache openly confesses and practices his creed of cruelty, whereas the Christian hypocritically professes mercy and honesty and at the same time surpasses the Apache in deeds of dishonor and brutality."

Albert had never heard her speak thus. Across the campfire, the expression in his eyes changed, like an illumination.

She knew he loved her, but he also saw her as the enemy sometimes. She was female and white, both of which he associated with weakness. Yet her simple statement in defense of the Apaches had knocked down one of his many walls. She still had so much to learn. Especially about her own son.

"Hobble the horses for the night, Albert," she told him. Keeping his hands busy also kept his mind busy, too busy to brood.

Bingham stood, picked up his rifle and stared down at her. "'Reproofs for discipline are the way of life, to keep you from the evil woman, from the smooth tongue of the adulteress. Do not desire her beauty in your heart, nor let her catch you with her eyelids. For on account of a harlot one is reduced to a loaf of bread.' So sayeth the Lord. I'll take the first watch."

Beauty? Bingham had called her harlot and adulteress often enough, but surely he did not associate that word with her. Not beauty. Puzzled, she watched the preacher stride away from the circle of firelight to take up sentry in the hills above.

Mattie shifted and picked up her plate once more with the intent of cleaning the supper mess. However, mere movement of her ankle shot pain through her. Her face must have shown it, because Gordon stood up and came toward her in that easy, coordinated stride of a man who is centered in his body, who knows both its strengths and its weaknesses well.

She was unsure of his purpose and nervous as he knelt over her, but he merely lifted her skirt's fringed hem. "None of us ever thanked you for what you did back there at the cornfield. You were brave." He gave her a crooked grin.

He felt along her ankle. She winced. In response to her flinch, he eased his grip.

The creek bed's stones had gouged and bruised her feet more than she had realized. She felt his eyes on her. She met his gaze and saw confusion there, as if he were trying to understand this wild creature that she was.

"Come on," he said, gathering her up into his arms and standing. "We're going to work on the swelling again. One more time in the cold water, and you should be ready for the famous Halpern hot foot-wrap."

She could not equate his humor with the barbaric sport of foxing that he practiced. But then, neither could she equate his artistic nature with it. His sophistication contrasted with his impoverished background. Truly, he danced with the paradox.

Fully knowing she was making her situation all that much more difficult, she nevertheless gave into this moment of being cared for. It wasn't the same as being cherished, but she could pretend, couldn't she? If only for the moment.

She put her arms around his neck and rested her head against his shoulder. She could smell his own particular male scent. She liked it.

Before Nantez had taken her captive, she had not noticed someone's skin scent. Oh, if someone wore too much toilet water, her sense of smell might be offended.

But life with Nantez had made her very much aware of scents. After a while she could identify different ones in the dark. Nantez's skin repelled her. He bathed as often as his two squaws, but it had a definite and distinctive odor.

She nestled her face deeper into the alcove created by Gordon's muscled neck and shoulder and inhaled even more deeply. His scent was an aphrodisiac. Incredibly, she felt the first stirrings of desire.

Oh, so many years had passed since Reginald first carried her to their marriage bed. Her sexual excitement had soon been doused. There was no meeting of their hearts or even their minds. Only of their flesh. Within a month or so, their lovemaking had become perfunctory and impersonal. He had seemed to be striving only to get her with child, and she strove only to get her uxorial duty over with.

Gordon lowered her to the bank again. Reluctantly, oh so reluctantly, she released her arms. He hunkered his big frame next to her legs and lifted her injured ankle. "You know, Mattie, your son doesn't trust me."

She knew he talked to take her mind off the chill of the mountain creek. She diverted her gasp into a "why?"

He looked over his shoulder at her. His pale brown eyes twinkled. "Because he's watching us. From behind that clump of underbrush off to the left behind you."

She was tempted to glance behind her but didn't. "In some ways Albert's a typical white boy. And then in other ways . . . ."

"Where did the name Albert come from?"

"Me great-grandfather. A wily old man. He was chief of clan Chisholm in the Forty-Five Rising, and he sent one son to fight for the Jacobites and one for the Hanoverians. That way old Albert ensured that the family would not suffer as they had done after the Fifteen Rising. No matter the outcome, someone would be on the winning side and forfeiture of land and wealth would be averted."

"A true Scotsman, your great-grandfather was. You might try reminding your son that he also carries Scots blood."

"He prefers to remember his Indian blood. Still refers to himself by his Indian name even. *Baishan.* It means knife in the Apache language."

"Knife. Are my suspicions right—his name comes from Nantez's free use of the knife?"

"Aye. I so named me son so as to remind me how much I hated his father. I thought I would hate me bairn, being Nantez's seed and all, but after he was born there was no way I could."

"You are an incredible person, Mattie McAlister."

She smiled. "Aye that I am. And I imagine ye find me a bit strange, too."

"Aye, that I do," he said, gently mocking her Scottish accent.

A sliver of a moon had risen, and by its wan light she peered at his face. "I tell ye straight now, Gordon Halpern. 'Tis drawn to ye, I am. For all your bizarre dress and your effete eastern ways. There's no denying it."

The hand cupping her foot stiffened ever so slightly. "I am married, Mattie."

"Ye don't have to remind me. A part of me wants to throw your fifteen hundred dollars in your face and go back to Fort Lowell. Why should I help ye get back what can only hurt me?"

He took her foot from the water and began to lightly stroke the chilled flesh with his big hands. Without looking up at her, he said, "Mattie, if I . . . if I shouldn't get Diana back from Nantez, I'd still . . . ."

He didn't finish the sentence. Nor did he have to. She understood. "You'd still not be interested in me as a woman. Is that it?"

Now he looked at her. "I admire you, I find you extremely interesting, but I . . . I am not attracted to you."

"*Glaikit!*"

"What?"

She drew her foot away from his grasp. "*Glaikit.* Idiot. Fool." With the majesty of good Queen Victoria, she pulled herself erect. "Do ye not see that ye fell for a . . . a . . . doppelganger."

"A what?" He was staring at her as if she really perplexed him.

"A doppelganger. Your wife is a ghostly image of a real person. Ye are missing the real thing, *glaikit!*"

She swung away and began to stalk back toward the camp. Hobble was more like it. Her ankle hurt terribly, but she wasn't going to ask for his assistance.

Of course, it had to happen then. Of all times, with him still staring after her. Her ankle collapsed beneath her weight. As she stumbled, she gave a small cry.

At once, he was springing up, sprinting the few steps' distance, catching her, even as she fell forward. Somehow, he rolled the two of them so that he was under her, his body serving as a cushion for her own.

Dazed, she lay atop him. "'Tis a grand thing ye—"

"Mattie, by damn, if you aren't the stubbornest, most headstrong creature I've ever—"

"That's all I'll ever be to ye, isn't it, Halpern? A creature!"

Startled by her vehemence, he stared up at her, his mouth open. "You know what I meant, Mattie."

His voice was low, as if trying to connect with her with his tone, if not his words. God's blood, it was like the way a horse breaker talks to a wild horse! She drew back her fist and slammed downward.

Her action was so unexpected that he didn't have time to dodge the blow. His head jerked to one side with the impact. His hand came up to his jaw. "You have a wicked punch there."

"I know what ye meant, all right. I also know that I wouldn't have ye even ye were served to me on a platter like flambéed pheasant. A man who's as foolish as ye, who doesn't know real quality when its beneath his nose, isn't worth my time."

He laughed, and she vibrated atop him with the rumble in his chest. "Does that mean you are reneging on our deal to find my wife?"

She braced her hands on his broad chest and pushed herself to a sitting position astride him. "Of course not. With my half of the three grand, Albert and I are going to Scotland to live."

"Scotland, is it!" He reared upright, so that he was face to face with her.

A very erotic position, she thought, what with her knees braced beneath his armpits.

"You have high hopes of locating a lost title there and becoming a grand lady?"

"I *was* a grand lady. Here."

"Then act like it, Mattie." He hefted her off him and drew her up to stand before him. "I'll help remind you if you can't remember. For one thing, ladies don't cuss."

Her hands balled, and she was sorely tempted to punch him again. "On such foundations of quicksand are opinions like yours built. Bastard! Goodnight to ye. And sonofabitch, also!"

This time, when she stalked away, she meant to keep walking on her own even if she had to hop on one foot. His beastly laughter, she ignored.

10

Mattie's left moccasin required immediate attention. All Apaches, men and women, knew how to make moccasins, since it was necessary to repair or replace the footgear often while on a raid. Consequently, each warrior always carried an awl and some sinew thread.

Mattie, likewise, practiced the habit. As she sat stitching the leather by early morning's light, Halpern painted her. "Ye make me nervous, staring at me like that."

Over the top of his sketch pad, which was braced on one knee, he frowned at her. "Don't talk. You disturb me."

"'Tis the whole problem, Halpern. If I were commonplace, I wouldn't disturb ye. As it is, I stir your creativity."

"Commonplace, no. Colorful, yes. Now tilt your

head slightly. Yeah, like that, so the sun slants across your right cheek."

"The same could be said about yourself. Colorful. I'd wager, though, that your Diana isn't colorful. Beautiful, mayhaps. But colorful, no. The two qualities aren't compatible. Beauty is boring. It conforms to the standards of the times. Conformity is commonplace."

"For someone who has such a low opinion of beauty, you are certainly loquacious."

"True beauty has its own fire." She tied a knot in the thread. "Whereas stylishness, often confused as beauty, is mere conformity."

"Will you shut up."

"There, I'm finished," she said, holding aloft her repaired moccasin.

"Well, I'm not. Hold still."

"Ye'd do well to paint the West, Halpern. Nowhere else are there such sunrises and sunsets, such richness of color. The West has an unbounded opulence of sunshine that—"

Bingham strode into the clearing. "Did ye find any game?" she asked him.

"Plenty of game. Turkey, deer, javelin. Some wild horses even."

The way his hand rubbed his rifle stock as he talked, she could tell he was agitated. His next sentence confirmed her suspicions.

"I've scouted as far as the bottom of the mountain. Found a dozen or so wickiups that look abandoned. As if the owners had to leave in a hurry. Came upon a cabin still trailing blue plumes of wood smoke. Empty, too."

Albert was whittling on a mulberry sapling for a bow he was making. He glanced up quickly. The sun, just peaking the mountain ridge, caught the gleam of hope in the boy's eyes. The same gleam of hope reflected in the adult eyes of Gordon.

Mattie dashed that hope. "The wickiups could belong to any band. The abandoned camp could be as old as year or so."

"And the cabin?"

She didn't have an answer.

"It's a start," Gordon said, putting away his pad and charcoal. "Let's follow the trail."

Bingham went down to the river to wash the cook pans. Gordon had already strapped his saddlebags on his bay and had returned to roll his blankets.

She began to get her own things together, squatting on an ankle still swollen, despite the heated blanket Gordon had wrapped it in. At the sound of hooves, she looked up, just in time to see Albert, riding bareback, trot her spotted pony from camp. "Albert!"

He kneed Pepper into a gallop.

"He's headed for his father!" she cried. There was no time to think. She was the one closest to the horses. She dashed to the nearest mount, even as pain exploded in her ankle and shot up through her leg. She swung up astride the gelding and dug her heels into the its flanks.

Pepper was already far ahead. It easily scaled the rocky banks of a low bluff. This was country in which the pony was at home.

The gelding could win hands down in a long stretch. These short bursts of convoluted clearings, devious ravines, and treacherous rock-strewn hills made up for a landscape as alien as the moon's to the gelding.

The figures of Albert and Pepper were diminishing. Her only chance was to use the Winchester sheathed in the saddle scabbard. It was a terrible decision to have to make. She drew out the rifle, took aim, and pressed her thumb down on the hammer.

The shot was deafening and the rifle recoil jarred her shoulder. And jarred her heart with its ghastly effect.

The pony tumbled. Albert somersaulted. His body landed in a grotesque heap.

Días muire, what if he had broken his neck? If God listened to mere mortals, then surely that Divine Power heard her heart's cry. A pathetic petition. *I know I am unworthy. That I could have done better, but . . . oh, please let him live!*

At a speed that would break her own neck and that of her mount's, she galloped toward the two prone forms. She reached Albert first. Before she could bound from the saddle, he was already struggling to push himself upright to a sitting position.

The pain in her ankle was secondary to the relief in finding him alive. She grabbed him to her and began rocking back and forth. "Me bairn. Achh, me wee one."

He stared past her at the lifeless horse. Her cherished Indian pony. "Mother . . . Pepper . . . ."

She felt the tears in her throat. She cupped her son's face, making him look at her. "Understand me now. I will not give ye up."

In silence, they returned to camp with Albert riding postilion.

Why did everything have to be so complicated?

She only wanted to heal and be healed. To love and be loved. Yet she had destroyed one of the very things she loved.

Gordon took the reins from her, and she fell into his arms. "Me ankle." It was throbbing so badly she felt sick to her stomach and dizzy. She feared she might pass out from the pain.

"This time you may have indeed broken it in the bargain."

"No." Even breathing was difficult. "I don't think so."

Back in the cold water it was for her ankle, at which point Gordon pronounced the bone sound enough. "No breaks," he said, examining it. Her flesh was pink and goose bumped.

"I say we bind it," Bingham muttered. He knelt on the other side of her.

Albert, in charge of the horses, watched. His eyes, large and anxious, said what he couldn't say: how awful he felt to have brought all this on.

"Bingham's right," Mattie said. "My chemise will have to do for binding strips."

The two men glanced at each other, then rose to wander away discreetly. Even Albert, a big boy now, led the horses beyond the concealment of the eight-foot canebrake.

She pulled off her shirtwaist and, still sitting, tugged her chemise up out of her skirt band and over her head. Once she had rebuttoned her shirtwaist, she began tearing her chemise. Being as threadbare as it was, the muslin gave way easily.

"Here, let me," Gordon said, rejoining her. He hun-

kered down next to her and began to bind her ankle.
His profile looked stern. From that angle, his Roman
nose didn't appear so obviously broken. Strength of
purpose was etched in his prominent chin.

Then he surprised her by withdrawing something
from his jacket pocket—her jar of glycerin and rose
water. Gently picking up her good foot, he began
rubbing a glob of the unguent into its bottom.

"Where did ye get that?"

"Off the saddlebags strapped to your pony," he
replied, his attention fully focused on her foot.

She was embarrassed. Her feet weren't pretty, not
with all their calluses and cracks and scars. "Not the
feet of a lady, are they now?" she said.

"Depends on how you define a lady." His gaze was
steady.

She closed her eyes, hiding herself behind her lids.
His fingers stroked her arch with firm, steady pressure
that was at the same time light. She sighed. Tension
eased from her. *"Días muire,* but that feels grand."

It felt more than grand. It felt wonderfully erotic.
She couldn't let herself feel that way about him,
much less think that way.

Her eyes snapped open. He had switched feet, and
his thumb was gently exploring a spot near the ball
of her injured one. On most people that spot was soft,
but hers was bony. "Deep scar here," he commented.

"Nantez's work. Or rather one of his squaws'. At
his instruction."

At once, his thumb ceased its exploration. The
horror in his eyes was like a slap across her face.

She felt defiled. Like a leper. She jerked her foot

from his grasp, then winced again at the sudden pain. "We'd best be going. The day is getting late."

When at last they rode out, the trail Bingham had found turned out to be too old and too rough to follow.

She finally gave up when the terrain ceded the remnants of its earth to solid rock and they stood on the brink of grand canyons. "This is where Nantez roams," she told Gordon.

In awe, all four of them stared out at the purple haze with mouths open at the sight of canyon after canyon looming in front them.

Somehow, somewhere in those almost inaccessible recesses of the Sierra Madres, she and Bingham were supposed to locate Nantez.

There was nowhere to go but down the precipitous walls of the gorge. At its bottom, a rapid river coursed, a tributary of the Yaqui. From that far above, its areas of white water looked like lazy swishing foam.

They checked their cinch straps. As an extra precaution, Mattie secured her own mount's strap through the ring of girth with an extra jerk. One by one, the expedition's horses fell into line and picked out a path of sorts that obviously hadn't been used recently. It zigzagged down the steep mountain.

Behind her, hooves dislodged small rocks that went tumbling out of sight; their pinging sounds likewise diminished into the quiet void. The loosened rocks were a danger to those ahead on the trail.

She missed Pepper. The pony would have handled the dangerous terrain even better than Bingham's stout mule or the pack mule. As it was, the dun mare belonging to the Mexican soldier shied nervously with every step.

She glanced back and saw Albert's face. For all his expression of bravado, his little hands clung tightly to the saddle horn of the other Mexican's big iron gray.

The descent down trails carved into impossible slopes took half a day. There was no doubt in Mattie's mind that a lot of mules had been lost by slipping over the sheer precipices. Despite the awesome view of chimneylike peaks and porphyritic pillars, taut nerves made her back and thighs and fingers ache even more than her ankle.

They halted for a midday meal on the narrow plain banking the river. Briery buckthorn made for less than ideal picnic conditions.

Gordon swallowed a bite of hardtack and asked her, "What do you think? Anything look recognizable?"

She stretched a cigarette paper between fingers and sprinkled tobacco flakes onto it. "Halpern, look around ye. Do ye see anything that isn't rock or water? It all looks the same."

Bingham knelt on one knee beside the rushing water to fill his canteen. "Our main worry is to find a crossing. Or we go back up the way we came."

Locating a safe crossing took two hours. The other side had a shallow landing that forced a virtually vertical climb up the canyon's striated wall. It was a tiring day, especially for the horses.

When Mattie thought about the succession of canyons beyond this one, she contemplated pulling out of her agreement with Gordon. Yet her nature was such that she would see the venture through. She had to.

Besides, why not enjoy the opportunity to spend as much time as she could with Gordon? He was the one man who had the power both to awaken her dormant passions and to break her heart, if she weren't careful.

Eventually, they neared the summit. Where the trail ran parallel to the ridge, her mount began balking at proceeding ahead. She held her breath, as if that small act would lessen the chances of soaring out onto a gulf of thin air.

In front of her, Bingham's mount danced nervously. When its hooves drew perilously close to the trail's curving rim, he reined hard on the horse. "You son of Satan," he cussed, "I'll strip the worthless hide from your flanks!"

Mattie scanned the trail immediately beyond Bingham and saw nothing—until she looked up, and up. "Sonofabitch," she whispered.

The plumes projecting from navy blue hats were only less ominous than plumes from Apache war bonnets. A score or more of rifle barrels winked wickedly in the sunlight. They were trained on her and her fellow travelers. Even if they could outrun a hail of bullets, the trail was too narrow in which to turn the animals.

"Federalistas!" Bingham said.

"Aye," she agreed. The grim image of being lined up against an adobe wall and executed by the Mexican soldiers did not improve her attitude. "Any suggestions?"

"Given the alternatives," Gordon said behind her in that dry voice of his, "it would seem there's nothing we can do but brave it out."

Her heart thumping, she kneed her horse onward.

The four of them and their caravan cantered on up the steep, pebble-strewn slope.

By the time they crested the canyon's rim, it looked as if a whole company of Mexican soldiers were lined up to greet them. They wore less than friendly smiles and appeared eager to test their bayoneted rifles.

Gordon rode up beside her and said sotto voce, "Our only consolation is that none of the three soldiers whose horses we have stolen is among our official welcoming committee."

An officer in charge sat astride a magnificent white stallion. He nudged his horse toward them. Closer, she could see that he had the bulbous nose and florid coloring of a heavy drinker. *"Buenos días."* He nodded toward Gordon. "You are Americans, eh?"

Gordon rested his hands over his saddle horn, as if making himself comfortable. "That we are, colonel."

"And I am Colonel Morales, prefect of the district." He flicked a leather gauntlet-clad hand toward their string of horses. "You have a large remuda for so small a party, no?"

Unsure of what a remuda was, Gordon glanced at Mattie. At that same moment, she noticed that the horse her son rode sported the brand of the Mexican cavalry—and knew that the colonel had also spotted the brand.

"They're not all our horses, Colonel," she said with what she hoped was an easy smile. "The two I and my son are riding we found grazing in a cornfield. Empty saddles and all."

The officer's raisin-brown eyes narrowed on the saddle. She realized then she had tripped up. All three saddles clearly had the stamp of the Mexican army engraved on their saddle skirts.

"I think," he said, "that you four will enjoy the hospitality of our *hacienda*. It is not far from here. Maybe two hours' ride."

"We have other plans—" Gordon began.

"We'd like that very much," she broke in.

Gordon turned one of his black looks on her, clearly annoyed by her contradiction of him. Obviously, he didn't realize that if they didn't accept the offer, the colonel would enforce it.

She returned his glower then flashed the colonel a gracious smile. "We *are* very tired, colonel. We lost two of our horses in a sandstorm and were afoot until we recovered them. We would very much welcome a respite at your *hacienda*."

She could only hope her story satisfied him. As they fell in with the troops, she glanced at Bingham and Gordon. Both wisely said nothing to dispute it.

The two-hour trip required crossing the Plains of Janos, which were peppered mostly with dull sagebrush. Tired and annoyed by her aching ankle, Mattie rode lax in the saddle. Her muscles felt as stiff as new leather.

Quail scattered as the company of soldiers passed by and wild geese took flight. Albert surprised everyone by drawing a bow and letting fly an arrow he had fletched with an eagle feather. While he rode the dozen or so yards to retrieve the bird, the colonel watched him with eyes that did not reflect amicable feelings. "The goose will be welcome at the dinner table tonight. The boy is adept in the ways of the Indian, eh?"

She knew he was suspicious about Albert's heritage. "My husband and I," she deliberately nodded at Gordon, "felt that our son should be raised to hunt game on his own."

Gordon's hands tightened almost imperceptibly on his reins, but he did not betray her.

"Ahh, then you, *señor,* are an avid hunter?" the colonel said.

Beneath the flow of his mustache, he smirked. "Unfortunately, Colonel, I do not have Albert's remarkable skill."

"The four of you have been in Mexico long?"

"Not very," she replied quickly, deciding to use Gordon's recounting of his travels as a basis. "We've been visiting mining towns in the Southwest for investment purposes. Mr. Bingham here is our guide."

"Then you are familiar with Mexico, *señor?*" the colonel asked the preacher.

This was coming close to being an inquisition.

Bingham cleared his throat. "A little. I had a vision of the Virgin. It led me to seek her out here in Mexico's pastures." He finished by genuflecting. "I never found the virgin I was seeking."

The colonel slapped his thigh and chortled. "Ah, very good, *señor.* Very, very good!" But the stony expression in his eyes stated clearly that he didn't buy the story. Mattie could almost feel the adobe wall at her back.

11

When it came within sight, the hacienda appeared to be more a fort, or presidio, than home. The presidio and the outcropping of baked adobe homes composed the pueblo known as Tres Amigos.

The hacienda's high adobe walls were pockmarked by age, their mud brick exposed. They were capped with shards of glass. A cannon's snout poked from a guard tower.

However, inside the walls the main building was a handsome old home with a span of lovely arched arcades. A cool retreat from the beating rays of the sun, directly overhead.

The colonel led his company of straggly soldiers on past a line of hay racks to the stable yard, where wagonloads of beans and corn were corralled.

Mattie forgot to favor her injured ankle when she

dismounted and would have fallen had it not been for Gordon. For one timeless moment, the feel of his arms around her waist, supporting her, was something wonderful. A respite from the bleakness of her world.

"My sergeant here will find some sort of accommodations for your guide and your son," Colonel Morales said to her and Gordon, "and relieve him of his dead goose. If you two will come with me, I will provide a room for you."

Gordon's arms stiffened, and he released her at once. She was afraid he would make a protest, but the colonel walked on past them.

With misgivings, she watched the little man lead Albert and Bingham off in another direction. What if Albert made a bid to escape without her watchful eye upon him?

After they collected their saddlebags, they followed the officer across a colonnaded courtyard that contained a large fountain in its center. The air was cooler and scented with hibiscus and oleander.

They passed through a portal that opened into an office of sorts. The colonel picked up a hand bell from the cluttered desk and rang it. "Liliana will show you to your quarters," he said with a smile that would indicate only the most congenial of hosts.

In only a matter of seconds a gnome of a woman appeared. Her face was as brown as a prune and almost as wrinkled. From her features, Mattie concluded that she was either of the Tarahumara or Yaqui Indian tribes. She appeared to be middle-aged, and the legs that showed from beneath the fringe of her knee-length deer-hide skirt were heavy.

After receiving instructions from the colonel about dinner time, they followed Liliana down a cool, tiled corridor. She admitted them to one of the small wooden doors opening off it.

The room was as proportionately small but, surprisingly, comfortably furbished with, among other pieces, a staved hip-bath, a copper-paneled trapadero for clothing, and a dressing bureau.

Its mirror revealed to Mattie just how unkempt she looked. Dear God, any man would be repulsed by a woman whose hair looked like snarled barbed-wire, whose clothing was as stained and torn as the town beggar's, and who hadn't had a full bath in weeks.

Her gaze drifted from the mirror to the bed. The large four-poster bed draped with jute netting stared at her like a corpse risen from the dead. She might just as well have eaten jimpson weed, so crazy she must be to pretend she and Gordon were husband and wife.

After the old Indian woman departed, Gordon turned on her. "Mattie, what in God's name prompted you to lie to the colonel? You've gone and gotten us in a—"

The way he balled his hands low on his hips and glared at her through the thick fringe of lashes infuriated her. "I saved our hides, Halpern!"

Despite her statement, he was backing her into a corner, with only the bed on one side of her and a shuttered window on the other. "Did you now? Or did you have another motive?" He looked so fierce, so brutal, so angry.

"Ye ever heard of adobe-walling? That's what the Mexicans do to their prisoners. They blindfold you and put you up against a wall. Then they fire bullets into you, execution-style. The three horses we took from those three infantrymen all sported Mexican army saddles as well as brands."

He towered over her now. The muscle that twitched in his jaw frightened her. He was big enough to do anything he wanted to her. "Your explanation was superb, Mattie. And sufficient." His voice had dropped to a quiet tone; much too quiet. "You didn't have to make us out to be husband and wife in the bargain."

"As if I'd want to be your wife," she said, hoping her tone was more defiant than her cowardly heart. She felt as if she actually was up against a wall. She could back no farther.

"Then why?" He canted his head. "Unless, now you are figuring on double-crossing me. Tie in with the Mexicans. I don't know. Something isn't right, here."

"It's Albert," she blurted.

"Albert?" His scowl relented, if only a little. "What does he have to do with this?"

"The arrow he shot . . . the way he looks, all Indian . . . I was afraid the Colonel would realize Albert was . . . the Mexicans would as soon kill an Apache child as squash a worm . . . I had to. . . . " She knew that she was babbling, but she couldn't help it. "I'm so bloody tired of battling enemies on all sides of me, Halpern!"

How much pain was enough? When would she be able to say to herself that she knew all of sorrow and no longer chose it as her own. She had built barricade after barricade to halt the fire of fear, to save just a small portion of herself. Was there no stopping or escaping the burning?

Gordon's hands dropped. He sat down on the bed and stared at his open palms. "Look, Mattie. Don't burden me with the kid. Any kid. I don't have any background to draw on for being responsible for children. I got by on my own. You're just going to have to let Albert do the same for himself."

She stepped in front of him. "Never. Do ye hear me, Halpern? Never. As long as I am alive to watch a sunrise, I'll be there for me son!" She paused. "That's what loving is," she said more softly. "Seeing only the love in others and giving only love."

He took one of her hands that hung at her side and turned it over, palm up. His fingers traced the calluses and scars. "It hasn't been easy for you, has it, Mattie McAlister?"

She stood rigid, hardly daring to breathe. "'Tis never easy. For anyone. You know that."

His eyes darkened to a deep black, as dark as a mine. "Up until Diana was captured, I would have said differently. Her life seemed to be one eternal moment of whimsical self-indulgence." With that, he released her hand. "Speaking of self-indulgence, a warm bath would be wonderful. Do you think we could persuade that old Indian woman to bring us warmed water?"

"You're going to bathe? Here?"

A slow smile twitched his mustache. "Mattie, I told you I'd help remind you that you're a grand lady if you couldn't remember. A grand lady should bathe regularly."

The flush of mortification heated her cheeks. "Circumstances don't always make that possible, Halpern. Unless nature fills Tucson's arroyos, one has to have money to use the public shower bathhouse."

He came to his feet. "Well, today we have been blessed by circumstances. In place of nature and an arroyo, that old Indian woman can fill the tub. While I go in search of her, I want you to undress."

"But—"

Grinning, he shrugged out of his coat and tossed it to her. "Shroud yourself in that if modesty overcomes you."

He left the room, and she stood gaping after him. The man was quite clearly serious. She could refuse. What would happen? She was coming to know him well over the past fortnight. Despite his brutal profession—well, one of his professions was brutal, anyway—she doubted that he would force her. That sensitive, passionate side of him—his other profession—would not permit it.

So what would he do? And what should she do? Playing the coy maiden would be preposterous for her. Yet, despite all she had been subjected to, there was still that core of modesty within her that Nantez's crudity had never been able to obliterate.

Considering the repercussions of this coming bath, she began to disrobe. Her clothing was stiff with grit and dried mud and sweat. Just in time she peeled away her shirt and slid into his jacket, which hung well past her knees. The jacket must have cost a fortune. It was lined with satin, cool to the touch, and had black jet beading edging the lapel.

With only a brief warning knock, he entered, followed by old Liliana. She carried two pails of steaming water. At the sight of Mattie, clad only in a man's jacket, she grinned. Her mouth reminded Mattie of a jack-o'-lantern's.

Liliana dumped the water into the staved tub, then padded over to the *trapadero* to take out a wash cloth and soap for Mattie's use.

It was then that Mattie noticed the welts on the back of the woman's thick legs and heavy arms. Some appeared to be recent. "Liliana? Have the soldiers been mistreating ye?"

The woman looked at her stolidly, and Mattie repeated the question in Spanish.

"Pendejos," Liliana replied. "Their raping and murdering will not go unpunished. One day my people will turn on them."

Mattie said something in Spanish to console the woman. She could understand the hate that blazed in those Indian eyes. But it would take more than her people's revenge to make a difference. The fire in the heart would have to be put out first. Mattie still had her own fire of hate to quench.

After the Indian woman departed, Gordon closed the door and turned back to her. "What was that all about?"

She told him about Liliana's mistreatment by the soldiers. "The Tarahumara and Yaqui warriors can be crueler than the Apaches. The problem is that they burn their anger in the marihuana weed. They loose themselves in its mists as they try to recall centuries ago when they lost their glory with the arrival of the mounted white man. But one day, they'll rebel, and no one's scalp will be safe."

A wicked gleam graced Gordon's eye. Apparently, he knew she was delaying. "Well, Mattie? Are you ready to be scrubbed down like a baked potato?"

"Like a baked potato?"

"Maybe that's not a good analogy. How about like a sacrificial virgin?"

At that, she laughed aloud. "A virgin? Aye, that is good, Halpern! I tell ye now, if the town of Tucson sacrificed virgins to ensure rainfall, I'd make bloody certain its good citizens knew I was the town tart."

He chuckled. "Well said." He strode up behind her and took the coat's dusty lapels in his hands. "Quit stalling, Mattie. Give up the jacket and get in the tub. I'll close my eyes, if that's a problem for you."

She glared at him over her shoulder. "Ye know it is." It was a problem for her with him standing so close.

Obediently, he closed his eyes, but the twitching of his mustache betrayed his amusement.

She lifted her arms from the drooping sleeves and, free of the jacket, quickly stepped into the tub. "Christ thorns, Halpern! This is the devil's cauldron! Did ye want a boiled potato?"

"Oh, quit grumbling."

Glancing around at him, she realized his gaze was on her backside. At once, she slid down until the water topped her breast. Still, the steam offered little coverage. "Ye are a blackguard, Halpern. Soap? A wash cloth? Do ye mind passing them to me?"

"Oh, I plan to do more than that."

His tone was suggestive. She turned her head again to see that he was rolling up his sleeves. "Oh, no ye don't! I can wash meself, thank ye."

"Your dirt-smeared chin and leaf-bedecked hair doesn't indicate an affinity for water." He advanced on her with soap and cloth and purpose.

"Why are ye doing this to me?"

He swished the cloth in the water and briskly buffed it with the bar of soap. She noted that the soap was made not from the harsh lye used by the fort laundresses but herbs and soft tallow. "Maybe to pay you in coin for your own devilish deeds."

"Me devilish deeds?" He was unsnarling her matted hair with his fingers. "What about your own shenanigans? Ach, what are ye doing?"

"For instance, flicking your cigarette ashes in my Scotch." Without warning he dunked her head beneath the water.

She came up sputtering, "Ye bloody—!"

"Hold still." His powerful hands massaged her scalp with the sweet-scented soap.

"Ahhh." Was that her, purring like some tamed household cat?

Another dunking!

"Damn ye, Halpern!" she gasped, coming up for air, her hair rinsed free of soapsuds.

A wash cloth swooped down between her breasts. They were small, but fully rounded, looking to him as if God had taken two pomegranates and appended them to her chest. They were hard little knots, maybe because they were untouched. Unnoticed. Unheeded. They yearned to be stroked by a lover, though she would deny such a thing. Mattie McAlister didn't need any man to make her feel better.

Gordon scrubbed her shoulders vigorously. The cloth worked its way down her spine and upward to her nape, then slid under each of her arms. Next, it swooshed down past her navel.

"I can do that meself, thank ye very much!"

"Oh, but I insist."

She could tell he was taking great pleasure in tormenting her for a change.

Then, he knelt beside her, his face even with her own, and worked the cloth between her thighs. "For all that you're small-built, you're perfectly formed, Mattie McAlister."

In his eyes she could see the ember of passion glowing, growing, filling his green-rimmed pupils.

Her eyes closed against that sudden flare of desire she saw deep in his eyes. The heat simmering in the pit of her stomach, far down, bubbled over, flooded her veins with a rushing, swelling desire. That desire thundered its need against her eardrums.

Common sense, logic, conscience were drowned in this passion. It was alien to her, and since she had never experienced it, she did not know how to deal with it. To fight or to yield.

After being a captive all those years, she had committed herself to becoming autonomous. In doing so, she had given up her right to intimacy. She had disassociated herself from the chance of having a loving man for her mate. All these years, she had fought. For just this one moment, she would yield.

She sighed. Without quite realizing it, her legs

parted farther. His fingers, covered by the cloth, were allowed entrance. Her hips shifted, swayed, created their own current within the water.

Then the fingers were gently withdrawn. Her eyes snapped open. Gordon was slipping his hands beneath her arms, raising her from the water, cradling her against his chest. His body warmed hers.

"I'm dripping all over your shirt."

His savage mouth silenced hers. Still holding her lips prisoner, he carried her across the room and lowered her onto the bed. Only then did he set her free—only long enough to shrug out of his wet shirt and shuck his dusty pants.

He was built so beautifully, she thought, watching him from a pillow that was becoming rapidly soaked by her heavy, wet hair. She couldn't even remember Reggie, who apparently had been an average specimen of the male. Nantez reminded her of one of the Grimm brothers' trolls. Squat, ugly, prehistoric.

Gordon was long of limb and roped with muscles. Articulate, too. "The heart only lives when it loves, Mattie. Give into love. You won't be hurt."

But 'tis not me ye love, she wanted to scream.

Of course, Gordon Halpern was talking of that passion of the bodies. Something she had never quite understood. Romance and chivalry, such as her literary diet had yielded—Dante, Boccaccio, Shakespeare—those things she could understand. Even be excited by. But this primitive passion. . . .

Yet she gave in to the mystery of his passion. She raised her hands to cup the dark face leaning over hers and draw it down until their lips touched once more. She would have sworn her action elicited surprise in him, but then her eyes closed and she gave into the wonderful feeling of . . . feeling. Just feeling.

Of itself, the act of kissing was wondrous. Of lips touching each other, then touching here and there on the face. The underside of her chin, his eyelid, her earlobe. Then their lips returned to claim one another, as if in need of replenishment.

His tongue tip, stroking her lips, sought entrance to her mouth. His hand glided over the rising mound of her breast, paused, then moved on to claim her rebellious little nipple.

The shock of both, his hand and his invading tongue, made her tense for a fraction of a second.

Then, incredibly, her body overrode her brain. Her repressed passion overcame her caution. With a moan, she responded touch for touch, kiss for kiss, murmur for murmur. "Halpern, me dear, ye are so grand . . . there."

He chuckled. His weight eased partially down over her. "And you are so small . . . there."

A furious blush heated her skin. "I am made like other women?" It was a hopeful question.

"Made like other women? Commonly so." His mouth covered her breasts with kisses in between breaths. "But think like other women? Impossible."

Her disappointment was followed by nervous curiosity. "How so?" Catching his jaw, she stopped his kisses. Lifted it so that she could see into his eyes. "Do I not think . . . think properly enough? Have I been too bold?"

Another chuckle. "No, no. You are free-spirited.

You have a mind—and will, I might add—of your own. An entrancing conversationalist, you are, Mattie. No discussions of knitting and babies, but ribald stories of poker games and Indian tricks and—"

"But I love babies and . . . "

He was still kissing her, had worked his way down to her navel. " . . . and you are a wonderful mother. I see this in things you do. You are there for Albert. Always. No matter what. Whether it's pain or fear or lack."

A part of her mind wondered what they were doing talking while their bodies were making this fantastic pleasure.

Gordon, shifting his weight full atop her, gave her that answer: "It's because of all this that I am drawn to you, my charming renegade."

She looked up into his face, so close to her own. "You are drawn to me? To me? To the wild, wanton Mattie McAlister?"

"Oh, yes," he whispered against her ear. His breath made her feel all tingly; his mustache tickled in a most pleasant way. "Very much."

His weight was heavy. She felt him, too, large and heavy between her thighs. Seeking, prodding, entering slowly, slightly, withdrawing, then once again nudging.

"You are like no other person. I've met the low-born and the high-born. You are neither. And yet both. Forever Mattie."

She peered up at him through narrowed eyes. Was this a compliment? She pushed at him. She managed to roll from beneath him. "No, Halpern. Ye are merely satisfying your dark side."

He jackknifed upright. "What?"

"Ye heard me." She levered herself up onto her elbows. Her breasts sloped forward to pouting points. Naked, breathing hard, she and Gordon faced each other. "Come to me with love in ye heart. Not just in your head."

"Did it ever cross your mind that I am married?"

"Did it cross yours?"

That black scowl of his took over. "Too often, lately."

She was paradoxically pleased by his admission. "Ye will stay with her if we find her?"

"Yes." His blunt reply stole her hope. "To do otherwise would make less of me."

Had she only been so loved. Urbane, charming Reggie, in his flight during the Apache raid, had not even paused to look back and make sure she was safe. But Gordon, the killer of men, was gentle of heart. How could that be? Had she been so socially deprived during her captivity that she had failed to grasp the concept of what the Netdahe shaman had called the "True of Heart?"

She rolled away from Gordon, pulling the spread with her to cover her nudity. "Halpern, a terrible thing has happened. I have fallen in love with ye." She saw that beastly twitch of his mustache. Her oddity must indeed amuse him. "I could refuse to help ye find your wife, but I know ye would barter with the devil himself to help get her back. So I'll help ye in your quest. But be warned. Once we find her, you're on your own."

"For God's sake, Mattie. I told you, I'm married. I don't have any choice."

She picked up the bar of soap and hurled it at

him. He ducked. It knocked over the statue of the Virgin in the niche. "Ye made the choice to make love to me!"

He lunged across the bed and grabbed her arm, jerking her back down onto the mattress with him. "Don't put all this on me. You admitted you were drawn to me."

She squirmed beneath him. "But ye acted upon it. I won't be an incident in your life. Or anyone's for that matter. I am worth too much for that."

His iron-strong grasp stilled her flailing hands. "Don't you think I know that, Mattie McAlister. You're unforgettable."

"I tire of this sparring with words."

"You need to be made love to. We all do. Men and women were made to be loved. To be touched and held and stroked and caressed."

His voice was a caress in itself. She was yielding to its mesmeric tone when a rap at the door interrupted them. From the other side, a masculine voice delivered a message in Spanish.

At Gordon's quizzical look, she explained wryly, "The colonel requests our presence now for dinner. It would appear your sacrificial virgin has been spared."

"For the moment. And I much prefer the town tart."

12

Heat from the dining table's candles, as well as those in the wall sconces, flushed Mattie's cheeks. Or mayhaps erotic memories of an hour earlier were responsible for her "uncommon good looks," as Colonel Morales put it upon seeing her. Indeed, the two sergeants also present eyed her with . . . surely, it couldn't be admiration.

Her skin glowed from Gordon's rigorous scrubbing. Its natural rose undertone was due to her Scottish heritage.

True, her hair, though clean and lustrous, looked like a bird's nest according to Gordon. She had refused his suggestion to draw her heavy hair up into a neat cluster of curls and coils.

She still wore the rank leather skirt but had changed smocks. The black velveteen blouse she had donned had a scooped neck and was fringed with tiny seed-shells sewn by one of Nantez's squaws.

Wearing the blouse set off a line of questioning that was leading in a dangerous direction. "Your *blusa, señora,*" the colonel said. "It looks Indian tailored. Apache work, if I am not mistaken."

Across from her, Gordon shot her a veiled look of concern. All she could think of was the tender, raging passion his touch engendered in her. She forced herself to focus on the officer.

"Aye, that it is, Colonel Morales. We bought it off a blanket Indian at Fort Bowie. An old Apache, I am told." She leaned forward and flashed the little man a warm, disarming smile. "I would love to buy more. Can you tell me if any Apaches live in the area?"

He fingered one end of his mustache, as if trying to make up his mind about her. At last, he said, "You do realize, *señora,* that they are very dangerous people?"

"Savages. Subhumans," Bingham said. He abstained from the wine but stabbed at the baked *pozole* and Albert's goose with a gourmand's relish. "'They seize bow and spear; they are cruel and have no mercy.' Thus sayeth the Lord."

"I've heard that they are indeed dangerous," Mattie said, accepted the *bolillos* proffered by a Mexican servant boy. "But the Apaches we saw at Fort Bowie seemed so tame."

"One of their principal chiefs in our area is far from tame, *señora.* Nantez is cruelty incarnate."

At the mention of his father, Albert perked up. Thus far he had been silent, downing his food like a starved wolf cub.

Before joining the soldiers in the sala, Mattie had warned him to say nothing about his father. "There are those who would want to harm you if they suspect you are Nantez's son," she had told him. If Albert had been brought up in the security of civilized society, she would have had qualms about being so blunt with the child. But Albert was well acquainted with murder and violence.

Did she really think she could introduce him to what she had once considered the white society's civilizing influence? After four years at Fort Lowell, she wasn't so certain that white society was any better. Human nature was human nature wherever one found it.

She leaned forward, resting her forearms on the edge of the massive mahogany table. It was so old, it had been worn smooth by both hand polishing and diners' arms. "You said this Nantez is in the area?"

"His base camp is deep in Cusarare Canyon."

Cusarare Canyon. The name was familiar. "How far is this place?"

"At the edge of Terra Incognita . . . the Void of the Canyons. You will never find your way there without a guide. Nor would you want to, *señora.*"

"Terra Incognita?" Gordon asked, twirling the fragile stem of his fluted glass between his powerful fingers. "Is that on any map?"

"No. No one knows where it is but the Indians who roam it. The Yaquis, the Tarahumaras, the Apaches."

"Colonel?"

Everyone turned toward the *sala* door that had been opened by a nervous-looking soldier. He spoke in rapid Spanish. Mattie pretended to be occupied with the breaded goat meat, but the private's message rang an alarm in her: two soldiers, afoot, had wandered into the compound.

"Perdónenme," the colonel said to those at the table and placed his napkin beside his plate. "I have a matter to attend to."

The other two officers did not speak good English, and in the colonel's absence, the conversation fumbled along in a horrendous combination of the two languages. Mattie desperately wanted to alert Bingham and Gordon. Maybe the three arrivals weren't the same three they had unhorsed back at the creek bed, but her intuition warned otherwise.

At last, the colonel reentered the room. She watched his face closely for any telltale signs of change of disposition. Were those black-beaded eyes more suspicious than earlier?

"My regrets, *señores, señora.*" He reseated himself, placed his napkin on his lap.

She breathed easier—until he snapped his fingers, telling the hovering boy to fetch the two soldiers, then said to her and the others, "Some visitors have arrived whom I think you may know."

She gave Gordon a frantic look. His brows met across the bridge of his nose in a perplexed expression. She gave a little warning shake of her head, and he nodded.

Then she flashed Bingham the same warning glance. He looked from her to the doorway.

At that moment, the boy entered the dining room. He was followed by the very two she had dreaded.

The rotund sergeant was the first to recognize her and the others. His fat finger pointed like a pistol at Bingham. *"¡Allí!* That's the one," he cried out in Spanish. "That's the one who held us up and killed Diego and stole our horses!"

Colonel Morales spread his hands. "My very own guests at our supper table. They break bread with me, drink my wine, and all the time they have betrayed me."

As if a message had passed on telegraph wires between them, Gordon and Bingham shot to their feet. They turned the table onto its side. Dishes, glasses, serving utensils crashed to the floor. Glass splintered. Candles sputtered hot wax.

Mattie and Albert jumped back from the flying debris.

At the same time, additional soldiers poured through the door. A total of fifteen rifles were aimed at the four guests. Faced with this, they all froze.

"¡Basta!" the colonel said. "Enough." He turned to the fat soldier, Gordo, and motioned toward them. *"¿Éstos son?"*

The soldier nodded, his chins quivering like pudding. *"¡Sí!"*

The colonel smiled. "Well then, we now have ourselves a child and three thieves. And what does one do with three thieves?"

One of the sergeants answered in Spanish, "Crucify them, *mi coronel.*"

She didn't bother with translating. Their fate was obvious.

"Boy. Come here." Colonel Morales said.

Albert flicked her a glance. What choice was there? She nodded. Tentative steps took the nine-year-old toward the officer.

He put his fist beneath Albert's jaw and tilted the little face upward. *"Sí,* this one does look like an Indian, sergeant. He will make a good servant."

The breath eased out of her. At least, Albert would not be killed. There was a chance for him. He could find a way to escape and make his way back to his father. Even life with Nantez was better than death. This philosophy was what had sustained her when she was with Nantez.

However, the colonel wasn't finished. "The boy's ears will fetch a good price in Mexico City."

"No!" she bellowed. She charged forward like a berserk buffalo enraged at her young being harmed. Short of being shot by all fifteen rifles, nothing could stop her. The sheer foolishness of her act caught the soldiers by surprise.

In less than an instant, her act communicated itself to Gordon and Bingham. As one, they hefted either end of the overturned table and stormed forward with it as a shield. A formidable ploy.

The startled soldiers did not know whether to fire or where to fire if they did. A few turned and ran. At the door, they jammed up. The table pinned several soldiers against the wall, and Colonel Morales among them. Dropping his end of the table, Gordon swept up one of the abandoned rifles and spun toward Colonel Morales. The officer was trying to push his way clear of the table.

"Stop!" Gordon ordered. "Now!"

The colonel and the other soldiers still pinned all halted. If they did not understand English, then the rifle's menacing snout spoke to them clearly. Of the dozen still in the room, all raised their hands. Weapons clattered to the floor.

In accord, Bingham and Albert began collecting them. Hastily. The soldiers looked as if they were just realizing that their superiority of numbers had had the advantage.

Gordon nodded at the table. "Move it. Out of our way."

At once, three soldiers nearest him complied. Then all the soldiers stepped away from the door. Absurdly, they appeared to form the parallel lines for saluting couples wedded in military ceremonies.

She and Albert hurried through the human hallway. Gordon and Bingham, weapons in hand, followed, walking backward, their eyes and rifles trained on the soldiers.

At the last moment, Gordon pointed his rifle at Morales. "You're going with us. If your men attempt to stop us, a bullet stops your heart."

So that everyone understood, Mattie translated Gordon's order into Spanish.

Morales's helpless fury was replaced by a fear that manifested in his darting gaze. A trapped rat. Then, he managed a nod and followed them down the corridor of upraised hands.

"Mattie," Gordon said, "you and Albert collect our gear. Meet us at the stables."

She and Albert sped down the colonnaded walkway. Albert ran into the room he and Bingham had been sharing. She dashed into theirs, assembled their strewn possessions. Arms full, she whirled to go.

Liliana stood in the doorway. Her flat face showed no emotion. In her arms was an antique musket.

Mattie's heart jumped up to her throat. After all she had been through at the merciless hands of the Netdahe squaws, she could not imagine dying at the hands of this Tarahumara Indian woman.

"I go," Liliana said. "I go. You go. We go."

Mattie tried to hold back her rising smile. She certainly wasn't going to argue with a musket. "We go."

Shouldering the saddlebags, she scooted past the Indian woman. Albert was not next door, but the room was empty of possessions. Hoping that he was already at the stables, she headed in that direction. She took a moment to lower the heavy bar across the courtyard gates behind her and the Indian woman.

Albert was already at the stables and mounted, as were Gordon and Bingham, along with their hostage, Colonel Morales. His hands were tied behind his back. "My men will find you and kill you in ways more hideous than any Apache could devise," he said.

"I doubt that," Mattie replied, swinging up into the saddle of her horse.

"Let's get out of here!" Bingham said. Nervously, he kept looking toward the courtyard. She, too, was expecting the soldiers to beat down its wooden gates.

Mattie gestured at Liliana. "She wants to go with us."

Gordon stared from her to the Indian woman and back to her. "Any more join us, and we could form our own parade. It would announce our presence in the Sierras to Nantez better than any trumpet herald."

"It might not be a bad idea," Bingham said and spit a wad of juice into the straw strewn across the stable floor. "Letting the woman go with us. The Tarahumaras and the Yaquis know the Barranca del Cobre better than the Apaches."

The woman must have understood that Bingham was on her side because she grinned broadly.

"What Bingham says is true," Mattie said.

"Get her a horse then," Gordon told Albert.

But when Albert opened the door to one of the stalls, the old woman shook her head. "I go. I go."

"I think she means she wants to walk," Mattie said.

"Walk?" Gordon repeated in dismay.

"Aye." Mattie had come to learn that the Tarahumaras, hardy survivors of the pre-Spanish era, were known as "the running people." "The Tarahumaras compete in races called *rarajipari*. It's sort of like several Greek marathons strung together. I have heard the Apache tell stories of watching Tarahumaras chase a deer until it collapsed and then finish it off with poisoned arrows or stones."

"Let's get on with it," Bingham said again and kneed his mount.

"Where to?" Mattie asked once they were outside the compound.

"Ask the Indian woman," Gordon told her.

In Spanish, she asked Liliana if she knew where in the Barranca del Cobre the Apaches lived.

The old woman grunted. *"Lugar del Aguilucho."*

"Place of the Eagles," she translated for Gordon.

"Does that ring a bell with you?"

She shook her head. "No."

"I think that's down river from a Tarahumara hamlet on the Rio Cusarare," Bingham said.

"Cusarare!" the woman said, a happy expression carved briefly into her face.

"The woman must be from there," Gordon said. He pulled back on the reins of his horse until he was even with the preacher. "How far is this Place of the Eagles?"

"From *Tres Amigos?*" Bingham fingered his beard. "After all these years, it's hard to recall. Maybe fifty miles as the crow flies."

"In this rock-jumbled land that could mean as much as three days by horseback or even more," Gordon said.

"Aye," Mattie said, "if that first day spent descending into a single canyon was anything to measure by."

By tacit agreement, they rode throughout the hours of darkness. With only a sliver of a moon to light the way, the going was slow and tedious. Morales maintained a furious silence.

Mattie swayed sleepily in the saddle. Fortunately, the sure-footed horses seemed to know instinctively where to place their hooves.

Ahead of her, Colonel Morales still sat ramrod straight. But so did Gordon. No further attention was needed at the moment. Mattie let herself doze off.

Toward dawn, a thickening mist made further travel impossible. Gordon called a halt. "Ask Liliana if she has any idea where we are," he told her.

She repeated the question in Spanish, but Liliana

shook her head. Because of the fog, identification of a locale was like looking for a gnat on a burro's rump. There was nothing to do but bed down for the remaining hours of darkness.

While Albert hobbled the mounts, the others stretched out bedrolls. Bingham removed his saddle blanket and offered it to Liliana for a bedroll. The thick woolen pad was rank, but Liliana took it and, wordlessly, lay down on it.

"Morales sleeps between you and me," Gordon told Bingham with a meaningful glance at the officer. "We don't want him to sleepwalk, do we?"

Bingham shook out his bedroll. "If he does, he better offer up a prayer to the Almighty first."

"Mother," Albert said, holding up Morales' saddlebags. "Look!" He fished out a bottle from one side.

"Gin!" Gordon said. "To warm the soul!"

"Set the soul on fire," Bingham muttered.

Not far from Gordon, she and Albert stretched out on the hard ground. She could feel the cold air penetrating her blanket. She should sleep, but thoughts and images and longings kept her awake. Every so often, she would shift her hips. She told herself it was her rocky bed that made her uncomfortable, but her continued squirming, she suspected, was a telltale sign of something more: the wanting of Gordon.

This wanting was relentless. Always within her, always prickling her. It was a physical thing. It was an emotional thing. It was everything.

There was something about Gordon that revealed to her another dimension of herself. A better. Because of him she had great longing—and great fear—but she felt more alive than ever. He was her sustenance; she wanted to taste him until exhaustion set in.

At last she fled the disturbing thoughts and images through sleep. A sleep that was far too short and interrupted by shouts and gunfire.

Instantly, she sprang upright. A ghostly form moved past her and Albert. She lunged for it, missed. Before she could scramble to her feet, the sound of horse's hooves hitting rock punctured her murky consciousness.

"Morales!" It was Gordon's voice she heard. "He's gotten away!" Gordon's tall form coalesced in her vision briefly and then as quickly dispersed as he streaked past her in pursuit.

"I'm hit!"

She identified Bingham's voice.

"Mama?"

"Albert, ye are all right?"

"Yes." But he huddled closer to her.

"Wait here." On hands and knees, she searched through the miasma, like a blind man, by feel. Here a jagged rock that pierced her palm; there a tuft of dew-damp beargrass thrusting between a fissure in the rocks, another place where a tiny prickly cactus thrust its spiny ridge into her left knee.

Bingham's pained breathing guided her. She reached his boot, moved forward until she could see his face. His agony was reflected in the rigid lines of his craggy features. "My ribs." He grunted. "They're busted by a bullet. From my own pistol. Morales stole it on his way out."

She felt along his torso until her probing elicited a sharp groan. "Good."

"Good!" His anger was weakened by his moan. "You are the devil's worker."

"Save your breath, Bingham, to torture those pure souls who believe in your hellfire and damnation. The bullet ye've taken is on your right side. Ye don't appear to be doing a lot of bleeding. Ye'll likely make it. Barring infection."

Behind her, she heard footsteps. Gordon's. "The man got away, but not with all our horses," he said.

"Good riddance," Bingham muttered.

"Morales has served his purpose—a safe conduct out of *Tres Amigos*."

"Can ye fetch me medicine pouch from me saddlebags, Halpern?"

"Don't touch me with those harlot's hands, gal," Bingham said.

"Ye're not in a position to do much about it, are ye now? Think about it! At last, I can take me retribution for all your worrying and worting of meself."

At his groan, she couldn't keep from chuckling. Fate worked so grandly, coming in full circle as it always did. She was relieved that no blood spittled his lips, though. That would have been a sure sign of punctured lungs.

By now, the rising sun was burning the fog away. Only wreaths of it drifted through the campsite. "Can ye start a fire?" she asked Liliana in Spanish.

The young woman simply stared at her.

Mattie didn't have the patience to deal with her. "Albert, gather some twigs and cedar bark for a fire."

Gordon returned with her pouch. After sifting through its contents, she said, "I don't have all that I need to treat a wound like that."

He, too, stared at her blankly. Then he said, "Any suggestions? I imagine the nearest field hospital is quite a walk."

She turned to the Indian woman. "Stay." She nudged her to sit beside the preacher, who eyed Mattie with bitter-bright eyes. She knew he had to feel a rage at his own dependency on her. And he didn't take kindly to Indians, as she well knew. "We'll be back shortly," she told him.

His dry lips tightened over his bared teeth. He had to be in a lot of pain. "To do your devilish deed, eh?"

She ignored him and turned back to Gordon. "You can help me."

She saw a smile lurking beneath his mustache, which was undoubtedly prompted by her autocratic manner. But he followed her into the fading mist. By the wan sunlight, they set out to scour the bare ground for specific herbs.

"Nettles?" Gordon asked her, groping through bristly underbrush clinging to a slope.

"For bleeding." On her backside, she was scooting ahead of him down a pine-stubbled embankment. Pebbles he dislodged tumbled down to ping against her back.

Closer to the bottom, the stubbly trees were more numerous. "And fir boughs," she added trying to reach one.

Being much taller than she, he reached and yanked at a coniferous limb overhead. "For what?"

"Inflammation." She was able to stand upright now. "A frog, too."

"A what!"

Over her shoulder, she grinned at him. "I don't know. The old shaman of the Netdahes insisted upon its addition."

"Well, I'll be damned."

"That arroyo at the bottom, we might get lucky and find a frog there."

She could feel his gaze upon her as she stooped to feel along its stony sides for gouges where a frog might retreat. No such luck.

He was hunkered down next to her. He looked at her as if he had never seen her before. "You are truly amazing."

She felt nervous. And breathless at the same time. "We'll have to resort to a pinch of hemlock in place of a frog."

She was afraid he might kiss her again. She wanted him to kiss her again. She sprang to her feet. "I can grind and boil all this together."

She hurried ahead of him back to the makeshift camp. Behind her, she could hear his heavy step. A part of her said she could turn back, recapture that lost moment. Another part of her warned that Bingham needed her care immediately.

Except for Albert, who hunkered over the fire he was building, Bingham was alone. As she had half-expected. "Where's the Indian woman?" she asked her son.

He shrugged. "When I returned, she was gone."

Apparently, Liliana had taken the opportunity to strike out in search of her own people.

The fire-blackened tin coffee pot served as Mattie's cauldron. When the poultice was ready, she bent over Bingham. A sheen of sweat across his broad forehead indicated he was already feverish. "The bullet needs to be removed. Do ye understand?

He only nodded. Those gray eyes looked as lifeless as ashes.

She unsheathed her knife from its resting place at her thigh and passed it to Gordon. "Hold it over the fire until it is blackened, then wipe the blade so that it shines like silver."

While Gordon fired the knife blade, she and Albert stripped Bingham—not without a rounded volley of curses on his part—of his outer shirt and an inner woolen one, which was stiff with sweat and dirt.

When she was ready, Gordon passed her the knife. "You know what you are doing?" he asked.

"She damn well better know!" Bingham growled.

"Give him some gin, Halpern."

After Gordon left to retrieve the gin bottle, Bingham fixed her with an eagle's eye. "Why are you doing this, gal? Why are you rendering me aid?"

"You're one of God's creatures, are ye not now?"

"After all I did to you?"

"Why, ye didn't do anything to me that I didn't let ye. I did it all to meself, don't ye see?"

He was looking at her, and at the same time staring past her. All at once, the sunlight scattered the remnants of fog. It was as if both he and she were given insight. Into themselves. Into their fellow creatures. "How did we allow this to happen?" he muttered.

From behind her, Gordon nudged her with the bottle

of gin. She passed it along to Bingham. "We believed it," she said. "We allowed ourselves to believe what others said and thought."

He swallowed a wee draught, then another. "Get on with it."

She made the first insertion with the knife. He flinched, his shoulder jerked. "Hold him, Halpern."

Gordon knelt above the preacher's shoulders and braced them. "Take another deep swig, Bingham."

The man did so, then focused his slightly glazed eyes on her. "It wasn't you I hated, Mattie. It was myself. I hated what I thought I had become. The worst of sinners."

She noted he had called her by her given name. It was first. "An illusion, the Apaches say, Bingham. The ghost of our dark side."

She made a deep incision. Her knife grated against either bone or bullet, she wasn't sure which. It sounded to her as if Bingham sighed. She glanced at his face. He had passed out.

She felt squeamish herself. A little more probing, and she determined she had located the bullet. Her fingers squished in the pulpy tissue of his flesh and retrieved the deadly piece of metal. "The poultice," she said to Gordon and realized her voice sounded faint in her ears.

Before he could hand it to her, she felt herself falling from a great height. Sliding into an abyss. Her last recollection was slumping over Bingham's inert body and hearing her son's fearful outcry.

When she came to, she was lying once again on her bedroll. Bingham was stretched out on the far side of the fire. He was alternately singing a lewd ditty and muttering Bible verses. His wound had been covered in a makeshift bandage of strips of fine linen.

Albert squatted Indian fashion beside her. His full lower lip was pressed flat. She knew he was worried. He had never seen her demonstrate physical weakness. In all of Nantez's blows, she may have fallen or reeled, but she always got back up or regained her balance.

She raised upon her elbows. Her blouse fell open, revealing the valley between her breasts. Her fingers flew to the buttons. "What happened?"

"You fainted," Gordon said from somewhere beyond her vision. "I took the liberty of relieving you of some of your uhh . . . constraints."

"What the hell does that mean, Halpern?"

He came into her view. "I made it easier for you to breathe, damnit, Mattie. I didn't know what else to do. I certainly wasn't going to take advantage of you, not with your son sitting here guarding you like a Wells Fargo agent does a strongbox."

At that she had to smile. She had a fleeting sense of feeling cherished. She glanced over at Bingham. "How is our patient doing?"

Gordon frowned. "All right for now. But we'll never get him down and up canyon walls. Not in that condition."

She thought for a moment. "Liliana's people. The Tarahumaras. They can't be too far—their village is on the Cusarare, Bingham said. At the head of the canyon. They could take him in. With Albert to stay with him, he will do fine until we can return. We should be back this way within a week at the most. By then, he should be fully mended."

The solution had come more easily than its actual accomplishment would. Mattie had liberally dosed Bingham with a quantity of mountain tea—white root, water brier, and unkum root. At Gordon's suggestion, she had added a liberal dose of the gin.

With jauntily delirious Bingham strapped to a litter pulled by the pack mule, the trip to the village on the Cusarare took half the morning. They wanted to jar him as little as possible, so the mysterious, challenging territory made travel slow.

Vultures and bald eagles were drawing high, lazy circles in the hot, blue sky by the time she and Gordon crossed a wooden footbridge over deep green pools. Birds twittered in jade green trees. An iguana, reminiscent of the prehistoric past, slithered away in underbrush.

They followed a creek to where Tarahumara Indian women were scrubbing laundry in the shade of orange trees. They were so shy they didn't look at her and her companions as they passed by. But the Tarahumaras' tittering could be heard, light as the mountain air.

The sojourners came to a halt in a dusty, rough-edged little village. It was a cluster of wooden huts with corn drying on their roofs in the sun. Besides corn, beans and squash as well as worms and insects served as diet for the hardy people.

The village was dominated by a seventeenth-century Jesuit mission. Its tumbled-down, deep-ochre walls were still graced here and there by a candle, a garland of flowers, amber beads, and other articles that testified to its continued, although maybe occasional, use by converted Tarahumaras.

The travelers' arrival must have already been communicated somehow, because Liliana stepped out from one of the huts' shadowed doorways.

Mattie gestured at Bingham. "Can he and my son remain with you for a week?" she asked in Spanish. "We will pay you to care for them."

The woman's shyness dropped away. She began talking rapidly with accompanying gestures toward the semiconscious Bingham.

Mattie couldn't quite believe she understood correctly. "Sonofabitch."

"Mattie!" Gordon said, "I told you about cursing. If you're going to be a lady—"

"Liliana says she will let them stay on the condition that Bingham marries her."

Gordon's brows shot up. "Sonofabitch!"

13

Mattie and Gordon were isolated from civilization by the intractability of the landscape of the Barranca del Cobre. The streams and torrents of the Cusarare that raveled through the barranca were their map. Jaguars, grizzly bears, mountain lions, and wolves were their traveling companions by day. By night the owl and the coyote.

That first night, she and Gordon made their camp where tracks of ringtail and deer bracketed the creek. A dozen yards farther, thin tresses of white water plunged hundreds of feet to a seething cauldron below. The thunder of the falls echoed away between cliffs and timbered crags.

The day's journey had been physically demanding. Often they had been forced to dismount and lead their horses up and down steep and narrow side trails.

The altitude rendered her breathless. Her calves had forgotten the ease with which she had once negotiated the surrounding terrain. Her right shoulder was bruised where her strapped rifle bounced against it.

She and Gordon slipped and slid down sharp switchbacks. They plunged on through loose rubble and dust. They pressed themselves against cliff ledges and picked their way over parapets of lichen-spattered volcanic rocks.

The rewards of the day's journey had been unbelievable views: cloud's-eye vistas of wooded mountains and coiling stony gorges. "My God," Gordon said in awe. "The view is every artist's dream."

The best reward of all was rest.

Exhausted and more dirty than she could ever remember, Mattie headed for a distant portion of the Rio Cusarare's banks so she could bathe in privacy. She knew that Gordon watched her leave. To her delight, she came upon crystalline geothermal waters, gushing from the north wall of the gorge. Heaven on earth, she thought!

She stripped off her clothing and waded into the warm water, which carried the faintest scent of sulfur and subterranean salts. To her surprise, she could float with very little movement.

Floating on her back, she gazed up through the last rays of the sunlight at the looming canyon walls. Above their high rimrock aeirie, hawks curved and soared. In front of her, the green river swirled between water-polished walls of stone. Butterflies with glimmering wings fluttered by on the warm breeze.

Feeling completely drained, she dressed and returned

to camp. Gordon had built a small fire. By its glow, his wet hair gleamed like highly polished ebony. Obviously he, too, had bathed.

No attempt at shooting game had been made, because they were afraid the noise might alert any nearby Indians. In place of game, Gordon had heated some of the tinned food. She took the plate of *refritos* and practically raw pork he handed her and wolfed them down.

A short time later, she lay beside the small fire, watching its smoke curl up toward the early evening stars. The day's trek, as well as the steam bath, had left her feeling too tired to talk.

Gordon wasn't. Stretched out in his bedroll, he turned toward her and propped his head on his fist. "So you don't think Bingham will be too happy about our arranged marriage between him and Liliana?"

She scooted farther down inside the cocoon of her blankets. At that elevation, the nights were cold. Even the stars looked like frosty snowflakes. "Hopefully, the concoction I told Albert to give him will keep him too sedated to give the matter much thought."

"And after we rescue Diana and get back to Cusarare? What then?"

"Then we rescue him next."

"Mattie, who's going to rescue you?"

The tone of Gordon's voice . . . she turned her head in his direction. The firelight cast a red glow over his face, throwing into relief his broken nose and scarred mouth and the wicked droop of one of his eyelids. "What do you mean?"

"I have this feeling that all your life you've been

taking care of others and that the core of you, beneath that scar tissue of your experiences, needs desperately to be rescued."

She stirred uneasily beneath the blanket. "Rescued from what?"

"From going unnoticed. Untouched. Uncared for."

She felt close to tears. Something about this man touched her inside. Compassion. And she knew that an important part of that word was *passion*. "Who's going to rescue you, Halpern?" she asked softly.

His eyes narrowed. "I don't need rescuing."

"Ye don't? I think ye need rescuing from yourself. You're one of those souls who keeps fighting even when fighting is not in your best interest. Me thinks that by not giving up, ye have survived."

He looked amazed by her statement, as if he had not given her credit for such insight. "All of which should tell you that I don't need rescuing," he said a bit too gruffly.

"Ye have a keen sense of justice, Halpern. Ye do right by instinct rather than choice—and the thing of it is that you're not even aware of doing so. I suspect you've got a sterling soul."

He turned over, presenting his back to her. "You are too trusting," came his voice in the darkness.

"Now what do ye mean? I weary of your riddles."

"I mean at one point the thought crossed my mind to make an exchange with Nantez: Albert for Diana."

She gasped. "How could you do that?"

"I'm not so sterling a soul, am I?"

"I don't understand, Halpern. I've never done

anything to hurt you intentionally. How could you—"

"When you love someone, you'll do anything for them. Anything. I loved Diana as much as you do Albert."

It took a moment for her to register exactly what he had just said. She pushed the blanket back and crawled over to him. "Halpern." She touched his shoulder.

"Yes?"

She was between the firelight and him and could not see his face. "Look at me."

He half rolled toward her. His eyes were like black sparkles. "What is it?"

"Ye said *loved,* Halpern. That ye *loved* Diana. Not *love.*"

He rolled away from her again. "Go to sleep, Mattie. We're both tired."

"No!" She climbed atop him, straddling him. She wore only a clean shirt, her body totally nude beneath. "No. I want an honest answer. If anything ye speak honestly. With brutal honesty. Ye don't love Diana, do ye?"

"I wish I had an answer for you. But I don't know. I just don't know. Right now, I don't know if I ever loved her." His voice sounded weary. Soul weary.

She slid down alongside him, seeking his warmth. Seeking his heart. His long, thick hair intermeshed with the wild, wayward strands of her own. "Wasn't it ye who told me that the soul only lives when the heart really loves? Then love me, Gordon."

It was the first time she had used his given name. He knew it, too. She could tell by the sharp intake of his breath. Or maybe it was what she had asked him to do. She repeated her question. Softly, but more passionately. "Love me. Oh, love me, Gordon!"

She felt his breath, slowly released, on her forehead. She felt his fingers touch her cheek. Find her cheekbone. Follow its line. Search for her lips. Trace the full curve of the bottom one. Linger in the indentation of her upper one. "Even if my heart's not involved?"

Her hand cupped the back of his neck. "You men are more romantic fools than women." She lifted her face and brushed her lips against his. "But it doesn't matter. If ye can't love me, then let me love ye. I am not afraid. I don't have your love, so I have nothing to lose, do I now?"

He was silent, and she heard the yip-yip of the coyote, calling its mate. Then he said, "Not until I have Diana back. Not until I know what my true feelings are. Maybe she and I will value each other more. I can't do that to you, Mattie. I know that I was wrong when I tried to coax you into—"

"Gordon—shut up." She began kissing him. Her kisses were filled with such hunger that it frightened her. *After all these years . . .* that was all she could think. *After all these years.*

His arm went around her waist, and he pulled her against him with a whispered, "Mattie." The whisper was a sigh she identified with regret. The sigh of the wind lost.

Her body's soft contours melded with his hard lines. Man and woman. Fitting so well, as complements, mirror images. She and Gordon were so opposite, yet so alike. If only she could make him understand this.

She tried. Tried with the desperation of someone who knew that at the end of the journey, she would come away with a handful of bank notes that would be frittered away. She would lose something that was abstract but all the more substantial, the love of a man for a woman.

"Touch me, Gordon." She took his hand and moved it up to her cheek. "See. I am flesh. I am real. I am ye."

A frown gathered at the outer corners of his eyes. Either he was perplexed by her statement or he didn't want to hear any more.

"Gordon, don't ye see that we are reverse reflections of one another's lives—rags to riches and riches to rags?" She turned her face slightly, so that her lips could kiss his palm. "But 'tis more than that. I am both your hopes and your fears. As ye are mine. To run away from this is to run away from ourselves."

"And if I let myself love you?"

"Stop trying to see the future, Gordon. Just love me as ye would another human being. Hold me against the darkness, the unseen. Tomorrow will take care of itself. I can love ye with all of me—and bless ye and send ye on your way with your Diana. So just hold me."

He did that. Held her. Throughout the night they lay enfolded together. And sometime in the night, he slept.

Mattie did not sleep. She loved him. Loved him so fully with all her will, and only her will.

Here was a man who had never been loved. Here was a woman who wanted only to give love. Here, deep in Copper Canyon, deep in their hearts, was love.

When, with the dawn and the chirping of the magpie, his eyes opened, she saw in them something new. Wonder? Serenity? Appreciation? She wasn't sure.

Slowly, he lowered his head and brushed her lips with his. "My medicine woman. You are indeed a healer."

That was enough for her. In silence, they dressed and prepared to leave the enchanted spot. Like magnets, their gazes were drawn again and again to each other. As she buckled the fleece-lined saddle strap, her eyes locked with his as he tied his bedroll to his saddle. They both smiled. *We have today,* she thought. *I cannot complain. We have at least today, and maybe tomorrow. Maybe.*

The journey continued: times beyond counting of traversing the rims of wild ravines; here and there, clearings and meadows in dense forest of pine, hemlock, and oak; thousand-foot descents that took a mere forty-five minutes and demanded all their horsemanship skills; boulder-strewn canyon floors.

They were so close to the Place of the Eagles, they did not want to spend the night on the trail. Without pausing for meals, they rode, and walked, leading their mounts where necessary.

The Place of the Eagles was at the dead-end of a trail in the depths of the Rio Cusarare. One could not go any farther.

When she sighted the hulking, eerie stone monoliths shaped like mushrooms, parasols, and pagodas, memories flooded into her mind. "I came past these formations the night I fled Nantez."

Gordon studied her through the fringe of his incredibly long lashes. "What happened that night to cause you to flee? After all that you had gone through, why that night, Mattie?"

"There had been a celebration of a raid soon to be staged against the town of Galeana. A ceremonial war dance. Nantez and his warriors had gotten drunk during the festivities."

"A war dance?"

She kneed her horse, nudging it onward, but at a slower pace now. She was not anxious to arrive at the Netdahe camp before dark. "The purpose for the dance was to recruit volunteers for the raid of Galeana—and to stir up a fighting spirit."

Gordon's mount trotted alongside at the same slow pace. "With Nantez's temperament, I would imagine that war dances were a common thing."

"There was another excuse for the dance. It was for the benefit of young Indian boys who wanted to become warriors. They had to practice this dance as if it were a real battle."

"Ahhh." He said no more, but she knew he understood what she was trying to say.

"That night, everyone in camp had been invited to witness the exciting spectacle. A bonfire had been built that night in the center of a large cleared circle, around which the tribal members had gathered."

She could still feel the heat of the blaze. And the old terror. Whenever Nantez drank, he was abusive.

"Ten paces west of the fire sat four or five men who had thumped tom-toms and pounded a sheet of stiff rawhide. During this time, they sang a high-pitched, eerie chant. It reminded me of bagpipe music that me father used to play.

"From time to time, the drummers would call out the name of some prominent warrior, who would then step forth from the crowd and strut around the fire while the singers praised his bravery and deeds in battle. This was the signal for other men who wished to take the warpath to join this man in the promenade and later to serve under his leadership during the raid.

"Finally, when it seemed likely that all brave and eligible fighters had joined the war party, the men formed a line on the opposite side of the circle from the drummers. Then the warriors advanced toward the drummers in leaps and zigzag motions—as if in a real raid. Brandishing their weapons, yelling, writhing like they were possessed . . . then suddenly they stopped and shot their guns or bows and arrows over the heads of the singers."

"A grand finale of sorts, eh?"

"The war dance was very realistic and exciting, especially to the young boys like Albert. They loved to stage sham battles in imitation of their elders."

"Something happened with Albert, didn't it?"

She squinted her eyes against the afternoon's blinding sunlight. The limestone walls of the canyon intensified its brightness. "Nantez singled out one of the boys. Nah-de-gaa was fatherless and had a club foot. He rode horses with the skill of a plains Comanche. But Apaches don't need to rely on horses in mountains and canyons."

"So, this boy with the club foot was a hindrance to the Netdahes?"

"Not that much. But Nantez did not tolerate a weak body—or a weak heart. I learned that in me first month of captivity.

"Anyway, by the time the boys took part in the ceremony, he was quite drunk." Her voice dropped an octave. "He instructed them to practice their warfare skills on Nah-de-gaa. No one stepped forward to contradict Nantez. He would have smote anyone who dared. I watched the other boys rain half-hearted blows on Nah-de-gaa. Albert was among them."

"Oh, God."

"I became sick. Sick with the scene. Sick with meself for not interfering. At last, Nantez called off the boys. Called off the dogs, because that was how they were acting. Like camp dogs.

"And that was when you decided to run away?"

"I knew the warriors would drink themselves into a stupor. I waited 'til the entire camp was asleep. Then I roused Albert. He didn't want to go. He started to cry. I was afraid he would waken someone."

She paused, filling her lungs with air. "I . . . I gagged him with a headband. Gagged me own son. I felt so terrible doing this, but I could not bear to watch Albert become the animal Nantez is. I think I would rather Albert and meself both dead."

Gordon said nothing, but she noticed his hand tightening knuckle-white around his reins.

"I half-carried Albert, half-dragged him, from the camp. Then it seemed like I ran. Ran and ran with him in tow. Even though he was just five years old, he was no wee thing. A heavy burden, he was. By the light of dawn, I could see those formations we just passed. I kept them in me sight as a beacon. 'If I can just reach those,' I'd tell meself, 'then I can rest.'"

She allowed herself a slight smile. "I was so afraid of what Nantez would do when he caught up with me—for taking his son—I reached the formations and kept going. Running, walking, running again. Always moving. I tried to hide me tracks the way the Apaches did. Walking in water when I could. Trailing a small bush behind me. Walking backward in me footsteps. Whatever. As near as I can reckon, we reached the border two weeks later."

"I knew I picked the right person for the job."

She glanced over at Gordon. He was smiling. Admiration glinted in those warm brown eyes. "Did ye now?" she teased, glad to be finished with the story of her escape.

"I remember the first moment I saw you, Mattie. The way you entered Kee's dining room. You had a certain arrogance, as if you feared nothing and no one and knew your place in God's order of things. Your outspokenness announced your honesty. Your manners that bordered on crudity—"

At this, she laughed.

He went on. "I've been around, Mattie. I've learned to spot a sham. You are a sham. Your outer crudity protects your innate gentility."

His opinion touched the core of her. He was far more perceptive than most anyone she knew.

"I figured that there were a number of qualified people I could hire as a scout," he continued. "But if I had to spend several weeks in the desolate wilds of Mexico, I could think of no one as interesting as you were. And an excellent study for my sketches."

"Ah, then I was merely a diversion for ye?"

Before he could reply, she held up her hand for silence. A birdcall trilled. It was only one of the growing chorus that began at evening. But this one was different. She couldn't distinguish in what way. She just knew. "We may have been sighted," she whispered.

He drew a steadying breath. "Now what?"

She bit her lower lip while she thought. "Nantez is so unpredictable."

His breath expelled in a snort. "The entire Apache nation is unpredictable."

"I say we keep riding, casually. We might have the element of surprise."

"And if they've spotted us?"

"If they've spotted us, Gordon, there is nowhere we can run to." Just saying so made her scalp tighten. Now what, indeed? She had brought Gordon this far. Now how would they get Diana out of Nantez's camp? Alive. All three of them.

They rode through the deepening dusk. Neither of them spoke. She doubted if she had the voice required to do so. Her skin prickled.

Off to her left, a covey of white wing exploded from the brush, and her horse shied. When she regained control, she snapped, "I ask ye now, what am I doing? I have to be crazy, trying to rescue the wife of the bloke I love meself. Not to mention returning to the same vicinity as Nantez."

He hauled up on his reins. "What are you doing, you ask? You are doing what you have to."

"Says who?"

"Says a bloke who thinks there is a phoenix waiting to take flight from your sack of ashes."

"Ye must have a wee bit of the Irish blarney in ye, Gordon." Still, she felt pleasure at his remark.

By the failing light, she spotted a score or so of horses tethered along the river bank. Two or three whinnied and nickered as she and Gordon rode nearer.

He asked in a lowered voice, "Then we're near the Netdahe camp?"

She shook her head. "No. It's an old trick. Apaches drive their horses and mules a couple of miles farther down river and tether them there. Then the band packs everything on its back, climbs up the mountainside to a summit and makes camp there. If an enemy is trailing, he would spot the trail of the animals and would not notice the camp. By such measures, Nantez escapes surprise visits."

When they had gone a couple of miles without incident, she began to hope that they were undetected. Though why Nantez's guards should be so lax troubled her. A mountain lion's screech left her even more unsettled.·

She was looking for an easily accessible pass to a higher plateau. Her gaze scanned the smooth canyon wall on the opposite bank until she sighted what she had half-remembered—a slightly irregular staircase carved by nature into the limestone wall. "We leave our horses here," she told Gordon.

After tethering their own mounts, she started climbing. Gordon fell in behind her, and she knew the length of her legs above her moccasins was often exposed. They ascended the wall with a minimum amount of noise. Occasionally, a loosened pebble would clatter down the steps behind them. Or her rifle, strapped to her back, would thud against stone.

She stretched for foot- and handholds, scraped her fingers, lost her breath—and kept climbing.

A good ten minutes passed before she could see treetops. She heard the noises before she saw the fire's glow. Then she knew why she and Gordon had so easily approached the Netdahe camp. A ceremony was in progress. Not any ceremony, such as a war raid. But one so special that all else stops.

She remembered once before, when, in midflight from a troop of Mexican cavalry, one of the Apache girls had reached her womanhood. The warriors had separated from the women and children and older people, who had taken refuge behind a hill.

Right away, the girl's parents had arranged the traditional ceremony in her honor, even while the shooting was heard on the other side of the hill. The coming of age, marking the time when a girl was ready for marriage, was one of the most important events in a girl's life. The girls all looked forward to it eagerly. So the ceremony was never neglected, not even at a dangerous time like that.

That same ceremony was underway now. The sun had set beyond the spiraling tops of firs and pines, and the air was very cold. Before an open-sided lodge stood an old woman who was conducting the ceremony. She had spread out a blanket and was marking four footprints that led away maybe fifty yards toward a single eagle feather placed on the ground.

A girl still plump with baby fat was stretched out face down on the blanket. She was the candidate for the womanhood ceremony. Her dress was of the finest buckskin, decorated with small tin jingles and beadwork. Her long braids were laced with strings of colorful beads and tiny shells.

The old woman had returned to the blanket to perform a kind of high-pitched incantation over the spread-eagled girl. Behind the old woman were the girl's excited parents and an old man with a hawk face and fierce, kindly eyes. He had to be the sponsor—a close friend of the family. He jingled a rattle made of the hoofs of a fawn.

Mattie recognized the old woman as Pon-chie, one of Nantez's wives. Pon-chie's unpredictable and mercurial wrath had made Mattie's life in Nantez's household a living nightmare. The old man was one of the Apache's legendary men, Ramos, the tribal shaman.

Gordon crept closer, crouching in briar and brush that rimmed the camp. Beside him, Mattie scanned the Indians crowded in a circle around the ceremony's principal characters. Her blood congealed at the sight of Nantez, standing with other warriors. He was shorter, thicker, and uglier than she had even remembered.

His scrawny legs had an agility that matched any of his warriors. His eyes blazed with impatience, intolerance, and cunning. His hair, black, thick, and very coarse, was bound by a folded, red flannel band before it fell to his powerful shoulders.

Her eye sockets ached with the hate she felt when looking at him. The memory of being stabbed with his putrid flesh-sword burned in her brain. Another memory flashed before her: of trimming the hair at his forehead straight across at the level of his eyebrows. How many times she had been tempted to stab out his eyes! Only fear of the consequences at the hands of the tribe had kept her hand steady.

Gordon gasped. "Diana!"

Mattie followed the direction of his gaze toward the collection of wickiups. The tribe's women were clustered there, and Gordon's wife stood in their midst. She was taller than the rest, and easily singled out because of her silver-blond hair and extraordinarily light-colored eyes. Green or blue, Mattie couldn't tell from that distance. Looking refined and above the squalor surrounding her, Diana appeared to be unharmed and none the worse for being held captive for six weeks.

Upon seeing her Mattie felt jealousy, envy, instant dislike. All these powerful emotions thrust everything else from her mind. Here was Gordon's beloved. Not only had she survived, but she was unchanged by the experience. She was everything Mattie might have been.

Mattie felt her jaws tightening and forced herself to take several deep, restorative breaths. Now was not the time to lose control.

The girl being initiated into womanhood stood up and stepped successively in each of the footprints leading to the feather, which she then circled, picked up, and brought back it to the starting point at the blanket. Meanwhile, all the crowd watched closely.

This was a good time, in Mattie's opinion, to circle around to the far side, where the squaws and Diana stood. She signaled to Gordon to follow her and then moved past him, treading carefully, taking care not to disturb any branches.

Apache eyes were sharp. At points where the underbrush grew sparsely, she tracked a wider perimeter to seek concealment.

The drummers started up with a constant beat of their tom-toms. This was a sign for the second part of the ceremony to start: feasting and dancing, which could last as long as four days and nights.

Mattie knew that after the fire dance, everyone would join in a circle facing the fire, when the girl being honored would take a leading part in the dancing. During this diversion would be the time to extract Diana from the rest of the women. The problem was that before that part of the ceremony commenced two or three days might elapse.

From their vantage point behind the wickiups, she and Gordon watched the fire dance. Male volunteers, known as devil dancers, were dressed in the skins of animals. The dancers performed a series of intricate steps that consisted of moving sideways, north and south, rising alternately on toes and heels.

Mattie noticed that the men not dancing were passing around bottles, most likely *tiswin,* corn whiskey. Good. She could almost count on Nantez drinking enough to pass out. His propensity for drinking often impaired his judgment at critical times. This had been the biggest obstacle to his becoming a prominent Apache war chief, which was never a hereditary position.

Little by little, Mattie worked her way closer to the squaws, with Gordon following not far behind. As close as she dared get, she squatted on her heels, prepared to keep a night-long vigil.

He hunkered just behind her, so near she could feel his breath on her neck. She could only hope he had the patience now required of them. They had come so far, braved so many dangers.

No more than half an hour passed when, by good fortune, some of the women joined the dancing. The time was ripe for rescuing Diana.

But it also boded ominously for Mattie's plan because it meant that Nantez was not planning on staying long in that location. She had no way of knowing if he had selected the locale merely because it was a pleasant region in which to camp, with plenty of wood and water at hand; because it was a good rallying point and easy to defend; or because he was planning to go forth on another raid. If the latter were so, then he would not be caught unprepared for the chase.

But at this point there could be no turning back. She looked over her shoulder at Gordon. "Wait here for me."

"What?" he mouthed in surprise.

"Ye heard me." Dressed as she was, in buckskin skirt, she might be able to mingle with the score or so of women at the rear of the group; might be able to draw close enough to talk to Diana.

Gordon started to stand and she put her hand on

his shoulder. "No," she whispered. "I'll be back with your Diana."

She thrust her rifle at him for safekeeping. Head lowered, she stepped into the peripheral group of women watching the festivities. Diana was only two or three women away from her.

She edged closer. Now she was close enough to softly call her name. "Diana! Diana!"

The woman turned her lovely face and looked around, puzzled. She hadn't yet sighted Mattie, perhaps because Mattie was shorter than even the Indian women scattered around her.

"Diana," she called again. "I'm here to rescue you."

Diana noticed her then. She frowned, as if not quite trusting sight and sound. Her eyes were bright, like lurid, tropical flowers.

"I'm with Gordon," Mattie added.

At that, Diana began screaming.

14

The Indian women backed away from Diana. She wouldn't stop screaming. Not until Nantez approached her and backhanded her on her cheek. Then she staggered, blinked, and looked around her with the dazed glance of someone awakening to a bad dream.

At the same time, Mattie heard rustling in the brush behind her. She half-turned to see Gordon shouldering his way into the clearing. His anger had clearly overridden his reason—and her warning. That anger contorted his features into a frightening grimace.

Before he could aim Mattie's rifle, two warriors pinned his arms and wrestled away both her rifle and his own.

Nantez's ferocious gaze swung from Diana to

Mattie, then to Gordon. The subchief's slow smile revealed something Mattie had forgotten, how his teeth were blackened at the gums. On those bandy legs, he strolled toward her and the captured Gordon. The entire camp was so quiet that the falling of a pine cone sounded like an explosion.

Speaking in the Na-dene dialect of the Apache language, Nantez said, "You've come back. Where is my son?"

"Where you'll never find him," Mattie said, speaking in the same language. She had spoken boldly, knowing that to show fear was a weakness Nantez preyed upon.

Nantez raised his arm, as if he meant to strike her, and she flinched inwardly. Something else inside her reacted with an audible snarl.

"Tell him I have come for Diana," Gordon said.

"Who is this?" Nantez asked before she could translate Gordon's message.

"He is the brother of the white woman you are holding captive. We have come for her."

Nantez's grin grew broader. He glanced at Gordon, then back to her. "You plan to take her and just walk away. Just like that?"

Granted, the plan was farfetched.

"What did he say?" Gordon asked.

Mattie felt like a hot potato being pitched back and forth. "He's a bit amazed that we think we can walk in, take Diana, and walk out. Alive," she added, in case Gordon didn't get the gist of the remark.

"So am I," Gordon said dryly. "Amazed. Truly amazed."

"I have told Nantez that you are Diana's brother—
and me husband." Might as well unload the bad
news all at one time.

"You what?"

"Nantez will leave me alone if I am your wife. As
long as you live, that is. Why dinna ye listen to me
and stay put?"

Impatient, Nantez gestured to Diana, who stood
next to her. "Ask her if she wants to go," he said.

Mattie looked at her and in a calm voice repeated
Nantez's instruction in English.

The woman was beautiful. Even in her disheveled
state—her tawny hair mussed, the smudges beneath
her eyes, the faint bruise across one of her classical
cheekbones. Mattie noticed that she was a good half-
foot taller than Nantez. Diana shook her head. "No,"
she said in a mere whisper.

"Your wife has said she doesn't want to go with
us," Mattie relayed to Gordon.

"For the love of God, Mattie, she's afraid. Scared
stiff."

"Of course, she is. But we have to have her cooperation if we're going to get her out of here."

He started toward her, and she began screaming
again.

Once more, Nantez struck her. She crumpled to her
knees. Then, smiling, he stared at Gordon.

Gordon would have sprung at Nantez, but Mattie
stepped between the two men and told Nantez,
"We want to gamble for your captive, me husband's
sister."

Every Apache was a gambler. Man, woman, and

child. And there was nothing they would not stake, from their horses to their shirts.

Nantez's wily black eyes lit up. "What do you have that I cannot take?"

It was a good question. A great question. She needed a great answer.

"What's he saying now?" Gordon demanded. Only the greatest restraint kept him from pummeling the Indian.

"I told him we want to gamble for Diana. He wants to know what our stake is?"

"No wonder he's smirking."

"Exactly." She turned back to Nantez. With her eye on the masked Devil Dancers ringing Nantez, an idea came. "My husband is considered a great chief where he comes from. He will fight your best warrior for this woman here."

Nantez looked over Gordon in an appraising manner. "What's going on now?" Gordon asked.

"I told him you would fight his best warrior for Diana. The Apaches love wrestling matches."

"Good God, Mattie, I was a boxer, not a wrestler. There is a big difference! And what's our stake to be?"

She felt her heart turn to stone as she answered. "His son. Me son. Albert."

His eyes seemed to search hers. "You know what you are doing?"

"I believe in ye. Ye stand to lose as much as meself. We both stand to lose our loved ones. That gives us an edge."

He looked down at his hands, knotted in veined fists. "Set it up then."

She turned back to Nantez and told him what her stake would be. "Tomorrow at noon?"

A sly smile stretched his cruel lips. He motioned to one of the Devil Dancers. A big man, well over six feet and heavily muscled. "Martine. The man I choose to fight your husband tomorrow."

"I have no worry. Do you have a place for us to sleep tonight?"

Her audacity must have impressed Nantez, because after surprise crossed his face, he gave her a smug smile. "You and your man can sleep in the house of my wife's mother."

At once, she knew the reason behind his smugness. His mother-in-law could observe her and Gordon. If they did not behave as man and wife . . .

Nantez signaled that the ceremony was to continue and ordered one of his men to accompany Mattie and Gordon to the wickiup of his mother-in-law, Esqueda.

There was a banked fire in its center. In the dark recess of the wickiup, the old woman's eyes peered across the red glow. She said nothing but only nodded, giving her blessing that the two "visitors" might enter.

"You have gotten us into a hell of a mess," Gordon said, settling his big frame on top of a rolled animal skin, a brown grizzly from the looks of it.

"I?" She darted a glance at the old woman, then went to kneel before Gordon. With what she hoped was a loving smile, she began removing his boot. "Ye have gotten us into this bloody mess."

"What are you doing? Let go of my—"

"I'm removing your boot as a good wife should. And I might remind ye that if ye'd stayed put as I instructed ye to do, then we wouldn't be snared rabbits just waiting for Nantez's knife. Now kiss me."

"What?"

She began removing the other boot. "I said kiss me. Nantez's mother-in-law is watching."

"If this is a trick, I swear, Mattie, I'll—"

"Hush." Still on her knees, she leaned forward and wrapped her arms around his neck and kissed him gently but insistently.

At first, he didn't respond. She could feel his anger at her, and the situation, knotting every muscle in his big body. The steady pounding of the tom-tom outside didn't make for serenity. Instead, it seemed to fill the little wickiup so that there was nothing else, not even the watchful eyes of old Esqueda. There was only the throbbing music that compelled the heart to keep tempo with it.

Then Gordon's arms came up around her waist. She leaned into him, so that he was totally supporting her weight. His kiss deepened. His tongue conveyed inside her mouth the message of his body's desire. Excitement surged through her like a wind-whipped grass fire.

Somehow, he had lowered her onto the earth and was half atop her. He raised his head, and his long hair swung forward to brush her cheek. His eyes glittered. "Is this sufficient a demonstration of a happily wedded couple for our watchdog?"

Mattie heard the thickness in his rich baritone voice. It was clotted with passion as thick as Irish cream. "I don't think so," she murmured against his mouth. His mustache tickled her. "I think further demonstration is necessary."

He actually laughed. Here they were, facing imminent death unless she could produce a miracle on the order of the Virgin of Guadalupe, and spontaneous laughter was rumbling up from his deep chest.

She reached up and touched the side of his jaw, then his gold loop earring. "That's what I like about ye, Gordon. Your dark side is all there for anyone and everyone to see. There is no unknown, so nothing to be afraid of encountering. Your light side, however, is a marvelous mystery, a delightful discovery, that takes me by surprise."

"So, my dear, will this satisfy the old woman?"

He began unraveling her hair and spreading its heavy mass in a fan about her face. Perhaps he did not see the old woman slip away. Perhaps he did. Nothing really mattered now but this timeless moment.

With slow fingers, he removed her blouse and jacket, her skirt and moccasins. Next, he did something that took her breath away. He lowered his head and kissed her blighted feet, then bestowed light, tender kisses on each of her toes.

She did not try to cover her nakedness. It was her offering to him, all she had to offer. No wealth, no talents or gifts, no great beauty. Only herself, just as she was, imperfections enwrapping her spirit.

No words were needed, so mystical was the moment. Shedding his own clothing, he moved up over her . . . and into her. She felt alight, shining. More than she was. More than she had ever judged herself to be.

As he moved with her . . . becoming one with her, and she with him . . . she experienced the exhilarating sense of knowing she and he were creating something finer than either of them apart.

Then she surrendered to star bursts and sunflowers unfurling and snowflakes whirling and kaleidoscopic colors exploding, and she wanted to weep that he could not know this truth—that by uniting in loving they were transformed into something wondrous.

She did weep.

He raised his head and stared down at her with furrowed brows. "What is this?"

"The fire pit's smoke. It stings the eye."

His finger wiped the tear from the outer corner of her eye. "What happened to my woman of grit?"

"She was transformed from base metal into pure gold. If only for one soaring moment."

"I see. Or maybe I don't." He rolled to his side and propped his head on one fist. She averted her eyes from his enticing nudity. "I sometimes think women have the gift of insight, Mattie. Of seeing beyond reality."

"But men have the gift of making reality."

"And you don't? Look at what your resilience and ability have accomplished."

The embers' glow highlighted the mountains and valleys of his muscled body. She snuggled within the crook of his arm. "That resilience and ability better get us out of Nantez's camp alive."

"Will he hurt her? Diana?"

That he could think of another woman after making love to her enraged her. And affected her deeply. He was a man of great passion and compassion. "No,

I don't think so. Normally, when he drinks, he gets too drunk to be as cruel as he is capable of being."

He draped his arm across her waist and stared absently at the fire.

She stretched and yawned. "I'm tired. So are you. You will need your rest for tomorrow."

"What if I don't win?"

She cuddled up closer to him, savoring the warmth of his flesh, the crisp hair matting his chest, the hardness of his body. "Ye will. Your need to win is greater than Martine's."

It was but a platitude. Should Martine lose, he faced not only loss of face but loss of life. Nantez would see to it. "Go to sleep, me love. We're still alive. That is enough."

It is enough that I sleep in your arms, she added to herself. *If only for tonight.*

The next morning, Mattie awakened early to find Esqueda sitting at the feet of her and Gordon. The old woman twisted cords of beautifully decorated strands between her fingers.

"What is she doing?" Gordon asked, raising himself up on one elbow beside Mattie.

"Shhh." She lowered her voice. "Esqueda is a dreamer of dreams."

"A what?"

"She claims that occasionally a higher power works through her to tell her of future events. The Medicine Cords are considered sacred. Like a charm or amulet."

"Ask her if I shall win today."

She did. Esqueda took from a buckskin bag around her neck a palmful of powder. It was hoddentin, ground from the tule. She sprinkled her cords with the sacred powder, then mumbled a string of incantations that ended with the simple declaration, "The spirits do not say."

"Well?" Gordon asked.

"Esqueda says that the spirits do not say about the outcome of the match." Improvising, she added, "Esqueda says that ye must paint with your heart and not your eyes."

His eyes narrowed. "How does she know that I paint?"

Mattie shrugged. "Answers just come to her at the right time. At the right time, ye will know what she means."

"I suppose you do?"

"Aye. I listen for the answer."

"How is that?"

"When the need is so great that it silences the thunder of the outside world." But she doubted he would understand what she was trying to tell him.

When the appointed hour for the wrestling match arrived, she and Gordon were the last to join the crowd. From the yelling and laughter, it might have been a holiday. The Apaches were as boisterous as any ringside spectators.

The men were dressed in their white muslin kilts, loose shirts, and scarlet head bands. The women sported their finest jewelry of shells and beads and silver. Children peeked from behind their parents to watch the contest between the two men, red and white.

Gordon was shirtless and barefooted. With his long dark hair, he might have passed for one of the Netdahe, if it were not for the earring.

His opponent, Martine, wore only a breechcloth. He looked a good five years or so younger than Gordon, maybe twenty-five or thirty years of age.

Nantez gave the signal for the match to start. The two approached each other from opposite sides of the clearing made by the spectators. What Mattie knew of the sport was quite simple: each wrestler tried to out-maneuver his opponent in an effort to seize him and toss him to the ground.

The two circled each other warily. Martine was the first to make a move. He grabbed Gordon's ankle with one hand and used his body to drive him backward. A wild cheer went up.

Fear pinched her lungs. More than Diana's freedom was at risk. Mattie cursed her giving heart. She had been a fool to offer up her own son. Why did she think she always had to solve every problem?

Gordon was a big lad. He could handle his own problems. Except part of his problem was not only Diana but their own lives as well.

At the moment, Gordon wasn't doing so well. He stumbled, then managed to grip Martine's thigh. With the leverage, he pressed the Apache warrior back. Both still standing, they held each other in a tie-up of the head and shoulders.

The day was hot, and sweat sheened the two men. Muscles bulged and strained. Dust flurried.

Yet neither gained control. The Apaches watched in breathless silence. Many of them had wagered on the match.

Mattie scanned the crowd for Diana. Apparently, Nantez was keeping the woman under lock and key.

Martine grabbed Gordon's knee and forced him into a sitting position. All Martine had to do now was press Gordon's shoulders against the ground and the match would be over. Encouraging shouts went up for Martine.

Mattie realized that her fingertips were making indentations in her palms. *Come on, Gordon!*

Then Gordon made a sudden move. He flung himself backward. His body rotated quicker than the eye, it seemed. In a flash, he was on top of his opponent. His powerful arms forced Martine's shoulders back inch by inch.

The Indian struggled to escape. His eyes protruded. He gritted his teeth. Sweat poured from his pores. His hand dug into the dirt—and he threw it into Gordon's eyes.

Disapproval rumbled on the lips of the spectators. It was definitely an illegal move.

Blinded, Gordon released his hold. Martine took advantage of the moment. He rolled to a crouching stance and grabbed a fifteen-foot lance from a nearby warrior. He jabbed at Gordon.

Gordon jumped back out of range of the lethal lance tip, which was a blade from a cavalry saber.

Martine thrust the blade again. This time, Gordon didn't move as quickly, and the blade ripped a gash along his left lower rib.

"Gordon!" From beneath her skirt, Mattie withdrew the knife from its sheath.

He glanced in her direction and caught the knife she tossed him. Now the odds were even for the two men again.

Gordon dodged beneath the next swipe of Martine's lance and jammed the knife just below the warrior's right collarbone. Martine tottered but stood. Blood smeared his chest.

Then it was over. Gordon tackled the Indian, knocking him to the ground. He slung his torso across Martine's chest and pinned him to the ground, holding the knife against his throat.

Quiet reigned over the crowd. From their stunned expressions, Mattie could tell what they were thinking. No Apache could possibly lose a wrestling match to a white man . . . and yet, just that had happened. Worse, an Apache had cheated, broken the rules.

She released her pent-up breath from her dry lips.

Gordon staggered to his feet, wiped the sweat from his brow, then approached a grim Nantez. She didn't envy Martine. "Diana? Where is she?"

Nantez's gaze went past him to Mattie. "Tell him the woman can leave tomorrow morning."

She repeated the message in English to Gordon.

"I want to see her now." He was adamant. "I want to assure myself she is all right."

"It would be better to wait," Mattie said, "and not force the issue now. To make Nantez lose face, any more than you already have, would be unwise."

If only there was a potion to break the spell of

beguilement, Mattie thought. Hers with him. His with Diana.

Or mayhaps a potion to induce the spell.

"Can you arrange for me to see her later today?" Gordon asked.

"I'll see what I can do."

They ate a midday prepared by Esqueda, then went to see Ramos in his wickiup. "We wish to visit with Nantez's captive later today," she told the shaman. "Is this possible?"

His rheumy eyes studied the coals glimmering in the fire pit, as if they could give him an answer. At last, he answered, "This can be arranged." His gaze flickered from her to Gordon and back again. "I wonder if this is what you really want?"

Ye bloody well know 'tis not, don't ye, old man? Mattie thought. Aloud, she said, "It is what must be."

He nodded, his shaggy white hair dragging across his bony shoulders. "The woman will be here in the cool of the evening."

He owed her this much. They both knew that. "Thank you, Ramos."

Gordon followed her from the wickiup and back through the camp. Burros, dogs, and a chicken darted from their path. As she expected, all eyes watched them. Gordon was the new champion.

Children playing "toss the rock" cast curious glances at her and Gordon. Women in long cotton skirts peered from beneath lowered lids but continued with their work—grinding corn, tanning leather, carrying water.

"We're going to bathe," she told him.

"Are you crazy, Mattie?" he demanded. "Bathing at a time like this?"

"There is nothing else we can do. Besides, ye could use one after the match."

He wrinkled his nose. "I smell that bad, eh?"

She strode on through the short buffalo grass and down the steep slopes of a scrub jungle. "In addition, 'tis an opportunity to gather herbs."

"Gather herbs? You are crazy!"

"I don't trust Nantez, Gordon. He is not a man of his word. We can only hope he will let Diana go tomorrow morning because he doesn't want others to know that he has gone back on his word."

The creek she remembered emptied into the river that fed the waterfall downstream. The air was languid and fragrant, with mango and papaya trees and flowers like the crimson bougainvillea that plaited the forest undergrowth.

Wiry trees grew from in between immense slabs of limestone that sloped toward the creek. Its deep but clear water burbled along rapidly, scrubbing smooth those stones that might have been threatened by lichen.

With disregard for prying eyes, Mattie undressed for her lover's eyes on the bed of alluvial debris left by the battering river. In that pristine amphitheater, she waded naked into the icy cold, meandering current until the water washed her hips and the bottom inch of her unbound hair.

Despite all that had passed between them, she felt as shy as any maiden. She crossed her arms over her upper torso and turned back to Gordon.

Arrested by the sight of her, he had shucked only

his shirt and boots. He regarded her with bemusement that soon turned to something else.

She saw desire and longing there, felt it caress her flesh; but she also saw great fear and knew that they were both more alive than they had ever been. She smiled, blushing furiously.

His jaws tightened. In his expression was the pure admiration of a human being for something that was beautiful, the appreciation of something that was a divine work of human art.

"Come on in, love. I've something to show ye." So shy she felt, she didn't look at him once while she spoke.

"As sweaty and hot and dusty as I am, the Sixth Cavalry itself couldn't keep me from coming in."

She tried not to watch as he unbuttoned his pants and dropped them, but she could not help herself.

With the shedding of his pants, the hard, clean lines of his body were revealed in the shimmering, mist-dusted sunlight. He was fashioned by nature into a bronzed sculpture that rivaled Cellini's Perseus in grace, elegance, and sensuality.

She forced herself to turn away and wade in deeper. Behind her, she heard him groan. "Oh God, but this feels wonderful."

She smiled to herself. "I know something even more wonderful."

At that, he followed her with a much more ambitious tramp.

Forests and cliffs soared to the sky. Fifty yards around the river's bend, she reached the rock-walled chute leading to a pool of the clearest water before rolling down its gorge between cliff and timbered crag. She turned back to him. "Follow me, knave!"

She eased into a sitting position near the chute. The torrent of shallow water caught her and propelled her down the smooth rock slide and around a curve. Her laughter echoed between the limestone walls. When she hit the pool, a wave of water washed over her. She gave a shout of joy.

No sooner did she stand in the knee-deep water than the rushing water behind her pushed Gordon against her. They both tumbled, struggled to find their footing, then fell onto their backsides and laughed with the exuberance of children.

The moment passed and their laughter ebbed. Still, neither of them moved. Water sloshed around them. "You know I want you, don't you, Mattie? Again."

"And again and again, me love." She stood up and held out her arms. Water ran down off her flesh, as is she were a tropical fountain brought to life. She felt sublimely graceful, quintessentially female.

He gazed up at her through water-spiked lashes. Purpose was etched in his mouth and passion burned in his gaze.

She placed her hand on his wet shoulders. "I am yours, Gordon. But ye must choose it to be so time and again until ye realize that it could truly be no other way."

On his knees, he pressed his face against her soft triangle. His tongue stroked inside her in fiery, mute adulation. His hands stretched upward to claim her small breasts. In frenzy, his fingers rubbed her swollen aureoles and nipples.

Her knees sagged. She dug her fingernails into his shoulders. Paroxysms shook her slender body. She heard herself from a distance, offering up a string of Gaelic litanies.

At last, he rose, grabbed her wet body against his own, and took her mouth in a wild, fevered, unrestrainable kiss. Her heavy female aroma enveloped her. After a moment, she didn't notice that. She was so disoriented with the desire raging in her.

Sunlight poured over them like honey as they made love. Later, they washed each other. Their hands lingered, touching with a wonder that bespoke this was all new for each of them. His fingers combed through her wild hair, then tangled in her tresses to draw her face to his in a quenching kiss.

Her fingers traced the powerful line of his foot and marveled at its delicate webbing of vein and muscle and bone. Her hands explored his body to feel it tighten with his need of her. She learned the power of her femininity—and of her passion.

Reluctantly, they waded ashore to dress. They did not speak. To do so, to describe what they were feeling right then, limited the feeling of immensity, of infinity, of mystery.

Yet she wondered if he would heed her words about choosing to love. It was something one had to decide to do every day. She made herself face the fact that he might never realize the truth of her words, at least not in this lifetime.

When they reached camp, the sight of Kiko O'Neil in Nantez's doorway demolished all bliss—and all hope.

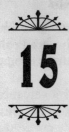

15

Kiko O'Neil was dressed in blue trousers and a brown canvas jacket. He grinned as he held back the animal-skin flap from the doorway. "Come on inside. Nantez and I have been awaiting your arrival."

Mattie strode on past him but did not miss the wrathful glance he shot at Gordon, who followed her into the wickiup. Nantez was sitting on the wickiup's far side, with an ugly smile on his face.

She dropped to the pine-needled floor Indian fashion. Gordon did the same. O'Neil let the animal skin close and squatted opposite her and Gordon. Every muscle in her body constricted. O'Neil was pack-mule wise; his presence did not bode well.

In the wickiup's dim interior, a faint movement behind O'Neil caught her attention. It was Diana's shadowy figure. Nantez beckoned for her to come forward. With the cautious step of a cornered cat, she edged around the wickiup's perimeter, keeping her distance from Nantez.

Mattie understood why. The woman's lovely face was swollen and bruised. But it was her vacant expression that was so awful to behold.

Rage exploded from Gordon. With a blue oath, he shot to his feet and started toward her. "What has he done to you, Diana?"

She shrank from him and averted her face. She raised her hands, either in supplication or defense, Mattie couldn't tell which. "No!"

Mattie knew that now was not the time to lose control. "Gordon, sit down."

He visibly battled with the urge to shield his wife from further violence. Self-restraint won. With a vein pulsing at his temple, he retraced his steps and seated himself once more.

"The man said he wished to see his sister," Nantez said in a taunting voice. "Now he has seen her."

She knew then. "Nantez does not plan to keep his word," she told Gordon. "He is playing with us, like a hawk does a snake."

Only audacity, only fearlessness, stood a chance against such malevolence. "There is a great sickness in your belly, Nantez," Mattie said.

"I have no pain," he replied.

"You will. Within two suns from now, you will die from the ghost sickness."

His eyes flared. He told O'Neil to summon Ramos.

"Even the shaman cannot help you," she told him.

At her side, Gordon said, "What's going on?"

"Playing on Nantez's fear of the supernatural. I told him he has a disease. The ghost sickness. That he will have pain in his stomach."

"You think you can make him believe it?"

"I can when his stomach starts hurting. I've just got to find a way to make it start."

"Grand. Just grand."

By this time, Ramos had joined them. Nantez told the shaman what she had said.

Ramos shifted his gaze from the subchief to her. The fact that he had often spoken to her of the Healing Way and even let her once watch a healing ceremony told her that he held her in a measure of respect, female though she was. "You have spoken about the ghost sickness to Nantez?"

She knew the Apaches believed in some supernatural force, a source of all power, that influenced the affairs of men. Whether for good or evil, they recognized its sway over them. "I have been given dreams. That Nantez would have the ghost sickness in his stomach. Now. At this time of the moon."

"You can stop this ghost illness yourself?" Ramos asked.

"I can. I have studied with the white men's doctors since I left the Netdahe."

Ramos made an expression of disgust. "They do not know about the body."

"They know about the mind. Nantez's mind will make his belly hurt. He has done a bad thing by taking this man's sister. He has done many bad things."

Ramos could not deny this.

Nantez did not try. He snorted. "I give you two suns. If I do not have this pain in my belly, then the man and you die."

"But if you do?"

He grinned. "If I have it and you cannot cure it, then the man and you die."

She tried making a flippant shrug. Behind him, Diana appeared not to realize the seriousness of the situation. She reminded Mattie of the half-wit boy who hawked newspapers at the corner of Calle Real and Pennington in Tucson. The Apaches would say that Diana had spiderwebs in her brain.

Mattie felt like she had spiderwebs in her own brain that night. She had talked heap big. Now she had to produce a heap big result.

Holding her close as they lay in the wickiup's darkness, Gordon asked, "What can you do?"

"I don't know. The answer will come." She was letting the question incubate while she slept. For her, there could be no question without an answer, no problem without a solution. The existence of one defined the existence of the other.

She had to believe it was so, because the only alternative was unthinkable.

When the answer came, just as she was stirring awake, still in that in-between world, it was so unbelievably simple that she was astounded she could have overlooked it. She had been fretting over her shortcoming in the face of Gordon's fastidious morning habits.

Habits!

By habit, Nantez arose at dawn every morning and, alone, would go to relieve himself at an arroyo some hundred yards from camp.

For her and Gordon to leave camp in hopes of taking Nantez hostage would be virtually impossible. But she could capitalize on his absence from camp to visit with Pon-chie. The old woman would be suspicious, but mayhaps her eyesight was still as poor as before. . . .

No one challenged Mattie as she left the wickiup. The camp was not yet astir, if she discounted the mangy dog trotting past. She walked a little ways into the brush. Without looking behind her, she knew she was being watched. She strolled on a bit farther, then squatted.

She picked her way back more slowly to the camp, then headed toward that of Nantez's, identifiable by his buffalo shield propped outside the wickiup. The first orange-pink flush of sunlight was tinting the eastern sky; he should be gone by now.

Pon-chie sat by the fire, preparing the morning's pozole. The old woman's wrinkle-clustered eyes glowered. "Why have you come?"

"I have come to break bread with you, Pon-chie. I cannot harbor resentment and be happy, both."

Pon-chie's eyes narrowed. Her knotted hands continued to grind the pestle in the pozole mush.

"I offer you my hand in friendship," Mattie said and extended it across the mortar.

Pon-chie knocked her hand away. "The way of the white man! Begone!"

She shrugged. "As you will."

She returned to the wickiup she shared with Gordon. Esqueda had returned and was preparing breakfast, the same breakfast over which Pon-chie had labored. "Where did you go?"

"To visit with Nantez's first wife. The old woman who presided over the coming-of-age ceremony the night we arrived."

He rubbed his beard-stubbled jaw. His eyes narrowed. "You're giving that secretive smile I've come to recognize as portending a problem for me."

At his mention of the word problem, her smile broadened. "Solution, Gordon. Not problem."

He flicked her an impatient frown. "Is there something you're not telling me?"

"Aye. I added me own herbs to the breakfast she was preparing for that beastly husband of hers."

"Herbs? Where did you get them?"

"I foraged for them when I went for my uhh . . . morning constitutional."

The bark of the cascara sagrada, the Strong Root— a mere dandelion, the sarsaparilla, the leaves of the pile wort, all were healthful individually. But concentrated and mixed, they produced nausea.

"'Tis like using the cause for the cure," she explained to Gordon. "For instance, the Indians claim that nothing is better for worms in children than the worms themselves dried on a red-hot tile and reduced to powder."

Gordon shuddered, and she laughed. "By midday, Nantez should be feeling a wee bit queasy."

He cocked his head and stared at her as if he were

trying to see within her. "Why didn't you just poison him, Mattie?"

"I've thought about it often enough, God knows. Deadly nightshade and certain toadstools would do it easily. But even if Nantez would have died, the squaws alone would have made life miserable for me and Albert. At least, Albert had the security of being his child. I don't think the outcome would be any different now. Should I have poisoned him this time, we three would still be captives. Maybe captives of Martine, should he succeed Nantez as chief. We both know how Martine must feel about you."

"Right now he feels a lot of pain." He pinned her with a searching gaze. "I noticed Nantez isn't missing any fingers."

"What? Oh!" She grinned. "So ye bought that story about the finger bone, did ye now? That bone is a wild turkey wing. I made up the story meself just after I arrived at Fort Lowell. Figured it'd keep me and Albert safe enough."

He chuckled. "Oh, Mattie, you're a rare find!"

She blushed, unsure whether that was a compliment or not. She meant to ask as much, but Ramos entered the wickiup at that point.

"Nantez has summoned me to cure his belly sickness," he said.

She knew that all hinged on her question. "Will you? Will you cure him, Ramos?"

His discerning eyes looked straight into hers. "I have told him that you have placed a curse on him; that you are the one who must lift it."

Relief seeped from her parted lips in a half-sigh, half-smile. "Thank you, Ramos."

"A return of the gift you once gave me. My debt is cleared."

In a low tone, she explained to Gordon what had transpired. "So, I need only to collect charcoal, a little wheat starch, and the bark of wormwood. In the meantime, go to the owner of that chicken we saw in camp and beg an egg. We will need its white."

"Beg? In English, I hope?"

"Pantomime. The owner will understand. Then, after I dose Nantez, Diana and ye and I will be on our way back to Cusarare with any luck."

Nantez was stretched out on a heavy, red woolen blanket. His heavy wheezing sounded like a train at a depot. At his far side sat old Pon-chie. There was not a trace of meanness to be found in her concerned and protective gestures toward her husband. Back in a shadowy corner, a movement suggested that Diana was also present.

"Do you wish to be healed of your ghost sickness?" Mattie demanded of Nantez in the Apache language.

He gritted his teeth. Anger, and pain, burned in his eyes. He made an emphatic gesture. "Yes!"

She opened the beaver skin she carried and spread it wide. "Then I can concoct a potion for you—with the agreement if your sickness is gone by the sunrise, we will go free. With Diana. Is that understood?"

Again, the explosive, "Yes!"

Using Pon-chie's mortar and pestle, she ground

and blended the herbs she had collected, then stirred them with *pozole* in a wooden bowl.

At the same time, her eyes searched the darkness and distinguished Diana huddled against a stack of skins and blankets. The woman's slender, lovely hand picked absently at a lock of hair, which was clumped with grease and dirt.

Mattie passed Pon-chie the bowl. "Feed him all that I have prepared. By sunrise, his ghost sickness will be gone."

She turned to Gordon. "Ye go on ahead of me. Go to Esqueda's wickiup. I will bring Diana with me."

He nodded, and she rose, crossing to Diana. The woman stared up at her absently. As she took Diana's hand, the woman did not flinch as she had from Gordon's touch. Mattie well understood how the woman must have been cowed by her experience.

Leading Diana from the wickiup, she could feel O'Neil's knife-sharp gaze on her. She suspected the mercenary did not plan to let them get far.

She told Gordon as much when she entered their wickiup. "Furthermore, even if Nantez lets us leave camp, he didn't promise he wouldn't pursue us later. We're leaving ahead of his schedule. Tonight, after the camp falls asleep."

He barely listened to her. Hands dangling at his sides, he stared at Diana with eyes reflecting a compassion Mattie had never seen before. It was something that exceeded intimacy. Mattie turned away from witnessing the touching scene. "I'll find Esqueda and have her prepare us a wee bit of food."

"No!" Diana said. Her hand swept out to clutch Mattie's arm. "Don't leave me."

Mattie glanced from the clawlike grip on her sleeve up to Gordon's face, which was full of pain. "Gordon won't hurt ye, Diana."

"It's all right," he said. "She'll need to time to get used to me. I'll see if I can find Esqueda. It shouldn't be too diffi—"

Just then the hide covering the wickiup entrance was thrown back. Diana whirled and gave a cry that was like that of a frightened animal. The intruder was only Esqueda with their evening meal. She ladled it out into bowls and passed them around.

Diana only looked at her bowl and turned her face away. No wonder the woman was languishing.

Gordon took his bowl and stared at it in distaste. "Appalling. What is it?"

Mattie stirred her finger in the mush. "Looks like ground intestines. Most likely from a ringtail. Horrible tasting but good for you."

She was too nervous to sit and ate standing up. She forced herself to swallow and flash Esqueda a smile to indicate that she relished the exotic dish.

Gordon made a token effort at sampling the food without betraying his disgust. She could tell he was trying not to glance in his wife's direction.

Diana had slumped down onto her knees, the bowl of food forgotten at her side. She looked as if she had passed beyond mere weariness. Soul weariness. That was what the Apaches would have called her malaise.

When Mattie finished eating, she rolled out two

of the animal skins. Gordon gave her an inquiring look. "I know 'tis only midafternoon," she said, "but we shall need all our energy. We'll be traveling all night and day from here on until we have safely crossed the border."

She motioned for Diana to come and lie down on one of the furred hides. The woman looked back at her blankly but rose after a moment. Circumventing her husband as if he were a leper, she picked up the skin, sought out a darkened corner, and curled her lithesome frame upon it.

So this was the vibrant woman who charmed scores of men?

Wiping her grimy fingers on her skirt, Mattie peered through the wickiup's dimness at the huddled figure. She was pathetic, yet she still retained a semblance of elegance and refinement in her every move and gesture.

Hands clasped across his drawn-up legs, Gordon watched his wife also. An indeterminate yearning transformed his face to a picture of hopelessness.

Mattie turned on her side and closed her eyes. Was there no justice in the world? No hope of happiness? Always this struggle . . . to try to make things right for one's self and loved ones.

When she awoke, she could hear the burping of frogs, heralding nightfall. She looked over her shoulder. Old Esqueda was snoring lightly. Diana slept as though her body had ceased breathing and her soul already had winged its way to heaven. Gordon's eyes sparkled in the dim light. Tears?

"Ye can't sleep?" she whispered.

Silence, then he responded with a low, raw timber in his voice. "Why her?"

Anger at him flashed through her. She rolled toward him, coming to crouch like a cat over him. "Why me?"

His hand clasped her shoulder as if to shake it, but he didn't. "No. I mean why doesn't she have that . . . that survival instinct? That resiliency you have?"

Her lips curled in a sneer. "Better me than she? Is that what you mean?" She wanted to claw out his heart. She wanted to cry. To wail like a banshee. "That she deserves to live more than I do? Now tell me, me good man, just how ye come by that? Does beauty qualify one? Manners? Wealth?"

She struck at his cheek with her palm. He swiveled his head, and she could see that his cheek was mottled from the impact.

At the same time, she was spitting like a cornered cat, "Tell me! Tell me! What qualifies one as deserving to live?"

With the prizefighter quickness, he caught her wrist and yanked her down against him. "I don't have the answer to that."

Esqueda, disturbed by the heated voices, shifted her dumpy body, then settled in sleep once again. Diana moaned lightly, but never stirred.

Gordon leaned his face close to Mattie's. "God knows I should have been the boxer who died in the ring on the Rio Grande this year. The one who died . . . he had children. Two boys and a girl, I later learned. With the money, he was planning to bring his consumptive wife to the West in hopes of restoring her failing health."

"And ye didn't have your own dream that was just as deserving?"

"Sure I did. So why him and not me?"

"Mayhap 'tis true," she whispered. "That Divine Justice is at work and we cannot see its purpose."

He gathered her against him. She nestled her head against the curve between his neck and shoulder. His skin had the fresh scent of their earlier bath. "I don't know whether to believe that. It's not a good enough explanation. Only a cliché."

"But clichés mirror the truth." Mattie paused. "Is she still beautiful to you? Diana?"

Reflective silence emphasized the quiet, steady beat of the pulse in his neck. Then he answered. "She always will be beautiful. She is a work of art. A statue of beauty. A lifeless statue, albeit. All emotions turned inward. I never reached her. And now . . ."

"And now, mayhap 'tis not too late. Mayhap this has jolted her such as nothing in her sheltered life ever did. With time and love, she may be all that ye ever wanted in her in the first place."

Those words were the hardest Mattie ever had to say. But she felt they were true and had to make him see this possibility.

He made no reply, and silence enveloped them.

His long hair, coarse as any Indian's, tickled her nose. She rested her face against his chest, and even there found hair to tickle her. She may have dozed. She wasn't sure, but when she next opened her eyes, moonlight slanted through the aperture between flap and doorway.

She could have done no more than twitch a muscle or blink her lashes, but Gordon knew she was awake. "Time to be gone?" he asked.

"Aye. Leave Diana to me."

"Most willingly."

She rose, went to the sleeping woman and nudged her shoulder. Diana's eyes flew open. So did her mouth, but Mattie quickly covered it with her hand. "'Tis all right. We must leave now. We are going home."

"Home?" came the muffled whisper.

"Aye. Home."

That single word, home, seemed to have the power to make the woman cooperate. She rose and let Mattie take her hand. Like a sleepwalker, she permitted Mattie to draw her toward the door.

Mattie spared a departing glance for Esqueda who snored gently in oblivious slumber. Or did the old Mexican woman actually wink at her as she turned back toward the doorway?

Outside, the *ranchería* was quiet. A few campfires smoldered. Dogs dozed. To move among the wickiups unchallenged, she knew, would be relatively easy. To slip past guards stationed outside the camp's perimeters would be more difficult. She had no knowledge of where they were posted.

A cold half-moon lit the way for her. Using all her past experience with the Apaches, she slipped through the underbrush. She was careful where she placed her feet, and she gingerly moved limbs from her path and replaced them. She imagined herself gliding like a snake—the Indian symbol of rebirth and new life. Diana and Gordon followed in the trail she forged.

Always, her eyes scanned their field of vision, peering through the moonlit night for shapes and forms alien to the landscape. Mist curled up from the ground and wreathed around the trees like serpents.

Her ears listened for sounds not in keeping with the forest or those that were native to the forest, but might be coming at an inappropriate hour. A night bird's call. She stilled, tensed. After all these years, it was so difficult to recall what was natural wildlife and what were Apache tricks.

Resuming her steps, she kept her pace steady and slow, so that the urge for flight did not turn into a disastrous, blind running.

The density of trees thinned. Gradually, solid rock replaced soft soil and vegetation. She began to breathe easier. No call to halt. No sudden shaft and sudden pain between the unprotected shoulder blades.

She sensed they were nearing the canyon rim. How to find the path back down in that darkness where moonlight was deceptive? Yawning chasms waiting to swallow up their bodies at one misstep.

The shale beneath her foot began to slope. She had more a sense, a subtle feeling, than any substantial evidence of the ravenous rim just beyond mortal sight, aided by moonlight.

Then even that small concession by luck was withdrawn as Stygian clouds smothered the silver crescent. Her steps slowed even further. Rocks slid away and their sounds echoed. Then there was silence.

Her palm sweated. Diana's was dry and cool.

Time was pressuring her to hurry. Instead, she sat down, tugging Diana with her. Behind them, Gordon did likewise. Mattie slowly began to edge forward. That terrible fear of the unknown was magnified a thousand times in the thundering beat of her heart against her ribcage and the pounding of her pulse against her eardrums.

One heel encountered space. She froze and sucked in her breath.

Diana pushed against her.

"Stop!" she told the woman.

Diana nudged her again.

She slid, maybe a yard or so. Diana slid with her. Then her feet jammed up against something solid. A boulder.

Diana laughed.

Mattie's fear was like an acid, corroding her veins and bones. Feeling her way around the boulder's pitted surface, she veered off to her right. Despite the night's coolness, perspiration dotted her forehead and saturated her armpits. She could smell the odors of pine and cedar mixed with the odor of her fear. Did Gordon realize how precarious were their positions? Literally precarious?

Again, her foot struck emptiness. At once, she flung herself backward. Her spine collided with Diana's knee. The impact must have frightened Diana. The woman started flailing her fists against her. "No! No! Don't! Stop hurting me!"

Mattie warded off the woman's blows. Felt herself

sliding. Her feet scrambled for a toe-hold and encountered slippery shale. She was going over the edge!

Her hands grabbed only the air. She was falling.

How far she fell, rolled, tumbled, bounced was all a blur. She must have come to a stop on a plateau of sorts. The air was knocked from her. She felt bruised. Only Nantez had ever battered her this badly.

She tried sitting up, but the hand on which she braced her weight plunged on downward. *Días muire!* She must be on a ledge!

Suddenly, the moon blasted away the clouds and revealed the precipice spread before her. She was perched on a stob of rock not much wider than a table. Below and beyond, the white-rapids river coursed through the canyon like a thin stream of spilt milk.

"Mattie!"

It was Gordon's voice. With motion she could ill afford, she turned her head to look back. He stood off to her right, on the rim's edge. Diana was backing off. The woman was going to run back to the Apache camp!

"Mattie, look down," he called.

"Are ye daft?"

"Behind you. See the ridge?"

Carefully, she peered over the edge. Indeed, a bridge of rock, mere inches beneath the one on which she sat, connected the stob with the canyon wall. The upward slope of the bridge had slowed the momentum of her tumbling so that she had not rolled on over the table's edge.

Obviously, her guardian angel hadn't slept through this particular peril.

Cautiously, she swiveled her body around to face the rim and Gordon. She lowered her feet over the edge of the table top until they touched rock. She could not bring herself to stand, to cross the natural bridge upright, although it was more than a yard's width.

On all fours, she crawled forward. Her hands knotted on tufts on grass, as if they could support her weight should she lose her balance. It was absurd. She grinned and started to chuckle. She was midway across the bridge.

"What in the hell are you doing, Mattie?"

"Celebrating precious life!" She continued crawling, looking neither to her left nor right, but only down at the sandstone. An ant was her companion. It moved more quickly than she. Who ever said ants were slow?

At last, she reached the canyon wall. Drawing a fortifying breath, she looked up. And up. Stairstep ledges appeared to offer handholds and even areas wide enough to gallop a horse. But the distance between many of them looked higher than she could reach.

No wonder she had felt battered from the fall. She must have hit every ledge.

"Can you find footholds?" Gordon called.

She shook her head. "No." She was trapped!

"Shit!" Gordon cried out.

"What?"

He pointed off to his right, then grabbed Diana and tugged her behind him as he ran along the rim's edge.

Mattie looked off toward the direction he was pointing. O'Neil! He was taking aim with his rifle. *Sonofabitch!*

"O'Neil!" she yelled.

Caught off guard, he swiveled in the direction of the shout. The muzzle of his rifle found her. She flung herself flat against the canyon wall. A ping and a puff of dust half-a-dozen feet ahead of her. Then another scarcely a yard from her.

Just grand. Now the moon had to shine!

Cautiously, she leaned her head forward to peer up at him. A whiz of wind ruffled her hair, and rock crumbled from the wall just past her head.

The dust cleared—and she saw in that direction what she had not noticed before. The ledge she was on narrowed, but continued to parallel the upper rim in a slope spiraling in a gradual descent. She began to edge along this foot-wide lip of rock. Glue could not have stuck closer to the canyon wall. Its plunging drop-off revealed a breath-sucking view of a grizzly death.

More shots zinged around her. Grit stung one eye. Then, mercifully, a cloud absorbed the moonlight.

Or, perhaps, not so mercifully. One misstep . . . .

She had to force herself to take a step. Test the rock beneath. Would it support her weight? Then another step. And another.

Why hadn't she stayed in Tucson!

Because Albert had run away.

Because of that paradoxical man called Gordon.

Because she would not have missed this adventure even if at this very second her next step meant plummeting two-hundred feet.

Or, at least, that's what she told herself as encouragement for each successive step she took.

From somewhere, she heard thudding sounds, a muffled scream, a clattering. With the canyon's echo it was difficult to tell the direction exactly. Gordon? Diana?

Then, she heard the scuffling of gravel underfoot coming from somewhere, not more than ten or fifteen feet above her. The ledge and the rim must be converging. Then came a man's distinctive grunt.

Which direction was O'Neil going? She could wait, but if the moon came out from behind the clouds, she would be totally exposed. Better to move on. Listening intently, she scooted along the ledge. Now, the canyon wall she had plastered her back to was no higher than her hips.

Too late, she heard the rustling steps, the heavy breathing—and collided with him. A single hand grabbed hold of her forearm. She tried to yank free, but its grip was stronger.

"Mattie?"

"Gordon?" She could make out his face now.

"Let me go, please. Please." That was Diana's low, pleading voice.

"O'Neil's out there somewhere," Mattie told him.

He released her forearm and said wryly, "I thought that was the Archangel."

"More like the Angel of Death. Let's keep moving. I'm fairly certain this be the trail we came up."

Moving in the mist and darkness meant proceeding at a snail's pace for the three. Diana's docile demeanor was a blessing. Gravel rumbled underfoot. If the noise was echoed any distance, the same was not true of O'Neil; that is, if he made any noise.

Occasionally, the moon peeked from behind its black-cloud mask, and Mattie was given a glimpse of the steep slopes and treacherous maze of switchbacks awaiting them. Still, she was also assured that they drew ever closer to the bottom.

Of O'Neil's whereabouts, she could only guess.

The confirmation to her guess came forty-five minutes later, when they reached the canyon's bottom. By that time the moon had made up its mind to light the landscape. They found their mounts where they had left them, and then they found O'Neil. He had fallen onto his back from a precipice above, and his eyes now stared up at the moon lifelessly.

Mattie led the way out the canyon. She tried not to think of the couple riding double behind her. Might as well tell herself not to breathe. The woman cradled in Gordon's arms was the woman Mattie wanted to be. Where she wanted to be.

Now Gordon had what he wanted.

And she? Well, she could claim her fifteen hundred dollars once she reached Tucson. Was it that damned important? Would it change who she was? Who she was now? Would it really make Albert's life any better?

She doubted it. At least, that was what she wanted to believe. That she could ride away now. Leave Gordon and his woman to their own resources. And damn the money.

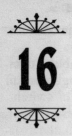

16

When William Bingham opened his eyes, he beheld Hell on Earth. The face of his nemesis was in the guise of a woman this time, but an Indian all the same. The same fierce visage: skin as dried as October's corn husks. A grin like a jack-o'-lantern's. Slanted eyes full of both fiendishness and ignorance at once.

He shrank back onto the straw pallet. "Get thee from me, Satan."

She thrust a wooden cup at him.

Poison? The blood of a sacrificial victim?

She nodded enthusiastically, indicating he should drink.

He peered dubiously into the cup. A dark, amber liquid swirled inside. He *was* thirsty. Tentatively, he sipped the concoction. He gasped. "Wine!" He sipped again. By God, it was a fortified wine. As good as any sherry or port, but definitely a home brew.

Later that day, using Spanish, he was able to communicate to the witch his desire to see the source of this nectar.

Again, that enthusiastic nod.

He was weaker than he thought. It took the assistance of both the Indian woman and the half-breed kid to get him off the earthen floor and to the hovel's crumbling doorway. He shook off their hands. The filthy hands of savages. "I can walk alone."

On legs weakened by two days of disuse, he followed Liliana over a stone-laid path that challenged his ankles. Tentacled, spiny cactus looking like some wild nightmare bordered the trail.

At the first pebbly incline, he almost slipped. The half-breed caught his elbow. William acknowledged the act with a brisk nod, the closest he could bring himself to expressing graciousness to the boy. After all, his birth wasn't his fault.

Then William looked out over a valley. On one side, high upon a slope that had the best exposure to the sunshine, was planted a vineyard. Large bunches of grapes were trained on crude pergolas.

The Tarahumara men were already harvesting the grapes into large, two-handled baskets. The women, looking like a string of ants, held the baskets on their heads and climbed the hill to disappear over the other side.

"Come!" Liliana took his hand. "Walk."

He allowed her to lead him back up the path. But

at the top, instead of returning to her house, she took another trail.

The trail came out at the ruins of the Jesuit mission. It had been built more like a fortress with stone-block rooms several feet thick. Now wildflowers and cactus grew in tumbled piles of stone that were once part of the wall next to the church.

Liliana passed under an ivy-draped stone arch and entered the church through a tile-faced doorway. They were in the north transept. Here, it was dark and cool.

Instead of going into the chancel, she led him and Albert on down a stone stairway worn by the passage of millions of feet, then into a cavernous room lit by torchlight.

Slowly, William's senses adjusted. First, he heard the sound of a reed flute, coming from another room. Then, he smelled the strange odor. At once, he identified it as peyote. The Tarahumaras held it in high regard, believing that it possessed the power to cure.

Lastly, he beheld a stone figure and recognized it as Chacmol, a heavenly messenger. It was said these people came from a culture far more advanced than even that of Cortez and his conquistadors, but he doubted this seriously. "A blasphemy!" he muttered.

Liliana took his arm and pointed at the darkened corner. There, perched on shelf after shelf, was a cache of raffia covered bottles. *"Vino,"* she said. *"Para la comunión."*

He shook off her hand and strode from the place of defilement and up the stairs like a man pursued by thirty demons. At the top, his recovering injury caught up with him, forced him to pause for breath and fight back the pain.

Ahead of him was the chancel. A portion of the caved-in roof emitted a waterfall of sunlight. A pepper tree flourished where once had been the high altar.

A burro chomped placidly at shoots of grass thrusting up from between the floor's broken tiles. The animal, its hooves clattering against the tiles, wandered closer to the pulpit in search of greener pastures.

Then William noticed the crude twelve-foot wooden crucifix behind the pulpit. Honey-gold rays of sunlight haloed the oaken Cross of Christ, which was carved with distinctly Indian features.

As he watched, a dozen or so Tarahumaras came and went, genuflecting, kneeling, lighting candles, leaving offerings of flower, corn, wine.

William stomped toward the pulpit and waved his arms, as if to scatter them like cattle. "You defile the Lord God Almighty!"

Worship ceased. The Indians whispered, "A crazed man." They fell back from his path.

At that point, the strangest thing happened. As he approached the pulpit, blood began to dribble from the wound at the crucifix's wooden feet.

Liliana's eyes were wise with the knowledge of the ancients.

Albert observed the long face of the man across from him, who studied the cards he held. A stupid man, this Bingham. He believed his white man's God would save him. Could he not see that the bleeding crucifix was, most likely, nothing more than wine spilt from one of the wine bottles?

"Five beans," Bingham said.

A stupid man. The eyes looked off, away from the five cards in his hand. He did not have anything. His God would not save him from Nantez.

"I call." Albert knew that his father, when he knew that his son was in the area, would track him down. Would kill whoever stood in the way.

This worried Albert. He didn't want his mother killed. But she was a woman. She still thought of him as her little boy. She couldn't understand that it was time for him to be a man.

Bingham's smile was serene. He spread his cards fanlike on the pigskin table. "Three queens, son."

Albert stared down at the cards, then up at the white man. "You lied. You said you had never played stud poker."

"No. I said I *don't* play the game."

He shook his head. "You hide behind words. A white coward." He shoved the beans at the man. His words were like shadows. Appearing, disappearing, reappearing. Without meaning.

Bingham was a coyote man. Furred face and hands, pointed ears, and eyes that shifted endlessly from side to side. A clever animal, this coyote.

But not as clever as Albert's father. His father would hunt, trap, and skin this coyote for sport.

He had been waiting for his father for four years now. Waiting for him to come for him, as this white man's god was supposed to come for his son, this Bingham. Stupid man. How could this god help his son when the god did not believe in fighting back? Nantez would fight for his son.

Those shifting eyes glittered. "Whatever you're thinking, son, you don't even know half of anything. Understand? Life is an illusion. Like desert mirages. When you're half-way across life's desert, you find out that black is white, shadow is really light, wrong is right and that you've been a fool most of your life. If not all of it."

More words. He shoved out another bean for an ante. Stupid coyote man. Now he would trap this animal at his own game. Albert dealt the hand.

After the Apache *ranchería,* Cusarare looked cosmopolitan to Gordon.

Diana slumped in front of him. He was concerned; she seemed more dead than alive. When he was fourteen, he had seen Union soldiers coming back from Gettysburg. Most of those who had survived had stumps for arms and legs. They all wore looks of shock, even the few who had been lucky enough to remain whole men. As if they had glimpsed the end of life. Diana wore that look now.

Liliana sat in the semishaded doorway of her mud hut. Her plump hands worked rapidly, weaving a pine-needle basket. She glanced up. The sunlight fell on her face, and its homely countenance beamed a smile that was beatific.

Riding next to him, Mattie swore under her breath. *"Sonofabitch.* Bingham must have gone and married her while in the haze of the sedative I gave him!"

"Or taken her to bed," he said.

Mattie shook her head. "No. Not even the sedative could bring him around to do that deed with her."

He laughed aloud, and Diana stirred in his arms. While she was still acquiescent, he bent and kissed her lips. They were perfectly shaped, with that enticing indentation in the center of the bottom one. But they were cold.

She turned her head away.

Another part of him died. Maybe, all of him would eventually die, so that his wanting of her would at last be ended.

Or maybe, as Mattie had suggested in solace, this life-threatening crisis in Diana's life would change her so completely, change her so that she could come to love. Love him.

But the deepest part of him, that part that knew truth, whispered that Diana would never be anything but the passive being that this horrible ordeal had made her. She had regressed to the mentality of a child not much older than Albert, and much less stable.

So. Here he was, saddled with a child for a wife. For the rest of his life. Somewhere, something inside him, an awareness, wept. His shoulders straightened. Everything had its price.

Mattie's boy materialized in the darkened doorway. His cold gaze could wilt a flower. "Get Bingham. We're leaving," Gordon told him. He had no idea how close Nantez was on their heels, but according to Mattie, the Apache chief would pursue them into hell if he had to.

Albert's gaze shifted to her. "Mother?" Before she could reply, he came toward her in a run.

She slipped from her horse and grabbed him. She nuzzled his hot, sweaty neck the way a mare nuzzles its colt.

A moment later Bingham staggered to the door. He looked like some shaggy mountain man.

"It must have been a hell of a romp," Gordon murmured to Mattie.

"Your wife?" Bingham asked, nodding toward the mute and listless Diana.

"Yeah. And your share of the fifteen hundred dollars. Get your gear together. A fiend worse than any Satan you've preached about is following our trail."

Bingham nodded. "So, we come face to face with our fears. Our shadows. The fiend becomes our savior." His grin, before he retreated inside, was spooky.

Or maybe, Gordon thought, *I'm just on edge. Maybe Bingham's right. I'm having to face my enemies. They are faces of myself.*

Liliana stood outside the doorway, her expression as vapid as the desert flats. Albert walked around from the staked corral behind the mud shack, leading their two horses and the pack mule.

When Bingham emerged from the shack with saddlebags and a rifle, Liliana looked up. He stopped and stared down at her. In the grizzly mass of beard, his mouth twisted. He turned away and stalked to his horse.

Liliana never said a word. Just watched them trot their horses out of the village.

Gordon darted a last look over his shoulder. She was still standing there. With her dark brown skin, she could have been one of those carved wooden Indians he had seen propped outside a sutler's store.

Bingham never glanced back.

Indian legend predicted that the coyote would be the last species on Earth. Albert studied the preacher, riding ahead of him. He doubted Bingham would fulfill that prophecy. The man was too stupid to take care of himself. No warrior rode with his carbine's muzzle resting in the saddle socket. Apaches carried the rifle in the hand, always.

Albert gazed past Bingham, at his mother. Her stirrups weren't hooded, providing protection from heavy brush, and her moccasins were falling apart at the seams, despite her efforts to keep them in one piece.

He remembered his first pair of moccasins. His mother had just made them for him, a fine new pair. She had told him to take care of them, when one of the neighboring women, Pon-chie, had come over to their teepee for a visit.

His mother had lifted him to the back of the woman's horse, saying, "Ride this horse down to the creek and water it. Don't get off while he is drinking."

Very proud of his new moccasins, he had ridden the half-mile to the water hole. As the horse stood in the stream drinking, Albert had been fascinated by the reflection of his moccasins in the water and had leaned farther and farther forward until he toppled over the horse's neck into the creek. All his pride had melted away, and he had run crying back to their lodge.

A group of women were sitting there laughing at him. Instead of whipping him for getting his new moccasins wet, his mother had slipped them off his feet, taken him in her arms, and comforted him.

He loved her very much and never liked it when his father beat her. But Nantez was like that when he drank. Always. He had even backhanded him occasionally when in one of his drunken rages.

Albert's eyes left his mother's small figure, and found the big one that belonged to the white man, Halpern. He had seen the man drink the firewater several times and had waited for the usual drunken rage that followed. But nothing had happened.

He could tell his mother cared about this man, and he didn't like that. He wished she would return to the Netdahe with him. He knew she wasn't afraid, not like the white woman Halpern carried. His mother simply hated Nantez. She hated him with the fierceness of a mother bear riled by an intruder messing with her cubs.

Albert smiled to himself, comparing the image of his mother, so small, clawing and roaring ferociously. He had seen her do this when Nantez attacked her or even himself. It usually earned her a blackened eye or busted lip. It would be better if she behaved like the other squaws and crept away.

In the lead, Halpern was riding north, keeping their trail within the protective folds of the mountains and their foothills. Considering that he rode double, he was riding fast. They all rode fast.

Albert smiled to himself again. Once Nantez had them in his sights, he would not let them get away.

All day they rode. No breaking for meals. His mother, Gordon, and the man's woman looked more tired than a Tarahumara Indian after a four-day run. Bingham didn't look too rested either. The way he held himself in the saddle said that his wound had to be smarting bad.

Even Albert felt tired. He shifted in the saddle. He had learned to ride a pony without a saddle. His legs felt stiff. He was thirsty, too. Occasionally, they watered the horses at a stream and passed the canteens around before refilling them. But his last drink of water had been hours before, and the sun was hot.

The cool forest of pines and oaks had given way to scattered madrona, sycamores, and colossal cactus. The horses rambled down dank canyons and up through natural rock tunnels. The ride was so bumpy that Albert felt as if every tooth in his head rattled.

His mother swayed in the saddle, as if too weary to even remain upright. Behind her, Bingham said, "I suggest we call it quits for the day. There is a silver mine not far from here. It would offer a good view of the surrounding country and an excellent defense position, if we need it."

The mine was located at the top of a hill overlooking a narrow valley. Anyone approaching could be seen from all but the rear side of the hill, which was on the north. An attack from the side would be unlikely.

The setting sun turned the clump of treetops to green canvas awnings over the entrance. A gondola track for hauling out ore faded into its darkness. Halpern peered inside. "Hades could not be any blacker."

"A lantern would help," Bingham grumbled.

Albert's mother took the hand of the white woman, who stood beside Halpern's horse. "We'll all feel better after we have a wee bite to eat." She led her over to two slabs of adjoining rock and seated her.

Albert stared at her. She was beautiful. Pale as the moon. Slender as a flower stem. Eyes like the precious bluish opals found in these very mountains.

"Albert," his mother said, "scout out a couple of stalks of dead cactus. We can improvise torches, should we have to retreat inside."

He lingered, pretending he was adjusting the blue wool webbing of his saddle's girth strap. Maybe this woman didn't want Halpern for her man. Albert held up a canteen before her, offering a drink. He was too bashful to speak.

She shook her head.

Well, she was only a woman. He turned away to find Halpern eyeing him with amusement. He flushed. "The cactus," he mumbled and went off.

Dinner was a collection of Liliana's dishes, all cold: bacon, potatoes, beans, and tortillas. Albert wolfed them down. He missed his mother's home-cooked meals. The others ate as hungrily as he. All except for Halpern's woman. She only picked at her food.

The day was almost gone. The sky was a dark indigo color. He was tired but not sleepy. By the faint half-light of evening he cleared rocks and pebbles from a flat surface of rock. Sitting with his legs folded, he began to play solitaire.

His mother, eyes half-closed like a dozing cat, leaned against a tree and smoked a last cigarette.

Albert knew she wanted Halpern and was hurting that he was interested only in the yellow-haired woman.

Halpern was trying to talk with his woman now. He hunkered before her and held both her hands. She seemed to be only half-listening.

"You could've put the red jack on that black queen there, boy."

He glanced over at the last column of cards. The preacher was right. "So, you want to play for me?"

Bingham spit a stream of tobacco juice. "The devil's game."

Albert flipped over another card, but the breeze caught it and sent it sailing. He lunged past Bingham. The card somersaulted across the dirt. He dived for it. At that instant, he saw the familiar slash of vermilion. War paint!

The Apache slinked from tree trunk to brush to rock, all the time moving in on Halpern. His back was to the warrior. Good, Albert thought. With the man dead, his mother would quit pining for him.

He returned to his position before the cards, but kept an eye on the warrior. Were there others? He glanced around but saw nothing. Maybe the Apache was an advance scout.

Or did the brush move over there? Maybe it was the tricky half-light.

The Apache was close now. Maybe a half-dozen yards away. Albert smiled to himself. Would the Apache give him Halpern's scalp?

He devoted his full attention to the game and turned over a joker. He shimmied his head, as if to clear it of spiderweb thoughts. Had he not taken the joker from the deck?

He muttered a resounding cavalry curse that brought his mother's sharp eyes on him.

There was no time for explanations to her about what the joker stood for, that a joker was held in reserve to escape from a predicament. He picked up a fist-size rock and played the joker: He hurled the rock into the skulking shadow behind Halpern and yelled, "Apaches!"

Halpern released the yellow-haired woman and whirled around, ready to spring. At the same time, Bingham swung his Winchester to his shoulder. He fired. In the darkness came the thud of something falling.

Diana screamed and fled inside the mine.

His mother backed toward the cave's entrance. "Albert, get over here!"

"Found the nasty devil," Bingham yelled out from the Stygian darkness. "Don't seem to be any more of them out here."

"There will be!" his mother called. She clamped her hand on Albert's shoulder, as if to restrain him from going back outside to seek out his father.

He didn't have to. He knew his father would find him.

17

"*I say we make a* run for it," Bingham said.

Gordon looked to her, and Mattie bit her lip. They all huddled in the mine's outer room. Cactus torches, anchored in metal clamps for lanterns, flickered uneven light across the timbers, where Diana crouched. Her eyes were wide, her lips quivering.

The dark blue of bornite copper streaked the walls. Silver glinted like stars in the rock. In its heyday, the mine had produced most of the silver that had propped up the finances of Spain.

"I don't know," she said slowly. "Nantez and his warriors have the darkness on their side. They know every wrinkle in the land blindfolded. If we're in headlong flight, we could ride right off a cliff."

"She's right," Gordon said. "It might be better to wait for daylight, when we have better odds. Should they attack tonight, Bingham has enough ammo to hold Nantez off until dawn."

"No!"

All heads turned to Diana. She had sprung to her feet. Her hands were clenched at her sides. A vein pulsed wildly at her temple. "No! Not Nantez. He will not get me this time."

Gordon said, "We won't let that happen, Diana. We—"

"It happened before," she said in her childishly high voice. "You didn't protect me. He did horrible things to me. He'll do them again."

He started to rise, his hand outstretched toward her, but she spun around and ran along the wooden cart track back into the mine's tunnel.

He grabbed the torch and started after her. Then he stopped, half turned. Mattie saw the horror that drained his face of its power. To descend into that mine had to be his worst nightmare.

She made to rise, but Bingham grabbed her arm. "Better begin loading our firearms to make ready for Nantez."

For the first time, she noticed no condemnation in his gaze. What had happened back there at Cusarare? She nodded.

He passed her a bandoleer of bullets and an extra revolver, a Smith and Wesson. She began loading it as fast as her fumbling fingers could manage.

"Mother. Can I help?"

Días muire! What was this? First, Bingham. Now her own son. She shook her head. "No, Albert. I don't want ye having to take sides."

"He already did," Bingham said. "Out there. When he threw the rock at the buck and warned Halpern."

She handed Albert her leather belt of cartridges. "All right. But ye can load. Only that. Do ye understand?"

He didn't get the chance to answer her question. A shot, fired by Bingham, rang in her ears. "Missed!" Bingham growled. "But they're out there. I'd swear on my missing scalp I saw one of those redskins."

She raised the revolver to eye level. The night was so dark, it was hard to tell which shadows were actually moving.

A shot burst near her, and shattered rock stung her forearm. Several more shots were fired, too close for their safety. Squatting, the three of them quickly withdrew several paces. She imagined they must look like crabs.

The exchange of shots resumed and went on for a good five minutes. Then all was quiet.

"Think they have gone away?" Bingham asked.

"Not Nantez."

She was right. The barrage of shots had been a cover for other furtive activities. Soon wisps of smoke drifted toward the mine's mouth. "*Sonofabitch,* the durty devils mean to burn us out!"

That old fear rushed over her, engulfed her, choked her. She was back in that dry creek bed with fire ringing her . . . and Nantez choking her baby. God damn, she hated him!

Soon, billowing smoke roiled toward them. Her eyes stung. She couldn't see a yard past the mine's entrance. Albert coughed. "I should have killed the bugger when I had me chance," she muttered.

Bingham glanced over at her. "Where's Halpern? He should have been back by now."

She didn't answer. She knew a mine could have dozens of tunnels that led to dead-ends. "Smoked meat." She coughed. "That's what we're bloody well going to be."

"Mother!"

She looked at Albert. He was pointing to the mine's ceiling. She looked up. The smoke was rising. A smoky cord drifted, coiled, then snaked along the upper rock toward the mine's depths.

"A draft!" Bingham said.

At once, she understood. The smoke was being pulled in by a draft. That meant there had to be another opening. It was not that unusual in mining operations to have several entrances. "Get the cactus stalks!"

She grabbed the one remaining torch and fled down the tunnel. The gondola track snaking along the damp floor and the smoke that rose to the ceiling guided her in her blind flight. Bingham and Albert sprinted after her along the descent that sloped gradually.

She passed two off-shoots. They were smaller than the main tunnel. She guessed that they were dead-ends. *Días muire,* what if Gordon and Diana had become lost in one of them?

To her dismay, the gondola track ended. She continued on. Then, even the main tunnel narrowed so that it was the same size as any of the dozens of others that branched off of it at that point. She stopped and peered out of her tiny circle of light. She was undecided. Which way to go?

"Gordon?" she called out.

"We're here!"

HERE. Here. here.

The answer bounced and tumbled off the walls, so that she did not know where "here" was.

Behind them came the echo of many feet and faint voices. So, Nantez had decided not to wait for his smoked meat!

"Mother." Once again, Albert pointed to the ceiling. The cord of smoke, much thinner now, drifted off to the left, along a narrow rocky corridor.

She plunged into its darkness. All three were forced to walk single file along a twisting tunnel. Mud squished beneath their feet. The dwindling cactus torch barely illuminated the way.

Occasionally, she looked up to determine if they were still following the smoke's path. Jagged black walls disappeared into evil shadows.

Then she made the mistake of looking down. A sheer drop to her left revealed a poisonous green river lurking fifty feet below. She averted her gaze and hurried on.

Ahead of her, she heard noise. A voice! Gordon's. "Gordon!" she cried.

"Stay where you are!" he shouted back. *ARE. Are. are.*

Her torch's light chose to die at that moment. It flickered once more, then was gone. Dank, cold darkness closed in on them. "Albert! Another cactus!"

The stalk prodded her shoulder. She could hear her son's breathing. It was rapid and shallow. He was as frightened as she. Where was Bingham? "Bingham?"

"I'm here," he said, coming up from behind. "You got a match, Mattie?"

She fumbled for her pouch, found its drawstring, and sank her hand inside. By touch, she felt amid the various articles for the phosphorous matches and found one. "Hold the stalk close, Albert."

Soon, a light spread among their three terrified faces. They looked at one another in open acknowledgment of their fear. Bingham voiced it. "The ceiling's too high for us to follow the smoke."

She didn't want to acknowledge the hopelessness of their situation. "Let's find Gordon and Diana."

Ahead, she glimpsed formations. Stalagmites? No. What she had seen was a sad, subterranean chapel, where miners had prayed for their lives to be spared. Its gilded Virgin was encased for all time in calcium-carbonate deposits.

She scurried past. Hurried along a vaulted catacomb. It emptied into a cavern where her torch light was all but lost. On the cavern's far side, beyond a field of inverted icicles, was another pool of light. Gordon's.

She, Albert, and Bingham negotiated the obstacle course of stalagmites. The three drew ever closer to what appeared to be two figures. Gradually, she could hear Gordon.

He was talking in a low, coaxing voice that shook slightly. "Diana, no one need ever know what happened."

"No. I am damaged goods. Do you think I would return to a society that would scorn a Diana Ashley?"

"You can start over somewhere else."

Mattie and the others were close enough now to see

the drama being played out. Gordon was at one end of a rope bridge. It swayed with every cautious step he took.

On the other side of the chasm spanned by the bridge, Diana was pressed flat against a moisture-sheened rock wall. She seemed to be unwilling to move any farther along a ledge that sloped upward into the darkness. "There is no place left for me!" she cried out. "Can't you see, Gordon? I have been defiled!"

"Listen to me, Diana! What Nantez did to you only changed you if you let it be so."

He took another step along the suspension bridge. It wobbled wildly. His free hand gripped the rope support. He never looked down but kept his gaze fixed on Diana. "Nantez can't defile your spirit! Do you understand what I am trying to tell you?"

"I can't endure myself!" Her beautiful face was a study of tortured agony. Tears spilled over her cheeks. "I can't endure this world! I can't endure the people in it!"

"Time will change your—"

The rest of his words never got past his lips, for suddenly, without further warning, she jumped.

"Diana!" Gordon screamed. He dropped his torch. It fell so far down that not even a hiss rose from the water.

Mattie ran to the chasm's edge. Far below, the river had swallowed up the human offering as it disappeared into the darkness.

Gordon had reached the bridge's far side. He knelt there, his hands over his face, his shoulders heaving. Mattie started across the bridge. Holding the torch, she had only her left hand to steady her as she picked her way across the rotting planks.

Behind her, Albert and Bingham followed. The

bridge swayed precariously, and she gasped. She couldn't get to the other side quickly enough. When she did, she collapsed to her knees beside Gordon and wrapped a free arm around him.

He dropped his hands. His face was wet.

"There was nothing ye could do. Diana made her choice."

"I know." His voice was like the rustle of autumn leaves. "But why couldn't she have chosen otherwise?"

Behind her, she heard a sizzling. She looked around and saw that Bingham was using his torch to set fire to the rope bridge. "The heathens won't be following us now."

They had literally burned their bridges. She could only hope that the chamber on this side of the subterranean river had an outlet to the top. "Let's get moving before we run out of torches."

Gordon nodded, rose, and took the torch from her. "I am in what Diana's mother would call 'my milieu.' I spent more of my time in the dark than I did sunlight. Now I'm ready to leave the dark. Forever."

The ledge widened into a path, and the ceiling lowered, so that it was easier to follow the smoke, most of which was coming off the remaining torch that Gordon held. At some points, the chiseled trail was steep and slippery. Mattie, third in line, could barely keep her footing.

The light of their last torch burned low. She glanced up at it, then out into the gaping darkness beyond its perimeter. At least, the torch's thin wisp of smoke still curled along, as if pulled by a draft. Surely, there was an exit ahead.

Her skin felt damp and moldy, and goose bumps prickled her flesh. Diana's death leap would be a horrible image in her mind forever.

Then her sight went as black as her thoughts. The torch. It had gone out!

"Damn!" Gordon said. "Now what?"

Closer to her, Bingham said, "We pray."

Her eyes played tricks on her. At first she thought that the pinprick of light was the after-image of the torch glow. However, as she moved slowly forward, the circle widened. The light came from a hole in the cavern's ceiling.

Ahead of her, Bingham intoned, "'Behold, bless the Lord, all servants of the Lord, who serve by night in the house of the Lord!' God is merciful!"

"Daylight!" Gordon said.

Drawing near that warm circle of light, Mattie felt as a soul must when it leaves the corpse and enters God's endless presence. The sight spurred her footsteps. A rickety rope ladder seemed to climb up, up, far upward into a small crack in the cosmos.

Albert reached the ladder first. He put his foot on the bottom rung. It splintered like a toothpick.

"Rotten," Bingham said. In the mass of his beard, his mouth curled downward. "I bet it's as old as Jacob's Ladder. The ropes will probably crumble to dust."

"The bridge's rope held," she said.

"You go first, kid," Gordon said. "It may hold your weight. Then you, Mattie."

She knew the two men could only hope that the ladder would sustain their heavier weights when their turns came.

She watched Gordon give her son a boost up to the second rung. Her eyes followed the boy as he ascended the rungs easily. The ladder swayed, but the wooden slats held. Within minutes, Albert blended with the blue of sky, then was gone from view.

"You next, Mattie." Gordon put his hands around her waist and lifted her until she could get footing in the first solid rung.

She tucked her revolver into her waistband and climbed rapidly. Out of fear. If she let herself think, if she paused and looked down, she was lost.

The higher she climbed, the more the rope swayed. Even looking up was dizzying. Suddenly, a rung cracked beneath her left foot. She slipped and clutched the rope sides. Her revolver fell from her waistband and a moment later thudded on the ground not a yard from Bingham's boots.

Her grip was sweaty. She slid only a few inches, but the ropes burned her palms. Still, she held fast.

When her heart quit pounding, she blindly felt around with her foot for a stable rung. She found one, then started climbing again.

When she could feel the warmth of daylight on her face, she began smiling. The hole turned out to be as large as a room.

At last, she emerged into the upper world. Calling Albert's name, she started hauling herself up over the rock ledge to which the ladder was anchored.

That was when she saw Nantez's vermilion-and-black war-painted face.

18

Mattie started to scream, and Nantez's hand clamped down over her mouth. Over his smothering, stinking hand, her gaze darted around, glimpsed only three other Apaches. All were wearing war paint. He must have posted the others at the mine's main entrance.

She kicked and pummeled, aiming behind her for his shins and crotch, but, held before him as she was, she was virtually helpless.

He hauled her down a pebbly slope toward a clump of cottonwoods, where Indian ponies foraged among the meager plants fighting for subsistence. He thrust her amid the horses, which danced out of the way.

Only then did she see Albert. He was struggling with a warrior, who had gagged his mouth with a red flannel rag and was trying to restrain his thrashing hands.

Nantez leaned toward her. His eyes were bright with malice beneath the Neanderthal ridge that hooded them.

She knew he wasn't going to kill her. Not yet, anyway. He would want to savor her death. So when he cuffed her on the jaw, she crumpled to the ground, as if unconscious. It was a trick she had learned early on in her captivity.

The blow hurt like hell. She wondered if she had lost any teeth.

He was already loping back to the cavern hole to intercept the next climber. She wiped away the blood that trickled from her nose and scrambled to her feet. Albert's captor was busy, binding Albert with a rope.

Nantez and two more warriors squatted on their haunches around the hole. Grinning in anticipation, Nantez waited for his next victim.

"Gordon!" she screamed out in warning. With her knife drawn from the sheath at her thigh, she charged toward Nantez.

He must have heard her coming, or maybe the warrior across from him had seen her and given a signal. Whatever, Nantez sprang upward and easily dodged her lunging knife. At the same time, he backhanded her with a fist that brought blood streaming from her nose.

He laughed.

She despised him at that moment so much that a fiery pit of volcanic anger erupted inside her. It was as if Mount Etna rumbled.

Before she could make another move, Albert darted between them. His face was red with anger, and the bandanna that had gagged him hung around his neck like a noose. "No!" he shouted at his father and rained punches at his stomach.

For an instant, there was surprise in Nantez's

expression. Then ruthless purpose set his malevolent features in stone. He grabbed Albert's little fist and jerked the boy to one side.

That one side-step took Albert to the rim of the hole. There was no where he could move now. He did a circus rope-walker's dance of balancing, arms flung wide, hands clutching at the air.

All this happened in less than a second. In that same second, Mattie lunged past Nantez, reached for Albert, caught her son's fringed shirt.

Then the fringe tore away!

She screamed and latched onto his hand as it was slipping through her sweaty fingers. She felt the weight of his body tugging her with him.

With a strength that could come only from desperation, she threw her weight to one side and collapsed half atop him at the rim's edge.

Beneath her, below Albert's head, she glimpsed Bingham rapidly climbing the ladder toward them and farther down, Gordon waited at the bottom. The juxtaposition of the three was enough to make her dizzy.

Next, she heard her son's grunt of pain from a kick delivered by Nantez. She felt Albert slipping on the loose gravel around the rim's edge. Her hands scrambled for anchorage to support both her and her son.

Then, she heard Nantez laugh again. That maniacal laugh combined with his attack on Albert . . . she was renewed with a frenzied energy she didn't know she was capable of possessing.

She rolled to one side and sprang upright, knife in hand. Again he laughed. He was so certain of himself, so cocky.

"The field mouse would nip the heel of the jaguar?"

She didn't bother to reply to his taunt. She thrust out her knife and charged forward in a drive that took him by surprise.

Unhindered by shame, she felt something light burble inside her. She recognized it as satisfaction. No amount of self-lecturing about the baseness of her nature could dissuade her from making that final thrust that disemboweled him.

He clutched at his stomach and stared down at his bleeding body.

She had staggered with the force of her drive. From where she had fallen on all fours, she looked up at him. She saw in his eyes that same wild, disbelieving, desperate glaze that could be found in the black eye of a landed trout. Then he fell to his knees and collapsed beside her.

Across the hole, she stared at the two remaining Apaches. Slowly, they rose. Eyes still on her, they backed away toward the grazing horses. Then they turned and leaped on two, and rode off as if a witchwoman was after them.

She laughed. Now she was indeed the savage.

This time, she did not cry afterward.

The adobe buildings of Fort Bowie could be seen from a southeastern bluff of the Chiricahua Mountains. The Stars and Stripes drooping from the post staff represented the completion of an arduous ten-day descent into Mexico.

And descent into our own private hells, Mattie

thought. For hours after she had killed Nantez, she had been filled with a remorse that had isolated her from Albert, Gordon, and Bingham.

"Stop ruminating, gal," Bingham said, riding up beside her. "What you did back there was the Hand of God."

Her smile was wan. "So, 'tis gone from Whore to Hand of God, has it, Bingham? No, me killing Nantez was not the Hand of God. Sometimes, we do things without thinking. And then we live with them. That's all."

Gordon detoured to the post sutler's store only long enough to cash a voucher drawn on Wells Fargo in Tucson for her and Bingham.

Could you come to love someone in a mere ten days? Mattie wondered. After all that had happened, the ten days seemed like ten years.

The Fourth Cavalry band practiced "Auld Lang Syne," and Company A drilled on the post parade ground as Bingham, Mattie and her son trotted their spent mounts past. Fourteen miles ahead was Bowie Station, where Mattie spent the first of her fifteen hundred dollars.

Bowie Station was a railroad town, so new that the lumber had that fresh pine scent. Even the boardwalks were still yellow and resinous. The four weary travelers tied their horses to the one hotel's hitching post and sought rooms to clean up.

Her nine-year-old had little desire for a bath and immediately afterward was off to explore the scattering of buildings around the depot.

She, on the other hand, spent an inordinate amount

of time at her bath. Settling back into the steaming water with a sigh that was close to a statement of bliss, she lit up a cigarette. Her last one. Forever. This time she meant it. FOREVER!

Too soon, she had to desert the bath. The east-bound train was due in less than an hour. Not that she would be on it. She had paid for a room for the night since she didn't want to start the trip back to Tucson by horseback this late in the day.

When she was at last dressed, in clothes that were less than clean, she sought out a bench in the shade of the station's eaves. Only Albert was there, walking the rails, his arms stretched out to balance him. She didn't doubt that his father's death affected him more than he showed. She could only hope that it was true that children were resilient. With his hair slicked back, she almost didn't recognize him.

In turn, he stared at her with rounded eyes.

She felt nervous. "Get off the track afore the train flattens ye like a johnnycake."

Eyes still on her, he did as she bade him and joined her on the bench.

With its back to the town and the mountains, the depot looked out over wooden ties and an empty treeless valley. In the distance, a dust devil whirled.

The afternoon was so quiet that if she listened intently, she thought she could actually hear the cholla and ocotillo withering in the boiling sunlight.

She glanced up to see Bingham coming down the platform. Sweat glistened above his beard, which was freshly trimmed. She forestalled whatever he might say by asking, "Well? Now that you've claimed your reward, is it off to that gold mine of yours?"

He shook his head and spit on the plank platform. "I've seen enough mines to last a lifetime."

"Mother?"

She looked down at Albert, sitting beside her on the bench. "I don't want to go back to school."

"Ye have to."

"The Netdahe children don't."

She sighed. "The Anglo children do."

"I can't be in both the Netdahe camp and the Anglo town," he said in a very mature tone.

She was too tired to explain that he would have to see value in both Anglo and Indian ways before fusing them into something unique for himself. He had already come so far.

With the reward money put toward a good education for both Albert and her, who knew? Mayhap, as old Sam Kee had often suggested, she could get her medical degree at the college that was being opened in Tucson.

"I'll head on out, now," Bingham said. "I want to get a good start before sundown."

"A good start for where?" she asked.

He smiled at her. The smile was like a benediction. "There's a church that needs restoring back in Cusarare. And a flock that needs a shepherd."

And an Indian woman waiting. Mattie chuckled aloud. "Good-bye, William."

He smiled again. In silence, she and Albert watched the man in the eagle-feather hat mount his mule and steer it southwestward toward deep and gloomy canyons.

She watched him until he was a mere speck. Watched and said nothing. Because what could be said at this point?

She heard the heavy steps of boots on the platform and turned her head. Gordon came around the corner with his saddle bags thrown over one shoulder.

As happened every time she saw him after an absence, if only minutes, her heart skipped a beat, her breath caught. Her gaze followed him the way sunflowers turn their heads toward the sunlight.

She stood.

His musketeer's rapier gaze swept over her, lingered at her face. "Your hair!"

Her fingers apprehensively touched a tendril that she had curled artfully at her temple. The rest of the mass was caught on top her head in a crown of lustrous curls. "Ye think I am ready for society?"

"Mattie, I think the question is whether society is ready for you. With your indomitable spirit, I feel certain you will continue to set it on its ear."

A faint train whistle reminded her that their odyssey together was drawing to an end. A plume of black smoke curled up from the foothills. Soon the Southern Pacific Rail would chug into view. And then a rail coach would carry Gordon Halpern back East, where a flourishing portrait-painting career awaited.

He surprised her by reaching out to remove a pin from her carefully coifed hair. Then another. "What are ye doing?"

And another. "Do you remember asking me what qualified one as deserving to live—and I told you I didn't know?"

Her hair tumbled around her shoulders. "Aye." Where was this conversation going?

The thunder of metal wheel against rail and the roaring clank of engine forced her to speak louder than normal.

He leaned his head near hers to make himself heard. His voice was low but distinct enough for her to understand every word. "This journey has taught me what that quality is. It's a nobility of spirit. Few have it. You do."

"That's what I've been trying to tell ye!" she practically yelled. "Not just about me. About all of us."

The train wheezed to a halt. She was still shouting. "Call it a wild heart if ye will. It makes us more than we would be otherwise. It makes us more than we appear to be!"

The engine hissed and spewed. The conductor was the first to step onto the platform. A tiny, old woman with a cane and carpetbag in hand got off. Next, two cowpunchers and an infantryman, most likely returning from leave.

And it was time for Gordon to leave. Apparently, he still didn't understand what she was saying. That she was trying to tell him how much she admired his honorable endeavors, his tremendous courage and deep loyalty. No matter what the appearances were, he was constant. When things seemed at their worst, he was most ready to give of himself.

"Mattie, I am a man of dour moods and fastidious habits. And tend toward physical expression when angry."

"Can ye not see that our dissimilar personalities mesh well into a union of complements?"

"I see that I could destroy your genuineness by trying to sophisticate you."

She turned her face up to his. "Do ye truly think anyone could do that to Mattie McAlister?"

She waited for an answer. She felt as if her skin was the only thing holding her together, a delicate husk. The fist of logic and reasoning squeezed her heart dry of life blood. Waiting to hear the words spoken—that he believed in the power of love—it was as if she had stood for thirty years with a rifle pointed at her breast.

She could see that he was struggling with himself. "Don't change yourself, Mattie. I want to remember you the way you look today. Wild. Uncommonly beautiful."

Well, if she had to beg him, then he wasn't worth her love. "Good luck with ye, Halpern."

He touched her cheek. "And all the best to you, Mattie. There is nothing that can stop you from having all that you want and deserve. Don't compromise. Make them accept you as you are."

His fingers lingered on her cheek, her jaw, as if he would say more. He didn't.

She did. "Good luck with your portrait painting." She stepped back, away from his touch, where she was safe from cracking apart, and turned to go.

"Don't you know it is the West I really want to paint? I want to paint this vastness, this wildness."

She turned around again. "What?"

He took her hand and drew her to him. "I want to paint you. To paint your eyes and mouth where I see the beauty reflected inside you."

Her lips parted in surprise. "Ye want me? Ye really want *me?* Wild, wanton Mattie McAlister?"

He lowered his mouth to just above hers. From the corner of her eyes she could see that the old lady was watching, as was the conductor.

"I want to be able to acknowledge my weakness, Mattie. I want to see the folly of independence and merge at the place of complete interdependence with you."

"All aboard!"

His finger touched her bottom lip. "I want to heal your every pain, if not heal, then share. I want to lighten my burdens by assuming yours as well. I want to sacrifice my pride, my self-esteem, fully and willingly. I want to give completely, free of the chains of return."

"Then you want to stay? With me?" She still couldn't believe it. "Ye are certain?"

"Remember what you told me? That we must choose it to be so time and again until we realize that it could truly be no other way. I want you as mine, Mattie."

"I want you two to make up your minds," Albert said. "The train is leaving."

The conductor called "All aboard!" for the last time. The train whistled its warning. Then it lumbered away without its passenger.

He was embracing a thoroughly disreputable-looking woman and kissing that beguiling beauty's mouth with a passion that brought a "humph" from the old woman and a "sonofabitch" from the grinning gap-toothed boy.

Bibliography

Betzinezy, Jason and Nye, Wilbur S. *I Fought With Geronimo*. Lincoln, Nebraska: University of Nebraska Press, 1987.

Browning, Sinclair. *Enju, The Life and Struggle of an Apache Chief From the Little Running Water*. Flagstaff, Arizona: Northland Press, 1982.

Dodge, Natt N. *Flowers of the Southwest Deserts*. Phoenix: McGrew Printing, 1951.

Elmore, Francis H. *Shrubs and Trees of the Southwest Uplands*. Globe, Arizona: Southwest Parks and Monuments Association, 1976.

Foster-Harris. *The Look of the Old West*. New York: Bonanza Books, 1960.

LaFarge, Oliver. *Laughing Boy*. New York: Houghton Mifflin Complany, 1929.

Lockwood, Frank C., *The Apache Indians*. Lincoln, Nebraska: Universtiy of Nebraska Press, 1938.

McLaughlin, David. *Wild and Wooly.* New York: Doubleday and Company, 1975.

Mills, Betty J. *Calico Chronicle.* Lubbock, Texas: Texas Tech Press, 1985.

Smith, Jr., Cornelius C. *Fort Huachuca, The Story of a Frontier Post.* Fort Huachuca, Arizona: 1978.

Terrell, John Upton. *The Apache Chronicle.* New York: Apollp Editions, 1976.

Thompson, Richard A. *Crossing the Border With the 4th Cavalry.* Waco, Texas: Texian Press, 1986.

Through Tucson's History. Tucson Branch, American Association of University Women and Arizona Historical Society, 1976.

Schultheis, Rob. "Mexico's Copper Canyon." *National Geographic Traveler,* (September–October 1992).

Wooster, Robert. *Soldiers, Sutlers, and Settlers.* College Station, Texas: Texas A&M University Press, 1987.

Tame the Wildest Heart by Parris Afton Bonds

In her most passionate romance yet, Parris Afton Bonds tells the tale of two lonely hearts forever changed by an adventure in the Wild West. It was a match made in heaven . . . and hell. Mattie McAlister was looking for her half-Apache son and Gordon Halpern was looking for his missing wife. Neither realized that they would find the trail to New Mexico Territory was the way to each other's hearts.

First and Forever by Zita Christian

Katrina Swann was content with her peaceful, steady life in the close-knit immigrant community of Merriweather, Missouri. Then the reckless Justin Barrison swept her off her feet in a night of passion. Before she knew it she was following him to the Dakota Territory. Through trials and tribulations on the prairie, they learned the strength of love in the face of adversity.

Gambler's Gold by Barbara Keller

When Charlotte Bell headed out on a wagon train from Massachusetts to California, she had one goal in mind—finding her father, who had disappeared while prospecting for gold. The last thing she was looking for was love, but when fate turned against her, she turned to the dashing Reade Elliot to save her.

Queen by Sharon Sala

The Gambler's Daughters Trilogy continues with Diamond Houston's older sister, Queen, and the ready-made family she discovers, complete with laughter and tears. Queen Houston always had to act as a mother to her two younger sisters when they were growing up. After they part ways as young women, each to pursue her own dream, Queen reluctantly ends up in the mother role again—except this time there's a father involved.

A Winter Ballad by Barbara Samuel

When Anya of Winterbourne rescued a near-dead knight she found in the forest around her manor, she never thought he was the champion she'd been waiting for. "A truly lovely book. A warm, passionate tale of love and redemption, it lingers in the hearts of readers. . . . Barbara Samuel is one of the best, most original writers in romantic fiction today."—Anne Stuart

Shadow Prince by Terri Lynn Wilhelm

A plastic surgeon falls in love with a mysterious patient in this powerful retelling of *The Beauty and the Beast* fable. Ariel Denham, an ambitious plastic surgeon, resentfully puts her career on hold for a year in order to work at an exclusive, isolated clinic high in the Smoky Mountains. There she meets and falls in love with a mysterious man who stays in the shadows, a man she knows only as Jonah.

The Trouble With Angels by Debbie Macomber

Shirley, Goodness, and Mercy are back and better than ever! Given their success last Christmas in *A Season of Angels,* they're eager to answer the prayers of troubled mortals once again, to ensure that this holiday season is filled with love and joy for all.

The Greatest Lover in All England by Christina Dodd

From the award-winning author of *Outrageous* and *Castles in the Air* comes a delightful romance set in Tudor England. "Settle down for a rollicking good time with *The Greatest Lover in All England.* A sexy, fast-paced romance filled with wry wit and bawdy humor. A winner!"—Kristin Hannah

The Green Rose by Kathy Lynn Emerson

A tale of love and deception in Tudor England. In order to be eligible for a vast inheritance, Sir Grey Neville needed someone to pose as his betrothed; and Meriall Sentlow, a recently widowed beauty, was the ideal choice. But when it was time to call off their charade, Grey wasn't ready to give up Meriall, despite the dangerous secrets that lay between them.

Heart of the Jaguar by Roslynn Griffith

Set in the Southwestern Territory in the 1860s, *Heart of the Jaguar* is a poignant love story that readers will cherish. Beautiful, rambunctious Louisa Jenks was sure that she'd never see Lieutenant Sam Strong again after he rode out of Santa Fe without even a goodbye. But when a series of grisly murders occurred in the New Mexico territory, Sam was back to track down the killer and save the woman he loved from a bloody death.

Knight Dreams by Christina Hamlett

A spellbinding romantic thriller involving a secret from the past which is linked to the ghost of a 15th-century knight. On a mission to bid for an ancient suit of armor in London, Laurel Cavanaugh finds herself propelled into a mysterious chain of events and into the arms of her very own knight in shining armor.

Marrying Miss Shylo by Sharon Ihle

From New York to California, a witty historical romance between a pair of crafty characters who never believed they would fall in love with each other. Shylo McBride was determined to find her mother. Dimitri Adonis was looking for a rich heiress. They wound up marrying, each convinced that the other's "supposed" money and status would come in handy for his or her own purposes

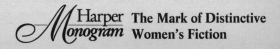

Harper Monogram The Mark of Distinctive Women's Fiction